PRAISE FOR MICHELLE SASS ALECKSON

RIGHT HERE WAITING

I've been *Right Here Waiting* for this book, and I didn't even know it! A hunky hero, a smart and sweet heroine, and lots of furry pups! There's so much to love in this satisfying story of hidden identities, secret romance, and chasing dreams. Grab a cup of hot cocoa and snuggle up to enjoy this captivating read.

— LIZ JOHNSON, BESTSELLING AUTHOR OF *THE RED DOOR INN* AND *BEYOND THE TIDES*

Right Here Waiting captivated me with cute dogs, fun characters, and a You've Got Mail type twist. The beautiful winter setting made me want to cozy up in front of the fireplace while I read, and the message of acceptance warmed me from the inside.

— ANGELA RUTH STRONG, AUTHOR OF *HUSBAND AUDITIONS*

CRAZY FOR YOU

With authentic local flavor, swoon-worthy hometown heroes, and gorgeous scenery, Michelle Sass Aleckson has crafted a heartfelt return to Deep Haven, Minnesota. This latest installment in the Deep Haven series will surely delight Susan May Warren fans and those who love sweet romances.

— GABRIELLE MEYER, AUTHOR OF *SNOWED IN FOR CHRISTMAS*

Michelle Sass Aleckson has created an engaging story with characters who keep you turning the page and a setting readers have come to love. Crazy for You will leave romance fans with a warm glow of happily ever after.

— TONI SHILOH, AUTHOR OF *AN UNLIKELY PROPOSAL*

RIGHT HERE WAITING

A DEEP HAVEN NOVEL

SUSAN MAY WARREN

MICHELLE SASS ALECKSON

sunrise
PUBLISHING

A NOTE FROM SUSIE MAY

You gotta love a guy who loves dogs. And when he's a handsome, strong adventurer and dog musher, say no more. The moment I met Nick Dahlquist, I KNEW he had to have his own story.

Nick, the guy who can survive in the cold, brutal winter... And his heroine? A woman who isn't thrilled with snow.

The concept made me laugh—but it's true! Deep Haven in the winter isn't for cowards. And while Jae, a petite helicopter pilot, is brave, she has no clue what she's in for when she joins the Deep Haven Crisis Response Team. Especially at the beginning of winter.

I also loved this twist on *You've Got Mail*. Michelle utilized so well today's online culture and the issues with revealing your heart online to strangers...while hiding yourself in person around the people you know and love. Such a great paradox and she nailed it in this story.

Michelle also nailed the winter beauty of Deep Haven. Probably because she lives in Minnesota and understands not only the brutality of winter but its deep grace and beauty. She brought this into the story—not only in the storyworld, but in the characters. I loved their romance, their challenges, and the grace-filled twists that Michelle wove into the ending.

This story is a charmer, from the puppies to the humor to, well, have I mentioned *Nick*? (If anyone deserved to have his face on the cover…) *insert deep hero sigh here*

You're going to love this story. Yes, you might get a little cold, but warm up with a crackling fire and dive into a world that's warm, despite the brutal wind outside the door. Frankly, the best place to be in winter is Deep Haven. It's right here, waiting for you. :) Enjoy!

Warmly,

Susie May

To Anders, Evie, Lucy, and Trygg

Long before I thought about being a writer, I wanted to be a mom. You four bring life, laughter, color, and richness to my days. Being your mother is my favorite "job." Love you so big...up to the stars!

PROLOGUE

March 15

LadyJHawk: Hey, sorry about the Iditarod. How are Bozwell and the rest of the dogs?

NixDogQuest: Thankfully Boz will be fine. I should've scratched earlier. I knew better. I really wanted to finish though.

LadyJHawk: What happened, Solo?

NixDogQuest: I'm sick. Stupid flu or something. I thought I could push through, but when I missed a turn because I was so out of it and the sled tipped over and bruised Boz's paw, I knew I had to scratch.

LadyJHawk: Well, yeah, your health is important. There's always next year, right?

NixDogQuest: That's what I said last time. I can't believe I've scratched two years in a row. Just once I'd like to finish a race well.

LadyJHawk: You'll get there. You did the Yukon Quest, right?

NixDogQuest: I finished second to last.

LadyJHawk: Emphasis on the finished. Hang in there!

NixDogQuest: You are so Princess Leia. Always the optimist.

LadyJHawk: Someone's got to keep hope alive.

July 8

NixDogQuest: Hey, Leia, how is C doing? Is he eating again?

LadyJHawk: Yes! Thank goodness. Seems like every time I move, he regresses.

NixDogQuest: Dogs are funny like that. And he's come a long way. Stick to the routine. As a former military working dog, it will help establish that sense of security he needs for the new surroundings.

LadyJHawk: I only moved to a different apartment here in the same city, but he's coming around. We're going to the same beach and dog park for runs. I think that helped. This time, it was only a couple days and he was back to his sweet doggy self.

NixDogQuest: Glad to hear it! How's the job search going, btw?

LadyJHawk: Meh.

October 5

LadyJHawk: So I found an amazing job possibility...

NixDogQuest: Really? That's great! You've been looking for a while.

LadyJHawk: Yeah, but this one is far away. I was kinda hoping to stick around here longer. I've got family nearby and I'm just starting to find some friends, BUT it's a pretty incredible opportunity. The job is perfect.

NixDogQuest: Then no question about it, go for it! What's the job?

LadyJHawk: Nice try. I thought we agreed to keep some level of secrecy. A girl's gotta have some mystery!

NixDogQuest: But you know everything about me. Even what I look like.

LadyJHawk: Yeah, but don't think I haven't noticed how you change the subject every time I ask about your family.

NixDogQuest: That's only because there's not much to say. But I won't pry. And for what it's worth, whatever the position is, if it's your dream job, you should go all in. Burn the ships! You've got this.

CHAPTER 1

*D*eep Haven in November was like a sad old man fighting for his life and losing.

Nick Dahlquist might not be an old man at the ripe old age of thirty, but it was hard not to feel like one with his throbbing leg. He looked up at the bleak sky. Sunlight was hemorrhaging fast. What was left spilled over the ridge onto his hometown and the bay below. Soon darkness would swallow it too. The wind off Lake Superior bit at Nick's exposed ears. His thermal shirt and down vest did little to fight it off.

If November was going to be this cold, it could at least have the decency to throw a little snow down.

Because without snow, his sled team was stuck.

Kinda like his life.

And if he wanted to get out of this rut, he'd need a good foot or two of the white stuff soon. Then he could start training in earnest for the Mush Puppies dogsled race. Thanksgiving weekend would be here in just under four weeks and he and his dogs needed to be ready. Sponsors would be watching the first race of the season, and if he had any hope of going back to the

Iditarod come March, Nick and his team had some convincing to do.

He released a long breath before yanking open the VFW door. The cheers and the smell of onion rings that used to beckon good times hit him in the face as he walked in.

These days he'd be okay if he never ate another VFW burger again. The flavor carried too many memories.

So why had he agreed to meet Darek Christiansen here?

He walked farther in, and aside from the people seated at the bar, he counted five long tables arranged in two rows, each with a bell in the middle all set for Trivia Night. The seats were filled with familiar faces, familiar teams with names like The Facts & The Curious, Nerd Herd, the Smartinis, Les Quizerables, and his old team, which had split off the Fellowship of the Quiz group when they grew too big to fit around one table. They were now the Huskaloosas, named after their high school mascot.

Chatter and laughter he'd once joined in on now grated against his nerves. The Huskaloosas were missing a few players, but his cousin Peter was still there with his girlfriend, Ronnie Morales, and her little brother, Tiago. Beth Strauss and Lena Larson were at the table, Ree Zimmerman and Seth Turnquist had their heads together, but no one was scribbling names down.

And of course, *they* were there. Also, together.

Nick watched Vivien Calhoun. Tall, willowy, brunette, blue eyes that dazzled on stage and a smile that turned him inside out. She looped her arm around Boone and tossed her hair back over her shoulder. Nick could practically smell her perfume. She turned her head toward him. He looked away before she caught him staring.

Nick should've insisted on meeting somewhere else. Or he could've ignored the resort owner entirely.

Well, not really. He could only evade so many messages from

2

a guy like Darek Christiansen, especially with the news yesterday from Licks and Stuff saying they were pulling their sponsorship due to budget cuts. Nick couldn't afford to lose any more support. Not with the foreclosure notice he'd received today.

His eyes adjusted to the dim lighting and made out Darek's tall form and dark hair at a table in the back. The man, who was wearing an Evergreen Resort hoodie, dwarfed the blue plastic chair he sat in as he nursed a bottle of root beer. At least he sat as far as he could from the Trivia Night event. Nick tucked his head and scooched past his old team without anyone noticing.

Now it was show time. Nick plastered on a big grin. "Hey, Darek. You folks staying warm enough out there at the Evergreen?"

Darek set down his bottle. "Yeah, but can you believe this cold snap? Sure could use some snow cover before our septic systems freeze."

Nick nodded. "No kidding."

As soon as he sat down, their usual server, Melissa Ogden, approached in her typical tight jeans, short dark hair, and a lot of makeup. He had played basketball with her older brother Anthony. But she must've been five or six years behind him in school.

"Hey, Nick. It's been a while. What can I get ya?"

"Just coffee."

Darek balked. "Coffee? Aren't you gonna eat?"

"Nah, not hungry."

"Suit yourself." Darek turned to Melissa. "I'll take a double cheeseburger and fries. And another root beer." After she left, his attention swung back to Nick. "I suppose growing up in the restaurant biz, a simple burger doesn't cut it anymore, huh?"

That wasn't the case, but no need to get into it. Unlike Darek, Nick had no desire or skill to take over the family business. The thought of being stuck inside the hot kitchen of his parents' restaurant all day long almost suffocated him. "I'm not too picky most of the time. Just full tonight."

Darek stared for a beat. "You okay, Nick?"

Nick's smile must've slipped. He shored it back up. "I'm great."

"So what's up with the hair and beard? You trying to grow them out like Peter?"

"Which NFL Viking running back rushed two hundred and ninety-six yards in a single game his rookie season?" Mayor Seb Brewster asked the trivia players from the band stage on the other side of the room.

"Adrian Peterson. 2007," Nick mumbled into the mug of coffee Melissa set before him. He took a small sip of the steaming hot coffee. "I'm fine, Darek. Don't worry about me. So, what did you need to meet me about? You said it was urgent."

The big guy looked him in the eye with unwavering concern. "It is urgent. I'm worried about you. Wanted to see you for myself."

Nick forced out a chuckle. "I told you, I'm fine. You really called me down here to talk about my hair and my eating habits? What are we? A bunch of girls?"

But Darek's intense stare held no humor. "I don't think you're fine. Regardless of your hair, this time last year you had dogsledding adventures booked for every weekend in December, January, and February. This year you have one. One time slot. I've had guests call because they can't get a hold of you to schedule and your website needs to be updated with the new online booking program. That's not like you, Nick. Usually you're great with the guests. I mean, you have like a million followers on Instagram. So, what's going on?"

It was nowhere near a million, but he *had* passed the 100K mark. Before he could set Darek straight, Seb cut in with another trivia question. "Which character in the *Star Wars* movies is partially named after George Lucas's son?"

Duh. "Dexter Jettster."

"What?" Darek asked.

"Nothing." Nick sneaked a peek at his old team. Peter shrugged. Ronnie wasn't even paying attention, and Seth and Ree were making puppy dog eyes at each other. They were clueless.

He faced Darek. "Hey, man, don't worry about me. I've just had a lot going on. I'm training hard and trying to get ready for the season." Everyone might think he was the joke of the town the way they plastered his failed attempts on the wall—every newspaper article a reminder of coming close and not quite making it—but he would show them. And, yes, he was a Dahlquist without a culinary degree or restaurant to run. But this was the year. He'd make his *own* legacy, grow his kennel into something impressive. And running the Iditarod was his ticket in.

"That's what you're doing hiding out in the woods? How do you train for dogsledding when there's no snow?"

One glance out the window showed the wind whipping a tattered flag out on Main Street and not a soul on the sidewalk. "You improvise. I have a wheeled cart I designed that I hook the dogs up to. It's not quite the same, but it helps. Sometimes I run them with the ATV."

"I understand you need to train, but you'd better find time to update your website and talk to your customers too. We have a deal. We sponsor you and you offer our guests their winter dogsled adventures. We both benefit from the advertising, right?"

Nick set down his mug. "I know our deal. I'll get the website updated. You can count on me."

"You turn in your Iditarod registration yet?" Darek waved to someone behind Nick.

"Yup." It was one of the big expenses he'd paid with the last bit of sponsorship money. But the four-thousand-dollar fee meant he was woefully short on his balloon payment on the second mortgage. And if he didn't run the Mush Puppies race at the end of the month, it wouldn't matter because he wouldn't have his third qualifying race done. And there would go his dream of actually finishing the Iditarod and being taken seriously as a full-time musher—the one dream he had left. He just had to limp by until then.

"In which film did James Bond drive a Ford Mustang?" Seb asked.

Nick whispered under his breath at the same time Daniel "Boone" Buckam shouted, *"Diamonds Are Forever."*

Nick glanced at him. How was it the man was tan even in November? His dark blond hair was perfectly styled, his fleece pullover a shade of forest green Vivien had always loved. She'd probably picked it out for him.

The team finally put some points on the board and cheered. Nick tried not to cringe as Boone swooped in for a victory kiss from Vivien.

He looked away. Nope, he never should've come here.

Nick gulped one last swallow of the bitter coffee and stood. "Look, Dare, I appreciate the concern, but it's not necessary. I'm just busy. I'll update the website and get caught up. Promise." He'd probably sell this whole charade and get the guy off his back if he sounded more like his old self, so he dug deep to find what he hoped was a lighthearted smirk. "I'll even shave and get my hair cut if it makes you feel better."

Nick turned to leave the table but only made it a step. Instead, he ran right into the woman haunting his dreams.

Vivien.

His radar must be off because usually he knew exactly where Vivie was in a room. Her wide blue eyes captured him. Her jasmine scent wrapped around him, almost strangling his breath. And, yes, once he'd smelled every perfume in the mall to find which one she wore just so he could identify the scent.

But that was a long time ago. Back in the day when they would skip their last class and go ice-skating or play video games or make late-night burger runs when her cravings hit. Yeah, he could admit it—he was a fool for whatever Vivie wanted.

Mostly because she was always up for his crazy ideas. She was the only one who didn't call him by that humiliating nickname after the fire.

But also because she was the prettiest girl in the class.

Deep in the back of his mind, he'd always believed they were made for each other.

Apparently not.

Nick backed up and smacked into his chair. Pain shot up his leg. Darek chuckled, still sitting at the table, watching them.

Vivien laid a perfectly manicured hand on Nick's arm. A sparkling diamond ring on her delicate finger sent a shock wave straight to his heart.

"Nick, why aren't you sitting with the team? We haven't seen you in weeks. What happened to our Mr. Life of the Party?" Her gaze turned concerned.

There were a lot of things from Vivie he wanted. Her pity was not one of them.

He cleared his throat. "Sorry, Viv. I was just heading out. I've got some work to get caught up on. Gotta update the website and all." He bent down and rubbed his leg. "Besides, I don't do trivia anymore."

She shook her head. "Don't do trivia—what are you talking about? You've done trivia every Monday night for the last fifteen years."

Darek speared him with a pointed look. "Yeah, and he knows all the answers too."

"And since when did you start growing a beard?" Vivie asked.

7

Nick shrugged. "Things change. No more trivia, and I don't shave anymore. I'm getting ready for the Iditarod."

Before Vivie could respond, the most unwanted change of all walked up to them. Boone slid an arm around her waist. "Do you want me to order you some more fries since you ate all mine?"

She shot him an almost believable expression of innocence. "I don't know what you're talking about. But you look like you want some onion rings. And a burger too. With extra pickles." She sent him off with a flirty wink and the unmistakable look of longing.

A longing Nick understood all too well.

This summer when Boone had showed up, Nick kept hoping he would join Vivien's long list of two-week boyfriends. The few guys that stuck around more than two weeks were the relationships Nick had worried about over the years as he waited for her to leave New York City and come back home. When she finally did return to Deep Haven, he took a cue from his cousin Peter. Watching what he and his girlfriend Ronnie had had given Nick the courage to take a chance and ask Vivie out.

And Vivien had thought he was joking.

So he'd laughed it off too. Then Boone swept in and took the spotlight. The ring on her left hand and the sinking feeling in his gut said Nick had missed his chance forever. She obviously had found her leading guy.

And it was time for Nick to bow out. Now.

He left with a wave and burst out the glass doors into the cold night. He jabbed his fingers through his unruly mop. The coffee roiled in his stomach and burned his throat.

What was he doing here?

Maybe he should leave. For good. Start over somewhere else.

And where might that be?

Hopping into his truck, he drove out of town and up the ridge to his cabin in the woods.

Sure, it was just a two-bedroom log cabin he'd built with his own hands. Nothing fancy, but every rock on that stone chimney and fireplace had been placed by his own two hands. He'd designed and constructed both the custom-built Quonset dog kennel out back and another large shed off to the side. And it was all surrounded by a yard of towering pines, spruce, and other evergreens with a mix of birch and oak.

No. He couldn't leave this. There were miles of trail right outside his back door, perfect for training and outdoor adventure. He just needed to get over Vivien Calhoun and move on. This was never the kind of life she'd wanted anyway. Deep down inside, he knew that.

He did one last check on the dogs and went inside. Kasha, his lead Alaskan husky, met him at the door. She was a mix of gray and tan fur and had a drive to win that matched his own. Now that her leg was healed, she was anxious to be with the other dogs outside. He should probably board her with the rest of the pack now, but her presence helped fill a little of the hollowness that had invaded his cabin this fall.

Nick called for Kasha to follow him to the brown leather couch by the fireplace. After stoking the fire, he grabbed the jar of his special recipe salve off the mantel. The yellow ointment released an earthy, resinous scent as he rubbed it on Kasha's leg. It had already helped heal the wound on her skin better than the stuff his previous vet had given him. The vitamin E and coconut oil mixed with shea butter and some frankincense and tea tree oils did wonders. And Kasha needed to be in top form.

He scratched the dog behind her ear.

"We just need a little snow, huh, girl? Then we can get back on the trail. Shake this funk off."

She licked his hand and lay on her rug by the door, not convinced of anything he had to say.

That was it though, right? He'd get over Vivien and find a

reason to laugh again eventually. Some fresh powder and the trail would bring him back to life like it always had.

But Darek was right. At this point, he couldn't afford to keep ignoring his emptying bank account. He needed to fill those winter bookings if he was going to have the money to pay back his loan in time. And feeding almost thirty dogs was not cheap, even if eight of them were puppies.

Nick walked over to his kitchen counter where the bank notice lay. He picked it up and scanned it once more. Sixty days. Two months to come up with the loan amount or they were taking the house. The kennels. The property. Everything. He threw it back down on the kitchen counter and picked up his laptop from the coffee table.

Tonight, he had to get that program updated. Darek had sent him the instructions that would update the scheduling program and connect it with the Evergreen Resort website. He opened the link he needed, but the single-spaced instructions read like a foreign language. After he read the same line five times and still didn't understand it, he released a grunt and fisted the hair at his temple. It wasn't the program that was the problem.

That diamond ring on Vivie's hand kept interrupting his thoughts. It winked at him, mocked him. He should just toss the laptop into the fire along with the Iditarod registration now and save himself the heartache.

A ping alerted him to a private message. He opened up the app and read.

LadyJHawk: *Hey, loyal fans are beginning to wonder if you're lost on the planet Hoth. Should we send Luke and Han out on the tauntauns to find you? ;)*

The *Star Wars* reference about the furry snow creatures brought a smile to his lips—a real one he didn't have to manufacture for appearances. His fingers typed out a response.

NixDogQuest: *Nah. Don't want the Empire to find my hideout.*

LadyJHawk: *For real, you okay? Haven't heard from you in a while.*

For some reason, when LadyJHawk asked, the question didn't rankle so much. In chatting over the last couple of years, they'd developed an online friendship. It was easier to open up to someone he was never going to see. Not in real life anyway. And she probably deserved something after a few days of silence.

NixDogQuest: *Just busy. Thanks for checking. How is C doing?*

Kasha barked, needing to go out one more time.

"Oh, sure. Now you need to go outside? Just when I have a woman who actually wants to talk to me?"

Kasha barked again.

"Okay, okay. I'm coming." The boiler needed to be stocked for the cold night anyway and he could come back to the chat later. He closed the laptop and stepped out onto his front porch in his thermal shirt and jeans. Kasha sniffed around and didn't go far to do her business.

Nick stuffed more logs into the outdoor wood boiler and trudged back to the deck with Kasha on his heels. The darkness of the night closed in around them. A sharp gust of wind kicked up, rattling the branches of the bare oak tree next to the deck and carrying the howl of a distant wolf. Leaning on the railing, Nick released a long breath.

I could really use some snow, Lord.

He looked up at the moonless sky.

Stars.

No clouds. No precipitation. No snow. Just stars resembling diamonds all looking down and laughing at him.

❄

The only thing better than a clear starry sky was a fresh calendar page with thirty new days to look forward to. And tonight, Jae Washington had both.

Not only was she starting a new month, but she was also starting a new adventure in Deep Haven, Minnesota. The possibilities of all it could hold almost made her dizzy as she drove into town. It was right where she hoped it would be—parked on the edge of a dark and dangerous Great Lake, comprised of a handful of cute houses and shops, and holding all the adventure shown in NixDogQuest's amazing *Get Lost in the Woods* vlogs.

Home sweet home.

"Seymour, I think this is it," Jae said as she parked her Subaru outside of the VFW, a small building with a bright yellow and green pointed false front and a neon OPEN sign in the window. She gave the Belgian Malinois a kiss on his snout. "Wish me luck, boy. I'm going to meet Ronnie and soon we'll settle into our new life."

He barked in agreement and then hopped to the back seat for a nap. Jae stepped out and did a slow twirl on the sidewalk, taking in her new town. Lights twinkled in the chilly night, showing off the quaint shops and buildings and reflecting off the ebony water of the bay. The waves dancing along the shore couldn't be seen in the darkness, but they added to the music of the night. It would look amazing in daylight.

And to top it all off, the air smelled like snow. Or what she thought snow smelled like. Magical whiteness, grace drifting from the sky.

Bring it on.

She opened the clear glass door of the VFW and was met with bells and laughter. The bright neon signs and early Christmas lights added a festive touch to the dim room. It sounded like a full crowd for a Monday night. Hopefully she could find Ronnie in it.

A tall man with dark hair and a vest that read Evergreen

Resort walked toward her. He smiled as he approached the door, probably on his way out. He seemed friendly enough to ask for help.

"Excuse me, do you know Ronnie Morales? I'm supposed to meet her here."

"Sure." He turned and pointed to one of the middle tables. "See the woman there in the pink sweatshirt, long brown hair in a ponytail? That's Ronnie."

"Great. I'm Jae, by the way. Jae Washington. I'm new in town."

He held out his hand. "Darek Christiansen. Nice to meet you. I'm sure I'll see you around."

She shook his hand and he left as Jae made her way into the crowded room. Good thing he'd pointed Ronnie out. She was surrounded by people, every seat at her table taken. Next to Ronnie another tall, muscular guy—this one with long hair and a beard—jumped up and dinged a bell sitting in the middle of the table.

They must grow 'em big up here on the North Shore of Minnesota.

A man with a microphone standing near the bar pointed to Ronnie's group. "Answer from Team Huskaloosa?"

"Oliver Cromwell."

"That's correct. Five points for Team Huskaloosa." The emcee added hash marks to a chalkboard hanging on the wall. "Let's take a ten-minute break and we'll start the second round."

The man who answered correctly slapped Ronnie's hand in a high five and then fist-bumped the younger boy sitting on the other side of her.

They even let kids in on the trivia fun? This was exactly the kind of small-town camaraderie she'd hoped for.

Jae approached their table. Ronnie smiled at her and stood as some of her teammates scattered. "Are you Jimmy Washington's daughter? Jae?"

"That's me. You must be Ronnie."

The woman moved closer and looked Jae up and down. "You must take after your mom, because you don't look much like Big Jim. And that's a good thing. This town could use a little more diversity." Ronnie winked at her.

Yes, in more ways than her five-foot-two-inch height, Jae embodied her mother's Korean genetics more so than her father's all-American DNA. Like everything from Texas, he was taller than the average man and had a sturdy build. Jae, on the other hand, could still shop in the children's section if she wanted to.

Ronnie introduced her little brother, Tiago, and the tall guy at her side, Peter Dahlquist.

Dahlquist? Jae's interest perked even more. Now they were talkin'.

"So you're our new chopper pilot. Welcome to Deep Haven." Peter also shook her hand and pulled up a chair next to Ronnie for her. "How was the drive from Texas? You can stay a little while, right? You'll be able to meet a lot of the team if you do. But if you're tired—"

"Not tired at all. I can stay for a little bit." Seymour would be okay and she didn't want to miss the chance to start getting to know the place. "As for the drive, we broke it up into three days and explored some of the sights along the way, so it wasn't too bad."

"We?"

A blonde waitress approached their table and smiled at Jae. "What can I getcha, hon?"

"Dr. Pepper, please." She was too excited to eat.

Looking around, it was apparent that everyone knew everyone. Groups were chatting and laughing up at the bar. The emcee sneaked a quick kiss from the cute brunette who brought him a glass of fizzy pop. At the next table, a mom fed her toddler pieces of a chicken nugget as she talked with an older lady—maybe even her mother, given the similar shaped nose and eyes.

"So who else is with you?" Peter asked again.

Jae's attention snapped back to her own table. "I have my dog, Seymour, with me. He's sleeping in the car right now."

"What kind of dog is he? I have a husky," Tiago told her. "Her name is Blue 'cause she's got these big blue eyes. What does your dog look like?"

"Seymour is a Belgian Malinois, so he's dark brown and black. He used to work with the Army Rangers, but he's retired now." After having him for over two years, she could finally say that without the squeeze around her heart.

"Cool!"

Looked like Jae had found another dog lover in the brown-eyed boy with a dimpled smile. The guys left to order more food as another couple came to the table.

Ronnie whispered in her ear, "If you get tired, let me know and I'll get you settled in at headquarters. In the meantime, I hope you're okay with public displays of affection."

"You must be Jae! Welcome!" Before the words could register, Jae was engulfed in a hug. A blonde woman with big hazel eyes released her and then stepped back next to Cole Barrett. Jae recognized dark-haired, blue-eyed Cole from his typical military posture and a picture in her dad's office.

He held out a hand. "Sorry, Jae. I'm Cole Barrett. This is my wife, Megan. She's prone to big displays of emotion."

Megan rolled her eyes but offered a warm smile. "We're glad you're here. Looks like our rescue team is almost complete now."

Team. Jae loved hearing that word. Yes, she had been in the Army and a part of other search and rescue teams all around Texas, and a little in the Northern Pacific, but she wanted to be more than a glorified taxi driver, more than a troop carrier.

And after failing the Torres family, she'd vowed to do more.

That was one of the reasons this job was so perfect. This Crisis Response Team wanted a pilot who would still go out on calls even if the chopper wasn't needed. And maybe getting out of the pilot seat and working side by side to save lives with the others, she could for once be on the inside.

And the location was a downright sign from God. Everything she'd ever prayed for.

Jae sat down and fought to keep her eyes from scanning the room for a certain handsome dog musher as she met the others who trickled back to the table. The town vet, Lena, a shy woman named Beth, an honest to goodness lumberjack named Seth, and his fiancée, Ree, all introduced themselves.

Silly her. It wasn't like *he* was going to walk right up like one of the locals and shake her hand. He was a celebrity.

One more couple joined them at the end of the table as the emcee started Round Two. Ronnie nodded to them. "Boone you know from your online interview."

He reached over and shook Jae's hand. "Nice to meet you in person. And this is my fiancée, Vivien Calhoun."

Vivien. Of course the gorgeous woman would have an elegant name. She could be a model with that long dark brown hair, big blue eyes, and full lips. Bet she never had kids make fun of her when she was growing up. She seemed like the popular type. Maybe someone Jae should shy away from.

But as the game progressed, Jae forgot her first impression when it was Vivien who made sure Jae was included, letting her in on their team cheers and inside jokes.

They were all so nice, Jae hated for it to end. But Seymour probably shouldn't be out much longer in the cold. She had promised to take care of him. She couldn't let Matt's memory down.

Ronnie walked her out. "The Crisis Team Headquarters is just a few blocks over on the East Bay. I'm parked across the street. You can follow me."

The crisp night air was a bit of a shock after the cozy atmosphere in the crowded VFW. Jae got in her car and rubbed her arms as she waited for Ronnie to turn around. Seymour jumped to the passenger seat. She scratched his chin right under his collar where he liked it. "We're almost there, boy."

Ronnie pulled up and Jae followed her SUV to the headquarters. Even in the dark, the huge metal-sided building was well lit from the outside. The big roll-up doors had shiny windows at the top.

Jae and Seymour stepped outside. "Wow. This is amazing." Not just the building, but the night sky twinkled with millions of stars. The Milky Way's glow lit a path across the darkness. It almost seemed within reach, it was so bright.

Ronnie's keys jangled in her hands as she searched for the right one. "Sorry this is the only place we have for you now. As an HQ, it is amazing. They designed the building with state-of-the-art equipment." They walked around to a smaller side door, which Ronnie unlocked. "But as living quarters, it's not much. And some parts are still under construction."

Jae and Seymour followed Ronnie into the bay. An ambulance, a couple ATVs, snowmobiles, and other rescue rigs barely took up a corner of the soaring expanse. They could probably park the chopper right in here along with a small plane and Jae's last apartment building complex. Scaffolding was set up along one wall. Coils of wire and construction material along with boxes blocked a big part of the cavernous room. The crowning touch was the massive climbing wall in the back.

"Here's your new home," Ronnie said, unzipping her jacket and removing her gloves. "For now, anyway. Since it's getting kinda late, I'll show you the Bell 429 tomorrow. It's in a separate bay attached to this one." Ronnie led the way down across the bay, her footsteps echoing off the tall, open ceiling. "You must be tough to be a female chopper pilot. Especially if you can handle the cold with just that light sweater."

Jae laughed. "Well, I *am* tougher than I look. As my daddy says, we're Texas tough. But honestly, I didn't know it would be this cold yet. I think my hands are frozen, but I've been too excited to notice." She followed Ronnie to the other side of the bay. "And flying a helicopter takes guts, sure, but it's more coordination than muscle."

"If you're anything like your dad, I'm sure you'll do great. I flew with him quite a bit. The man had nerves of steel." Ronnie opened a door to a hall. "We have the offices and classrooms as well as the bunk rooms on the second story." She led the way upstairs, down a hall, and opened the door. Ronnie flipped on the lights to display a room with three bunks and a row of lockers. "Here are the women's quarters. There's a bathroom with shower next door. The kitchen, break room, and offices are down the hall. Those areas are all finished. But a lot of it, as you can see, is still under some construction. We're getting close to being finished and moving everything else in."

Jae dropped her bag on a bottom bunk in the corner. "This is great. I don't need much, just a place to sleep."

"You can stay until you find a place to rent on your own. But I should warn you, affordable rental units are hard to find around here. So, you might want to meet with Nathan Decker, the local real estate guy, as soon as possible. And the rest of the team is keeping an eye out for listings too."

"Really? They don't even know me."

"You'll find out quickly that this is a tight-knit community. But once you're in, we take care of our own. And Jae, you're in." She held up a hand for a high five.

The words warmed Jae to the core as she gave Ronnie's palm a hearty clap. "I think I'm going to like it here."

Ronnie grinned. "Good. We'll do our best to get you settled quickly." She studied her a moment. "Do you have warmer clothes than what you're wearing? Like real winter gear? You're not in Texas anymore."

Jae looked down at her favorite sweater. The vintage belted cardigan had more style than warmth for sure. "No. I didn't have a ton of packing space, so I figured I'd buy what I need here. Do they have any secondhand places? I'm always up for a treasure hunt."

"I'm not sure what you'll find at the little thrift store here, but I can check around and see what I can dig up. I'd lend you something of mine, but it would probably swallow you whole and get in your way."

Before Jae could respond, something metallic clattered to the cement floor. Where was her dog? "Seymour! Come!" Usually he was so well behaved, but lately he was becoming more unruly. The big moves always unsettled him. He came and sat at Jae's feet with a distinct look of guilt all over his face.

"Will he be okay in here?" Ronnie asked as she bent down to pet him. "There's still construction going on. I'd hate for him to get hurt."

"As I was searching online, I found somewhere that I think will board him until we find our own place. A Nick Dahlquist." Jae fought to keep all excitement out of her voice and maintain a nonchalant vibe. "Is he related to…uh, Peter?"

"Oh, Nick! Yeah, he's Peter's cousin. And that husky Tiago was telling you about? That's one of Nick's puppies. She's been great for my little brother. Nick helped Tiago train her."

"So you think Nick will be a good option to board Seymour?" Jae clasped her hands together and crossed her fingers.

"Of course. He's a great guy. Super fun. Loves dogs. Although, now that I think of it, I haven't seen him around lately. He's probably getting ready for the dogsledding race at the end of the month. I bet Seymour would love it up there with Nick's pack."

Yes! Jae held back from doing a fist pump. Just like she thought. Nick Dahlquist, dog whisperer and outdoor adventurer, was the real deal. A thrill ran through her from head to toe.

Ronnie stood. "I'll let you get settled in for the night. You have my number if you need anything, right?"

"Yep! We'll be great."

"Good. I'll see you tomorrow."

After Ronnie left, Jae unpacked the essentials she'd brought with her. She never did accumulate much, so it didn't take long. It was easier with all the moving to pack light and buy what she needed when she arrived somewhere. It made it easier to leave when the inevitable itch struck and she was ready for something new. Her mother always blamed growing up in the military for Jae's wandering lifestyle. But the truth was, she was still just searching. Searching for a place that felt like home. Where she could be herself and be part of something bigger at the same time.

And Deep Haven might just be the last stop.

Jae plugged her phone into a charger and opened the private messaging app that had started this whole thing.

Ronnie mentioned she hadn't seen Nick around much. He'd posted on Instagram and a few short videos of a new batch of puppies, but the last message Jae had sent him days ago was still unanswered the last time she checked. But maybe...

She quickly typed out a silly message about tauntauns and held her breath as she hit "send."

Ping. A response!

NixDogQuest: *Nah. Don't want the Empire to find my hideout.*

After days of silence from her online friend, his reply quickened her heartbeat.

LadyJHawk: *For real, you okay? Haven't heard from you in a while.*

NixDogQuest: *Just busy. How's C doing?*

So he wasn't ignoring her. He was just busy. C, short for Seymour, laid his head on Jae's lap, begging for more scratches.

They'd come a long way thanks to these chats with NixDog-Quest. She patted the bed but Seymour whined and walked toward the door. He needed to go out before he would settle in for the night. "Just a sec. Let me finish this and then we'll go." She picked up her phone and continued.

LadyJHawk: *Good. We've been driving for a few days so he's a little antsy.*

She waited for an answer. Just as she wondered if he would disappear for good again, she heard the notification sound.

NixDogQuest: *That's right. You took the new job. Hope the new adventure is all you dreamed of.*

LadyJHawk: *Me too. I'm ready for a new start.*

NixDogQuest: *I know what you mean.*

The thought of tomorrow made her smile as she took Seymour outside for a quick walk. She looked up at the night sky.

So many stars.

She drew in a long breath. Snow was on the horizon. She just knew it.

Yes, Deep Haven was all she had hoped it would be and more. And tomorrow it would get even better.

Tomorrow she was going to meet Nick Dahlquist in person.

Let the adventure begin.

CHAPTER 2

*N*ick stood in the frigid morning air as he watched Kasha bound to the tree line for her morning bathroom break. A steel gray sky to the east hinted at the upcoming sun. He used to love mornings like this. Fresh air. Adventure on the trail to look forward to. He never wanted to miss out on whatever fun the day would hold.

Not so much lately.

Especially when the first thing he saw was the bank foreclosure notice once again as it lay on the kitchen counter next to the coffee maker. He was up late chatting with LadyJHawk and could barely function as it was. To be reminded of all that he was about to lose before he could brace himself with caffeine almost sent him back to bed.

He opened up the calendar on his phone. The last weekend of the month had Mush Puppies in bright orange text. His only hope was to do well in that race and get new sponsors. And in the meantime, he needed to sell this litter of puppies ASAP for some income to tide him over.

Today's calendar square had "Lena 8:00 am" typed in it.

That's right. He had Lena Larson coming with vaccinations and dewormer later this morning.

Oh wait. She needed to be paid too.

Nick groaned. It kept adding up. He checked his messages. The puppies had been advertised on his separate breeder website for a few weeks now and still no takers. Great. Maybe he should use his social platform to advertise them and find buyers, but his policy of selling puppies only to people he could verify would be good owners for sled dogs held him back. The pups deserved to go to good homes, and he'd had enough issues with one crazy stalker. Nick didn't need to put his family or dogs at risk.

He slipped the phone back in his pocket. "Come, Kasha. You can go back with Mischa later." Nick called her away from the kennel where she pawed at the fence and barked at her sister, wanting to play. That was probably a good sign. Her leg was healed. Guess he'd have to get used to an empty cabin once more.

The dog listened and followed Nick inside. After leaving his boots on the mat by the door, Nick kneeled by the husky and sank his fingers into the fur around her neck, scratching behind her ears. "You're supposed to lead us to a victory at the Mush Puppies race, right? Then we'll get some new sponsors, pay off the bank, and everything will be fine."

Her only response was a slobbery kiss on his cheek—the closest thing he'd get to any affection these days. "All right, enough of that. You're going to make me blush if you keep it up."

He changed the water and scooped out food into her dish. "How about something to eat?"

She gobbled down her food and followed Nick in the kitchen as he made his coffee. After two cups, the sun was up and he was awake enough to finish taking care of the other dogs. He left Kasha by the fire and walked back outside. As he walked past the outdoor fenced-in kennel on his way to the equipment shed, the pack barked and howled, wanting their food.

"I know, guys. I'm late. Just give me a sec." He hopped on the ATV with a rack attachment and drove it over to the metal Quonset kennel. He checked the outside temperature and then calculated how much pork fat to mix into the batch of fish and venison soup. Colder temps meant the dogs needed more calories. With this cold snap, he would need to put in an order with the butcher soon. Another payment he would have to make. Everywhere he looked, the bills piled up.

Nick fed Tillie and the pups first. Then he filled five-gallon buckets with kibble dog food, soup, and a small pouch with his homemade treats and loaded them on his four-wheeler. He drove it down the line of outdoor kennels where a pair of dogs shared a simple wooden doghouse in each 5'x8' section. He made each dog follow a command before offering a treat and then filled each bowl with food. Their enthusiastic barks and licks lifted his spirits a little. This was worth getting up for at least.

After all the dogs ate, he released them to their open enclosure, where they'd spend most of the day with plenty of space to run and play. He leaned against the fence for a moment and watched his pack. Now if only it would snow and they could get back to training. Then they could do what they were so eager to do. Race. And maybe he could finally gain some traction in life. Put Vivien behind him. Show the town—everyone really—that he was a serious dogsledder and outdoorsman. He might not have followed the typical Dahlquist path, but his business was just as legitimate as any of the restaurants.

In fact, it was more than a business. It was a lifestyle.

The sound of a vehicle on the winding gravel road alerted Nick. He checked his watch. Lena was right on time. He jogged around to the front of the cabin as she pulled up in her truck.

The Pet Haven Veterinary Clinic logo and her name were on the side.

"Now there's a woman who's made something of herself," his grandfather had pointed out to him a few months ago. "And she's two years younger than you."

She was only a couple years out of vet school and had already started a thriving business back in their hometown. She had the kind of drive and business sense his dad probably hoped for in his only child. His mom just thought he should ask Lena out because they were both single and on the same trivia team.

Maybe if he was going to get over Vivien, he should consider it. It was time to move on.

Lena hopped out of the cab with her bag in hand. She wore a fleece and pants in drab khaki and green. She might be called average with her 5'4" frame and straight brown hair, but she'd graduated first in her class at Deep Haven High and had a way with animals that was downright magical. Not average in the least. It was, however, hard to get a smile out of her.

"Let's see this newest batch of puppies," she said as she walked over to him with her serious demeanor. She had all the humor of a math textbook.

Which was fine for a vet, but nothing he'd want in a date. *Sorry, Mom.*

"Yeah, and the follow-up for Kasha. I want to know if you think she's ready to train. The team needs her."

"Let's do the vaccinations and see the puppies first, then I'll take a look at Kasha."

He led her back to the indoor kennel, forgoing the small talk she didn't like and he didn't have the energy for.

She knelt down in the puppy kennel and picked up the first black and white pup. She looked it over, weighed it, administered the medicine, and gave it a quick shot then released it back to the kennel. She did the same for all eight. As she jotted down the last weight in a pamphlet, she looked over at Nick. "Are you okay?"

He shrugged. "Yeah. I'm great. Why does everyone keep asking me that?"

Her eyes narrowed as she studied him. "No. There's definitely something wrong. Usually you are annoyingly chipper, breaking my concentration, trying to make me laugh, or distracting me with ideas for your homemade dog treats. But you've been silent this whole time." She removed her gloves and stuffed them in a bag. "And you've missed Trivia Night the last five weeks. Something is off."

She may be right, but there was nothing she could do about it. "Are the puppies all right?"

She shook her head, probably at his evasion. "The puppies are fine. Healthy weights. Tillie is doing a good job. You're keeping these to train?"

He shook his head. "I need to sell this litter. Have you had any inquiries?"

"No, but I'll keep my ears open. These pups will have a lot of energy. They'll need the right kind of home." She scratched Tillie behind the ears, the lines around her mouth softening almost to a smile. Lena was always more relaxed with the animals than with people. "Let's take a look at Kasha."

Lena followed him to the back door and into the cabin, where she examined Kasha. Her eyebrows furrowed a little more than usual as she gently felt Kasha's leg. She used a stethoscope, listened to her heart and lungs, and checked Kasha's ears and mouth. She gave the husky one last pat on the head and looked up at him.

"Well, is she ready to train? Will she be ready for the race?"

Lena nodded. "Go ahead and start training but take it easy and start with a brace. She should be ready to run the Mush Puppies race at the end of the month and be in top form by the time you run the Iditarod. That's in March, right?"

"Yeah." Nick took a full breath and smiled as he rubbed Kasha's head. "Hear that, girl? You're ready to go." Finally, something was going his way.

Lena stood slowly, her eyes still on the dog at her feet. "Take it slow, though. Don't push her too hard." She looked at him. "Now, I hate to say this, but I need a payment today. Your bill is still outstanding from the first time I saw her when she broke her leg. I can't afford to do business for free."

"No. Of course. I'll get it. I just..." He looked into Kasha's big blue eyes. "I need to sell a puppy first. I had to drop one of my sponsors when I found out they were being investigated by PETA last year. So I'm a little short on cash at the moment. But I promise you'll be the first person I pay once I sell the pups."

She stared. "Fine. But the past due amount needs to be paid in full. I don't like being a stickler about it, but I have bills too. Employees to pay."

"And I'll get the money to you as soon as I can."

"Okay. I can't do anything else until your bill is paid off though. You better take it easy so Kasha doesn't reinjure herself."

"We'll take it slow. Promise." He did his best Boy Scout impression and saw her to the front door. "Thanks, Lena."

As soon as she left, he logged on to his checking account. No matter how he arranged the numbers, there wasn't enough to pay off his vet bill, let alone buy the next shipment of dog food. When he'd lost his main sponsor, he had been sure that taking out that second mortgage on the cabin to tide things over would've been enough. But with Kasha's injury, last spring's small litter, and having to scratch in the Iditarod and miss out on any prize money, he was sinking into the red fast.

Wow. At this rate he wouldn't be surprised if a bill collector showed up on his doorstep.

He needed cash. Now.

He could ask for some shifts at his parents' restaurant. Not cooking of course. No sane person would let him near the grill. But he could wash dishes and serve. As much as he hated the thought of it, he'd do it for the dogs.

But at this point, there wouldn't be enough hours available. This was their slowest season. His parents always cut the staff down this time of year with only locals to feed. There wasn't lawn work or snow removal work right now he could pick up either. And his next sponsorship payments wouldn't come until January.

How had he let things get so far in the hole?

Was there anything he could sell? His truck? No, he needed it, and being customized with the dog kennels on the back, it would be hard to find a buyer. He could sell firewood. A few cords sold could at least make a good dent in his vet bill.

But then all the other things he'd been putting off purchasing but still needed to buy added up in his mind. A new water heater. His next shipment of gasoline for the four-wheeler and skid loader. The list kept growing.

He dropped his head, his forehead sinking into his palms, fingers caught in his unruly hair. He needed to sell these puppies. Now. And he needed new sponsors.

He quickly sent another message to the two families he knew well who had shown some interest in the past but never followed through. Maybe if he could shoot some video footage of the puppies, show how cute they were in the cabin in front of a fireplace, he could get some takers. If he didn't do something, the puppies wouldn't be the only ones needing a home.

※

The winding dirt road climbed farther up the forested incline while the late morning sun played hide and seek with the clouds and tree branches overhead. Stark white birch branches waved high above the hood of Jae's Subaru while stately evergreens stood tall and resolute on the hillside.

Absolutely gorgeous.

Jae checked the navigation on her panel with a glance. Nick's vlog, *Get Lost in the Woods*, wasn't too far off. It certainly wouldn't be hard to do out here.

Everything surrounding her sang of fresh air and beauty— the perfect place to start a new adventure.

Jae's phone rang through the Bluetooth speaker, interrupting her reverie.

"Hey, Daddy."

"How's my Sugar-Blossom doing?" Her father's Texas twang came through the speaker loud and clear. "Did ya make it to Minnesoooota yet?"

She laughed at his awful attempt at the Minnesotan accent. She could picture him standing on her grandparents' front porch, leaning against the post and sipping a dark Italian roast coffee out of an enamel mug. His gray-streaked brown hair would be hidden beneath his favorite black Stetson, his plaid shirt tucked neatly into his Levi's and his cowboy boots caked with dust and dirt.

"I made it in last night."

"And how is it? Did you meet Ronnie and Cole?"

"Yeah, they were great. Just like you said."

"I tell ya, those two got more guts than you could hang on a fence. I'm glad they can watch over you."

"Daddy, I can take care of myself. I don't need watchin'." And there went her own non-twangy accent she'd worked so hard to cultivate. She rolled her eyes at her own slip. "So, how's Omma?"

"Your mama is just fine. Happens to be right here next to me making me the most blessed man in the great state of Texas. Mimi and Pap are in town picking up a few things." His voice became muffled. "What's that? ... Yeah. ... I'll ask her."

"Daddy?"

"Darlin', your mama wants to know if you'll be down here for Thanksgiving."

"I wish I could, but I won't have any vacation time yet. I'll see what I can do to get down there before you go back overseas."

"Maybe Christmas we can fly up there. Sure do miss ya, darlin'."

"I miss you too, Daddy. I think you'll like it up here if you come visit. Lots of forest and hills. And Lake Superior is incredible." A glance out her driver's side window showed a break in the trees. The sapphire lake horizon stretched wide, as far as she could see.

"Doesn't it get mighty cold up there? I'm still surprised you're trading the blue Texas skies for the frozen tundra."

"The cold isn't too bad." When she didn't think about it. Yes, she'd had to don her sweatshirt and bathrobe as well as her thickest socks before she could fall asleep last night, but the headquarters building was so big. Surely once she found a small, cozy apartment, she'd be fine. Besides, though people might try to treat her like one because of her size, she was no delicate flower. "Texas was okay for a while, but...I need to find my own place, Daddy. And I think this is it."

"I get you have to find your place, but did you have to sell everything? You could've kept your furniture in storage or paid rent on your apartment another month or two until you were certain it would work. Or taken a leave of absence instead of quittin' your job."

Jae remembered Nick's video he'd posted the day she was offered the Deep Haven job, his direct gaze coming through her screen as he'd pointed to the camera and spoken. *If you're going to do something in life, don't do it halfway. Give it everything. Don't leave yourself an escape. Burn the ships and move on with the conviction that your only way through is to move forward.*

She'd heard that and she'd known. She had to do this.

"No, Daddy. I needed to burn the ships. Go all in. I'm gonna make this work." She had to.

His deep sigh came through loud and clear. "Well, good thing you're Texas tough. I'm sure wherever you go, you will light up a room and bring the sunshine like you always do." A slurp sounded through her car's speakers. "So what's on your agenda today, Jae Hawk?"

"I'm on my way to meet someone." Her arms relaxed now that Daddy had moved on to a different subject.

"Who are ya fixin' to meet?"

"Nick Dahlquist. You remember, the one I told you about? The guy who does those videos."

"You mean that guy you're always goin' on and on about? The one with the dogs?"

"Now, Daddy, before you start—"

"Are you sure you should be meetin' up with him? You don't know him from Adam. Is Seymour with you?"

"Daddy, I'm fine. And I do know Nick. Just because we've never met face to face doesn't mean I don't *know* him. Besides, he really helped me with Seymour. You know how hard it was when I first got him."

"I don't know, Sugar. This Nick could be slicker than a boiled onion. It's easy to be somethin' you ain't online."

"I can handle myself. I made it through boot camp and six years in the Army. I can handle this."

"I know, but—"

"And I'm just going to meet him and see if he'll board Seymour. It's not a big deal. Ronnie said he was a great guy. He's Peter's cousin."

"Who's Peter?"

"Ronnie's boyfriend."

"Oh. Well, if Ronnie knows him, maybe he's okay. But you be careful, now, ya hear? Don't set your heart too much on something until you know for sure. I'd hate to see you get hurt again."

"I'll be fine." It had taken her a while, but she had healed. Moved on. She was ready to open herself up again to the possibility of a relationship.

"Alright. I'd better scooch. Your Mimi's gonna tan my hide if I don't get back to help Uncle Will with the fencing."

"Love you, Daddy. Kiss Omma for me."

"Love you too, Sunshine."

And she knew he did. He and Omma were always so supportive of her. But Daddy might be a smidge overprotective of his only child too.

Like she had anything to worry about in meeting Nick Dahlquist.

When she and Seymour were still adjusting to each other and she was researching ways to help bond with him, one random search on YouTube had brought up Nick's vlog. She had been instantly captured by those sparkling blue eyes, so bright against his golden skin. His dark wavy hair peeking out of his beanie and falling over his forehead. He'd smiled on the screen, one arm slung around a gorgeous white and gray husky in his profile picture.

She'd had to know more, so she'd hit Play. He'd given a short introduction to his dogsledding team, and then through a GoPro attached to his chest, she'd joined in on the dogsledding trek through the north woods on screen. His rich voice as he'd narrated had drawn her in. And when he'd laughed at a deer they'd startled on their run, that laughter had woken something inside her. She'd stayed up all night and watched every video on his channel.

The man was living life to the fullest—such a stark contrast to her first six months with Seymour. She had been barely existing. But Nick's laugh was the first thing that made her want to really live again. And to find joy.

He was a natural with the animals. And some of his techniques helped Seymour. He had a special tune he would whistle to spur on the dogs. They responded to him.

So did she.

She'd started to attend a support group and see a counselor weekly. She was more intentional about going out with friends and talking to her family. She'd started living again.

All because of Nick.

She'd wanted to reach out and let him know how much his videos and posts helped her. She'd found his NixDogQuest handle and sent him a private message. He'd responded to her message and they'd begun chatting.

Her only stipulation was to avoid talking about work. Her conversations with Nick were an escape, a vacation. According to her counselor, she needed to remember that there was more to life than her job, and so she'd instituted her no-shop-talk policy with Nick.

Whether it was that or simply that they'd clicked, it still amazed her how close she could feel to someone she'd never even met. But she knew his voice, the slight dimple in his right cheek, the corny jokes, and she was so tempted every time he signed off with his "Go get lost in the woods and find adventure!" to do just that. The man inspired her.

It's easy to be somethin' you ain't online.

Well, maybe. She couldn't deny Daddy had a point. Not that Nick was a swindler or anything, but maybe he wasn't the same person in real life. And then what?

No. She was just letting Daddy's doubts get to her. After a couple years of chatting almost every day—except for the last few days of silence—she knew Nick better than she knew anyone else.

"Your destination is on the right," the navigation voice said.

Jae pulled into the driveway, which led to a beautiful rustic log cabin tucked into the woods. It had a covered porch and a rough-cut stone chimney towering over one end of the metal roof. A gray truck with dog boxes in the back was parked in the driveway on the other end of the house. The small front yard was covered in brown grass and a multi-colored carpet of leaves. It was a little stark and could use a few potted plants or a cute bench on the porch, but then again, it was practically winter. Still, the place was so...Nick. It was just as she'd pictured it in her head, only this time it wasn't on a screen.

This was real.

Jae left Seymour in the car for the moment and walked up to the cranberry-red front door. She breathed in the scent of pine and crisp woodsy air and knocked. She couldn't hold back her grin. He'd probably think she was a weirdo, as big as she was smiling, but it couldn't be helped. She shivered and drew her sweater tighter around her. Ronnie was right. She needed some warmer clothes.

No one answered. She knocked again and waited. Nothing. Barks and howls sounded from behind the house. He must be here if his truck was in the driveway. She followed the stone path around the corner to the side yard.

And then, there he was—coming out of a fenced-in kennel area connected to a large metal shed. Nick.

Her breath caught. His dark brown hair was longer than she'd seen it in the videos before, strands hanging in tussled waves down to his eyes. A dark beard covered his jaw and chin. He was more rugged and handsome in real life. Even the bulky canvas jacket and hoodie couldn't hide his athletic and tall build. His head hung low as he marched toward his back deck, clearly oblivious to her presence.

She should say something funny. Something witty or smart. Something memorable for their first face-to-face encounter.

"Hi there." Her voice squeaked.

Wow. Really knocked it out of the park there, Washington.

Not that it mattered. Nick didn't even look up.

Jae cleared her throat and tried again a little louder. "Hi. I'm looking for Nick Dahlquist from Nick's DogQuest Tours."

His head snapped up. "Oh no." His blue eyes narrowed. "How did you find me?"

She just blinked at him. "Um, I—"

"Listen, let's not jump the gun too quickly here. You can tell whoever sent you that I'm good for everything. I've got things in the works. I promise." He shot her an obviously fake smile before he turned and hurried toward his cabin.

What? "Can I just talk to you—"

"Listen." He stopped at the top of his steps. "I know you're just doing your job, but I'm trying to make a living here. I don't have time for this." He turned away, fiddling with the phone in his hand, his voice distant. "I promise I'll get something to you as soon as I can. No need to hassle me here at my home."

Okay, what was going on? This was Nick. Nick Dahlquist. Why was he acting so rude?

"I'm not here to hassle you. I wanted to introduce myself. I'm—"

"Stop." He put his phone away and scowled. "I'm not your buddy or your friend. I'm not dumb enough to fall for charm and a pretty face. I know you're only here for the money, so stop pretending to be nice. There's a reason why everyone hates people like you."

She gasped. No. He did *not* just say that.

And then he simply walked inside, shutting the door behind him.

There's a reason why everyone hates people like you.

People like *her*? As in…Asian?

All the things she'd prepared to say burned like acid in her throat.

I'm Jae, as in LadyJHawk.

I know you.

You inspire me.

We have this crazy connection online and now we have the chance to see what it would be in person.

She was about to march up those steps to knock on the door and give him a piece of her mind. She'd faced storms and disasters and the repercussions of war. She would show him—what? Was there any convincing someone that rude, that blind, of truth? Of the meaning of basic human dignity?

His words came back to her, slashing her dreams of what could've been and scattering the shattered pieces on the wind.

I don't have time for this.

No need to hassle me here at my home.

There's a reason why everyone hates people like you.

No. There would be no convincing a racist like that of anything. She spun around and rushed to her car.

She drove away, kicking up sharp gravel of the dirt road. She couldn't get away from him fast enough. The audacity of the man! Jae ground her teeth and bit back a storm of words she wanted to unleash.

Something ice cold and sharp wedged in through the fury.

Oh no. What had she done? She'd sold everything and moved halfway across the country to meet a man she had fantasized about for the last year. And to think she'd thought the job here in Deep Haven was an answer to prayer!

Seymour whined from the passenger seat. He licked the tears off her cheeks as she sped downhill toward town.

She was an idiot. A complete idiot. Daddy had warned her.

Guess he was right.

Because the Nick Dahlquist she'd just met was nothing like the man she'd chatted with or watched on the screen. She shivered even more, and her teeth chattered. Jae cranked up the heat until warm air blasted through the vents.

This was what she got for putting herself out there again. For thinking she could have something real and lasting. She was an idiot to think Nick might be someone she could share adventures with. Maybe if she'd been a little more transparent online, had a profile picture instead of an avatar, she would've discovered the true Nick sooner.

She wanted nothing to do with the guy she'd just met. Obviously, his online persona was just that. A farce. A mask he wore for the screen and his audience.

And if she'd messed that up so badly, the rest of her ideas about Deep Haven were probably an empty fantasy too.

CHAPTER 3

*J*ae needed to pull herself together before she met up with Ronnie and Boone for her orientation. She pulled over in a little parking lot right off the highway next to a river. She watched the clear brown water flow between ice-crusted banks and empty into Lake Superior. The waves on the lake raked the pebbled shore in a relentless rhythm, and Seymour ran into the water to chase them.

What had she gotten them into? This was a small town. What if others felt the same as Nick?

She watched Seymour splash along the shore. His dark brown and black doggy face was pure happiness. Probably because *he* didn't realize what a colossal mistake she'd made.

She sniffed. Well, if her dog could still wag his tail and find something worth chasing, so could she. Jae swiped the last tear off her cheek and took a cleansing breath. She wasn't helpless. Like Daddy said, she was Texas tough. So what if Nick wasn't all she thought he'd be? She still had a job—even if it had lost some of its luster after the disaster of this morning's meeting.

Okay, a lot of its luster.

But this wasn't any ol' employment opportunity. She'd loved

flying ever since the first time Daddy took her up in a helicopter when she was five years old, and this was her dream job. It was also her chance to find purpose beyond moving people and supplies. She wanted to get in the trenches and save lives too. With the CRT, she could fly *and* use some of her first responder training.

Besides, no one else she'd met last night seemed to have a problem with her ethnicity. Everyone at the VFW had been kind and welcoming.

She might've made a mess of things getting caught up in a stupid romantic fantasy of being surrounded by blue-eyed babies and litters of puppies, but that didn't mean she would throw away her career. She would go back to Deep Haven, avoid the poser she'd thought was her best friend, and start her training.

And hopefully Nick Dahlquist really would get lost in the woods and she'd never have to see him again.

Her phone pinged with an incoming message on her app.

NixDogQuest: *Hey, just wanted to wish you luck on the first day of your new adventure. I bet you'll do great. :D*

Jae stared down at the message while the wind whipped her long dark bangs across her face.

Humph. He was only being nice because he didn't know what she looked like. Her fingers were stiff with the cold, but she quickly typed a message.

LadyJHawk: *I'm not so sure. I think I made a mistake.*

Jae paused. She had to end this chatting relationship now that she knew who Nick was. As she searched for the best way to word it, Nick's next message pinged.

NixDogQuest: *How can you make a mistake yet? It's your first day. You got this! Now me, on the other hand, I started the day off like a jerk having to scare some bill collector away. I tried to ignore her, hoping she would leave, but you know how they get, acting all buddy-buddy to get their foot in the door before they start harassing* *you. I had to shut the door on her. You've got to be doing better than I am.*

Jae paused.

Bill collector? Is that what he'd meant by "people like you?" And now he felt bad.

LadyJHawk: *A bill collector just showed up at your house?*

NixDogQuest: *Well, I assume it was a bill collector. I'm a little behind on things and the only people that show up at my door these days are people I know. This woman was a complete stranger. Who else would it be?*

LadyJHawk: *Are you sure she wasn't a tourist or fan? You have a pretty big following online.*

NixDogQuest: *I hope not. Then I'd feel really bad. But I doubt it. After my stalker issue a few years ago, I took my address offline and do everything I can to protect it.*

Stalker? Sheesh, a little dramatic there, Nicholas.

LadyJHawk: *Stalker? Was she that scary looking?*

NixDogQuest: *No! She was really cute actually.*

Jae's anger cooled. He thought she was cute? *Really* cute? That was...interesting.

Should she tell him she was the woman he'd scared away? Would they laugh about it and start over?

Daddy's caution rang in her mind. *He could be slicker than a boiled onion. It's easy to be somethin' you ain't online.*

No. A good soldier did recon. She needed to figure out who the real Nick was first.

Jae jumped back into her car with Seymour and continued reading.

NixDogQuest: *But I once had this crazed fan who became a bit of a stalker. She drove to my house from Illinois. Followed me around everywhere. For weeks.*

Jae gasped. He was serious about that?

LadyJHawk: *An honest to goodness stalker? For real?*

NixDogQuest: *Yeah. I tried to be nice, let her know I wasn't* *interested. But eventually I had to take out a restraining order and get the sheriff involved because she wouldn't leave and she started harassing my family. It was a mess. She said she moved here to Minnesota so that "we could be together."*

No wonder he hadn't been excited to see her—a complete stranger for all he knew—showing up out of the blue. He'd thought she was a bill collector or stalker. Her ears and cheeks burned. She could just see the "told you so" expression on Daddy's face.

But there was also a tiny sense of relief. She hadn't completely missed the mark. Nick really *was* a good guy. Distracted, maybe a bit paranoid, but not the racist jerk unwilling to give her the time of day she'd assumed moments ago.

Oh no. A sinking sensation filled her. There was no way she could tell Nick she was LadyJHawk now.

Or ever.

Because what had she just done? Packed up everything, quit her job, and driven across five states to move here. If she told him now that she also happened to be the woman he was chatting with online, he'd go screaming for the hills and take out a restraining order on her too.

But thinking back on all they shared, the idea of hiding the truth didn't sit well in her gut. That's not who she was. She would have to tell him eventually.

And she would. She only had to wait until he got to know her as Jae and see that she wasn't some obsessive, creepy stalker. That there was an amazing job and this cute town that had drawn her here to Deep Haven—not just him.

And maybe she needed some time to make sure he was the guy she thought he was. Charming. Funny. Kind. And more importantly, not racist.

If that was the case—and oh, how she hoped it was—once he

got to know Jae in real life, *then* she could tell him. But for now, she would have to keep it to herself.

She read over his message again and smiled at the screen. It didn't hurt that he'd called her really cute. It was enough to make her forget the bitter cold for a while.

NixDogQuest: *You still there?*

LadyJHawk: *Yeah, I'm here.*

NixDogQuest: *You've got me thinking. What if you're right? What if it really was an innocent woman who only wanted a tour of the kennels or something? I shouldn't have freaked out. Now I feel bad. She probably thinks I'm a huge jerk.*

LadyJHawk: *If you see her again, offer an apology and chocolate. Women love chocolate.*

NixDogQuest: *I'm supposed to carry a stash of chocolate everywhere I go?*

LadyJHawk: *You said it's a small town. If she's not a bill collector, you're bound to run into her somewhere, right?*

NixDogQuest: *I haven't been getting out much, but it's worth a shot.*

Jae's calendar notification buzzed. She was scheduled to meet with Boone and Ronnie in twenty minutes. She needed to leave now to make it in time.

LadyJHawk: *I've gotta run and start my new job now. TTYL*

NixDogQuest: *I've gotta go sell some puppies and find a lifetime supply of Hershey's anyway. I know you'll do great!*

He ended his message with a superhero emoji. It quenched the last flickering dose of anger. She stashed her phone in her purse. "Well, Seymour, the next time I see Nick face-to-face it will probably be awkward as all get out, but for now I have a job to do. We need to settle in, get to know the place. Like Nick said, it will be great."

Her passenger barked in agreement.

Pulling onto Highway 61, she headed back to Deep Haven and the Crisis Response Team headquarters. In the daylight, the building was even more impressive. The two-story structure sat at the edge of the downtown area with Lake Superior providing an even more impressive background despite the cloudy gray sky. Jae parked and led Seymour into the main bay, where Ronnie and Boone waited. They both wore black CRT shirts with a pine tree and lake logo on the front pocket.

Boone checked his watch. "Right on time, Washington. We'll just wait for a couple of the others and we'll be ready for our ride."

Jae halted. "Ride?"

"You met some of us last night at the VFW, but we thought we would introduce ourselves in a more professional manner and give you a tour of Deep Haven. From the air. You can fly us around, get to know the chopper, the area, and some of your team at the same time."

"That sounds great." Jae left Seymour in the tiled locker room with his food, water, and favorite toys, and a note on the door warning others of his presence and asking them to use the other facilities. She would have to set up a kennel for him later.

When she came back down, Boone had a parka on and Ronnie was bundled up in a black down coat and a bright magenta winter hat.

"You're going to need something warmer. I'll see if I can find something for you later today." Ronnie laughed. "Can't have you freezing your tush off your first day on the job. We want to keep you around."

Jae looked down at her layered look consisting of two long-sleeved shirts and a sweater under her sweatshirt. She was definitely underdressed for this weather and probably looked like a total rookie. This ride would be a good chance to show the team what she could do.

Boone led them over to the separate helicopter bay where more team members waited. He talked as they walked over. "So we met last night and on your online interview. But just to recap, I'm the CRT Coordinator and Operating Manager. You know Ronnie Morales. She's our paramedic and in charge of medical training and volunteers. And here's Peter Dahlquist, fire chief of Deep Haven."

Peter gave her a nod. "Glad to see you again, Jae." Instead of the CRT logo shirt, he wore a navy T-shirt with DHFD in bright yellow letters. And how he stood in the frigid air with bare arms, she couldn't fathom. At least there was a jacket and hat in his massive hands. She was tempted to snatch them from him for herself.

Before she could, Cole Barrett walked up to them in his tan deputy uniform. "Hope I'm not late for the chopper ride."

Boone shook his head. "Right on time. We're just introducing ourselves to Jae and letting her know what our roles are in the CRT."

Cole pointed to his badge. "Deputy Barrett here, as you know. Kyle Hueston, the sheriff, wanted to come, but he's still out on a call so he sent me. Since we have first responder training and can offer support, we go out on a lot of the CRT calls."

Another couple walked up, also wearing CRT logo shirts and carrying winter coats. The woman was young, maybe mid-twenties, a cute strawberry blonde. She laughed at something the guy beside her said. He was tall and muscular and had intense blue eyes. Jae didn't recognize either of them from last night.

"This is more of the crew. Colleen Decker and Jack Stewart are both flight nurses. You'll almost always have one of them in the back of the chopper on medical calls. We also have a team of volunteer EMTs you'll get to know who will often assist Colleen or Jack, but for now let's see what you can do. Here's the helicopter." Boone opened the huge bay doors and moved to the side.

Jae got her first look at her new "office." The Bell 429.

Talk about beautiful. The helicopter sat outside on the helo pad, gleaming bright orange and white in the sun that had decided to peek out from behind the clouds. The same logo from the CRT shirts graced the tail section. The white-and-red-striped rotors stretched out over the sleek body. The familiar excitement buzzed at the idea of flying her.

"What do you think, Jae?" Ronnie asked.

"She's amazing!" Jae opened the door and glanced at the state-of-the-art GPS systems in the cockpit with fully integrated touch screens. Everything smelled brand new. The Bell 429 model was an old friend, familiar and comfortable, but the extra sparkle on this one made Jae grin. "You weren't kidding when you said she was new."

Colleen gave a shaky laugh as she slipped her coat on. "Well, you definitely couldn't fly the old one. She was pretty banged up after the crash."

"Crash?"

Boone nodded. "Yes, there was an accident. Thankfully Colleen and Jack are okay, and the pilot will fully recover, but he's done flying. Thus, the job opening. We really looked for someone with extreme weather flying experience—which you have from your time in Afghanistan and the California mountains—as well as medical training for the times we won't need the chopper. Insurance paid for a brand-new helicopter, and now we have our new pilot. Ready to take her out?"

"Yes, sir." After inspecting the outside of the Bell and releasing the rotors, Jae hopped into the pilot seat, and Boone took the other cockpit seat. The rest of the group piled into the back.

Jae flipped on the battery and all the screens lit up. Bit checks on. Jae flipped on the FMS 1 and checked the gauges and then FMS 2. Rotor breaks checked out. She started the first engine, then the second engine and blades, before forcing the collective down to make sure the rotors responded. They did. In fact, everything responded with the slight movement of her hands. The hydraulics all checked too and restored to normal, and Jae finished her preflight procedures and checked with air traffic control.

Time to see what this baby could do.

With one hand on the cyclic and the other on the collective, Jae brought the helicopter up into a hover.

Boone directed Jae as they lifted in the air. "As you can see, Deep Haven isn't huge. Most of the shops, businesses, and such are concentrated on these blocks downtown and along the highway that runs through the city. There's the school and more houses up on the ridge." He pointed to the open football stands and Husky scoreboard as they flew north. "But as the main emergency response crew on the North Shore, we'll cover a lot of ground outside of Deep Haven. Cook County is over three thousand square miles and we're about a hundred miles from Duluth, which has the nearest trauma center. Our Crisis Response Team has been needed for everything from fires to water rescue and SAR."

As they flew higher, Jae looked beyond the wooded ridge and she could see why. "Wow, we're really out in the sticks, huh?"

"Welcome to the Superior National Forest and the Boundary Water Canoe Area Wilderness."

"It's beautiful." Jae drank in the sights. Trees as far as the eye could see. Lakes, some small, others large, were starting to form ice. Dirt roads and rivers broke up the landscape, cutting through the forests. It was all so different from the urban Galveston and Houston areas and flat plains of the Texas coast she was used to flying over.

And a lot colder.

But there was opportunity for the adventure that she longed for everywhere she looked.

After pointing out a few more landmarks and working their

way up the shore of the Great Lake, Boone twirled his finger in the air. "Why don't we head back to headquarters and we'll get you started on paperwork. And I wouldn't mind a cup of coffee."

Ronnie's voice spoke through the coms. "I'll volunteer for a Java Cup run since I happen to know who brewed the last pot of coffee at the HQ."

"Hey, I made the last pot. I thought you liked my coffee," a deep bass responded.

"Peter, you know I love you, but nobody makes a mocha like my girl Kathy at the Java Cup."

They all laughed at the lighthearted lovers' quarrel. Soon they were back in Deep Haven. Jae landed the Bell, and Jack helped her situate it into the chopper bay with the motorized wheeled tug. By the time they were done, Jae wanted a vat of coffee—not to drink but to soak in. The cold had stolen all feeling in her toes and fingers. She couldn't stop her teeth from chattering.

When she walked into the break room, where the others sipped from mismatched mugs, Cole offered her a fist bump. "Nice flying there, Jae. Welcome to the team."

Boone threw her a CRT T-shirt. "Welcome on board."

Her new team raised their drinks. "Cheers!"

Her hands and feet might be blocks of ice, but the warm welcome made it all worthwhile.

Now, to warm up Nick Dahlquist.

❄

Now this, Nick could get used to. Sunlight reflecting off Lake Superior in the distance. The smell of ice and the sound of boots and broomsticks zipping across the rink. This was what winter was made for. They might not have snow, but they could flood the municipal hockey rink and start their twice-a-week broomball games. There was only so much training he could do without snow, so he might as well enjoy the ice.

"Pete, I'm open!" Nick called across to his cousin.

Peter slapped the ball with his broomstick, sending it toward Nick.

Out of nowhere, Ronnie slid into the ball's path and blocked the shot. "No way, Hot Stuff." She swung her stick back, shooting the ball to her little brother. "Tiago, go for it!"

Ronnie said she'd never played broomball before. It was easier to pick up than hockey. The players didn't wear skates, just their normal winter boots, and they used a ball rather than a puck, but Nick had underestimated Ronnie's athleticism and drive to win. She might be as competitive as he was.

But he wouldn't underestimate her again. "Peter, I'll get the ball, you block your girlfriend. Be ready for the Dahlquist puck, tuck, and roll."

Peter gave him a thumbs-up, and Nick slid over to Tiago. "Dude, I thought you'd never played before. Or your sister."

Tiago grinned but his eyes didn't leave the ball he was dribbling toward his buddy Josh Barrett, who waited near the net that Darek Christiansen was guarding. "We haven't. But I started training for hockey already. And you know how much Ronnie hates to lose."

Nick laughed. "I like to win too. Better watch out, kid." With a quick flick of his wrists, he stole the ball from Tiago and dribbled it away. He glanced over to Peter, whose bright idea at blocking Ronnie was to pick her up and throw her over his shoulders in a fireman's hold while she squealed and laughed. So much for their famous Dahlquist move.

"Over here, Nick!" Kyle Hueston blocked big Seth Turnquist and had a direct shot at the net.

Nick swung and the ball sailed over to Kyle, who easily met it with a swing of his own broomstick and scored one for the team.

Yeah! After high fives from the rest of his teammates—Peter, his sister Abby, Kyle, and Tiger and Darek Christiansen—Nick moved to the center of the rink for the next face-off.

Adrian Vassos from the opposing team met him in the middle. He may have been a trust fund baby from the Twin Cities when he'd arrived last spring, but Adrian had put down some roots in their small town in the last several months as he'd helped his girlfriend, Ella Bradley, kick off her organic cleaning supplies business. And he was becoming a formidable broomball opponent.

"All right, Pretty Boy, let's see what you got."

Adrian narrowed his eyes. "Bring it, Dog Man."

John Christiansen, the ref, blew the whistle and dropped the broomball down to the ice. Nick's stick captured it and he sent it directly over to Abby.

Darek, as their goalie, shouted down the rink. "Tiger is open, Abs."

But Josh and Tiago were relentless. They managed to steal the ball and get a couple of shots off before Darek grabbed it. Peter and Ronnie were doing more flirting than paying attention to the game, so Darek sent the ball to Kyle, who shot it toward Nick. With a wide-swinging arc, the triangular end of Nick's stick met the ball with a satisfying smack and the ball sank into the back of the net Cole Barrett guarded.

Three to two, baby.

"That's how you get 'er done, Cuz." Abby held out her stick for a clap, her blonde braid hanging down from her aqua blue beanie.

"Time-out," Ronnie called. She rushed to the edge of the rink where some of the townspeople and families watched. They were halfway through the game, so it was a good time for a break, and Nick could use some water. He moved to the rink wall where he'd left his water bottle. Abby gulped her own drink down and Peter came over to them.

"Dude, are you playing or flirting? 'Cause you weren't a lot of help back there." Nick punched Peter in the arm.

His cousin shrugged but didn't look very sorry. "You said to block Ronnie. And I've learned a direct challenge only riles her up, so I had to resort to charm and distraction." Peter's gaze followed Ronnie with unmistakable desire.

Nick pushed aside the twinge of envy that rose and focused on how happy he was for Peter. His cousin was a stand-up guy who deserved a good woman.

So what if Nick's chance had passed him by? He glanced over at Ronnie, who was talking to Ingrid Christiansen and someone standing in the dark shade of the bleachers. Ronnie blocked Nick's view of whoever she was talking to as she pulled things out of a box. A long black parka, a down vest, a bright green hat, one of those fur-lined Russian hats with the earflaps. Yikes. He wouldn't miss anybody in that.

"Hey, did you sell any puppies?" Peter asked. "I saw your flyer at the cafe this morning."

"Yeah, I finally sold two pups just before I got here. The Symanski boys want to start skijoring and doing a little dog sledding, so they bought a pair, one for each boy."

Abby packed her water bottle away. "I'm not sure how you let any of those puppies go. They're so cute."

"I really wanted to keep a few from this litter, but I need the money more. But I do make sure they go to good homes. Alaskan huskies have a lot of energy, so they need people and families that will spend time with them and not just leave them chained up in the backyard all day long."

Peter twirled his broomstick on the ice. "Tell me about it. Blue outgrew the apartment so she's boarding with me. Ronnie and I take turns during the day running with her. And Tiago spends any free time he has with her too. She's never tired though. She's like the Energizer Bunny."

"That's a sled dog for you. You should have Tiago and Blue

come out with my team once we get some snow. We can hook her up behind my sled and she can start training."

"Tiago would love that."

"What would Tiago love?" Ronnie asked as she came up to them with the stranger she had been talking to earlier. But now the short woman—at least, with the long, silky dark hair blowing in the wind, Nick assumed it was a woman—wore the black parka, the neon hat, an ugly brown scarf, and pink-tinted ski goggles. There wasn't a facial feature to be seen.

And yet, she kinda seemed familiar.

Peter clapped Nick on the back. "Nick here is offering to help Tiago train Blue to run with his team."

Ronnie's face lit up. "He would love that." Then she and Abby started talking dogs.

Nick didn't catch any of their conversation. He was still staring at the woman, trying to figure out why it seemed like he should know her. He finally stuck out his hand toward her. "Hey, I'm Nick. I don't think we've met."

"Oh, I'm sorry. I should be introducing you to everyone," Ronnie said to her bundled-up companion. "Nick, this is Jae Washington. She's our new chopper pilot with the CRT. Jae, you know Peter, and this is his younger sister Abby—she's up from the Twin Cities for a little vacay—and this is their cousin Nick."

"Hi." A muffled voice sounded through the scarf.

Her voice even sounded familiar.

Cole slid over to their group. "Hey, Megan has some wedding emergency she needs help with. Can you guys bring Josh home later? He really wants to stay and finish the game."

Peter nodded. "Of course."

"Thanks." Cole rushed off.

Ronnie sighed. "Wait a minute. That means the game is done unless we get someone to replace our goalie."

"I can do it," Jae said.

They all looked at the petite woman resembling a mini

version of the Michelin man. How would she move with all the puffy layers?

But having a not-so-nimble goalie on the opposite team wasn't necessarily a bad thing. Right?

Ronnie adjusted her own hat, pulling it down over her ears. "Have you ever played before?" she asked the newcomer.

"No, but it looks like hockey. I would just take Cole's place as goalie and stop the ball from going into the net, right?"

"Then what are we waiting for?" Abby asked. "Let's play some broomball."

The teams spread out into their respective positions. John held the ball up while Nick and Adrian faced off again.

"You're going down, Dahlquist," Adrian said with a friendly grin on his face.

"No way, Vassos. In fact, maybe we should have a little wager going on. Losers take a polar plunge in the bay."

"You're on."

John Christiansen's shrill whistle stopped the banter. He dropped the ball, and Adrian got the first contact. But Nick was able to block his shot to Ronnie and send it instead to Peter, who apparently had decided to take the game a little more seriously and now had eyes only for the little orange ball he moved into enemy territory.

Josh and Tiago were on him in a moment, like buzzing flies on meat and just as relentless. Adrian tried to move in on Nick's assist, but Abby kept him busy. All Nick could hear was the clash of the stick handles and Peter's laugh. One of the boys managed to get control of the ball and sent it to Seth, who shot it over to Adrian.

Nick and Ronnie raced toward him. Nick couldn't get physical with a woman on the ice, but Ronnie must not have the same hesitation. She gave him a sharp elbow to the ribs as they crossed the center line. "I'm here, Vassos!"

Adrian sent the ball to Ronnie, but Tiger Christiansen

blocked the pass and it bounced over the ice to Nick. Everyone was covered, so he moved it back down toward the goal, waiting for Peter or Kyle to slip free of their opponents. Soon Nick faced down the bundled-up goalie, Jae, all alone. He couldn't see any of her face, but she was crouched and ready to pounce on any shot he made. She might be short and wrapped up like a mummy, but something told Nick not to hold back and underestimate her like he had Ronnie.

Nick pulled his stick back to make the shot when someone slammed into his back and another stick cracked across his shin and sent him flying into the net.

He landed on Jae with a whoosh of air puffing out of her coat. Through the pink-tinted goggles, he could see her wide eyes. Wow, she was little. And the more he tried to quickly get off her, the more he became tangled up in the net. They probably looked like those fake sumo wrestlers in the huge, padded suits trying to get up. It took the whole team to untangle and lift him off the poor woman and to get her back to standing with all her puffy layers.

As soon as they were both back on their feet, he rushed over to her. "I'm so sorry, Jae. Are you okay?"

She took off her hat and goggles and rubbed the back of her head, but shooed away Ronnie, who tried to inspect her for injury. "Yeah, don't worry about me. I'm fine. I'm tougher than I look."

Nick froze. Wait a minute. Those eyes. That hair. That voice. The bill collector-slash-tourist.

Jae was the woman he'd scared away this morning.

"I think you should let me check out your pupil dilation." Ronnie reached for Jae again and pulled her over to the side of the rink.

"Nick, are you okay?" Abby looked at him with the same concern Ronnie had looked at Jae. "Did you knock your head on the ice too?"

"Huh?"

"Your head. Are you okay? You're standing there like an ice sculpture with your mouth wide open."

"I'm fine. Really." He gave a tremulous smile to Abby. He *was* fine, but he might still be in shock. He'd never expected to see the woman who'd come unannounced to his cabin again. But not only was she not a bill collector or a random tourist or a stalker, she was new in town—had come to Deep Haven for a job.

And what a welcome he'd given. He had been rude to her this morning and now had plowed her over like a bulldozer. He groaned thinking of all he'd said to her this morning. What a jerk.

He had to make this right.

While the others spread out, declaring the game over for the night, Nick ran after Jae. "Hey, Jae, can I talk to you for a minute?"

She looked up at him with raised eyebrows but didn't say anything.

"I'm so sorry."

She shrugged. "You said that already. Don't worry. I'm fine." The corners of her lips lifted in a tight smile.

"No, I mean, yeah—" Oh, he was botching this big time. But as he looked into her deep brown eyes, he forgot all his words. He wasn't kidding earlier when he told LadyJHawk that the woman was cute. In fact, she was downright stunning.

But now, she looked back at him with suspicion or confusion. "You were saying..."

Right. Nick shook himself. "Do you want chocolate?"

"Chocolate?"

Peter snickered as he packed his stuff up a few feet away.

But Nick didn't care. And suddenly, his thoughts came into focus. "I'm really sorry. Not just about falling on top of you, but about this morning. I thought you were someone else, and I had a lot going on, but I shouldn't have brushed you off like I did."

"Oh." A slight pink blush bloomed across Jae's milky white cheeks. Her gaze fell. "I, uh, I should've told you who I was or called first. I was hoping I could board my dog with you, but so far he's been okay at the HQ, so I'll just keep him with me." She fiddled with the hat in her hands.

"How about if I make it up to you? Can I buy you a cup of hot cocoa or coffee? You look cold."

She finally made eye contact again. And wow, if it didn't take his breath away like the old cliche said. "I am. I don't know how you guys live here in this frigid weather."

Nick pounded his chest. "We have hearty Scandinavian blood to keep us warm. And it's not even technically winter. Just wait until the subzero temps of January."

She shuddered. "I can't imagine."

"Before you freeze anymore, how about that hot beverage? I insist. I'll show you that it's not all cold and ice in the north woods."

Her smile widened. "A hot beverage sounds nice, but actually I'm kinda craving pie. Know where I can get some?"

"There just so happens to be a little bistro that serves the best pie in town, and I know the owners. What do you say we go and help you thaw out a bit?"

Would the woman he'd scared away earlier want anything to do with him at this point? He twirled his stick nervously while he waited for her answer.

"Sounds good. Lead the way."

Yes! This might be more fun than broomball.

CHAPTER 4

*T*he guy holding the door for her to the Trailside Bistro was the Nick that Jae always felt like she was chatting with online. This was NixDogQuest.

But she needed to remember that, for all he knew, they'd just met.

They chose a front corner table by a window overlooking the marina and the bay. He took her coat and hung it on the back of her chair before sitting in his own chair. The pine siding on the walls was decorated with sepia-toned pictures of pioneers and early settlers, a big Swedish flag, and pairs of old snowshoes and skis attached to the wall.

"Wow, this is cool. I wonder how old those beams are?" Jae asked as she followed the length of the thick logs overhead.

"They're over a hundred years old. This building was originally a town hall." Nick nodded to the older guy behind the lunch counter.

"Really? So you know the history of this place?"

"I'm kinda *related* to the history of this place."

"Oh yeah, you said you knew the owners." Jae scanned the

opposite wall. Was that a picture of Nick with Jimmy Fallon? Jae pointed to it. "And that?"

Nick waved it off with a shrug. "That's nothing."

"That's you! Right? You met Jimmy Fallon? That's definitely something."

"It wasn't a big deal. He interviewed me and a few other mushers when we did a North Pole expedition. But he only had me come because I had a litter of puppies at the time and he wanted to bring them on the show."

Jae looked around and saw other newspaper articles featuring Nick.

Deep Haven Man Goes on Arctic Expedition

Dahlquist Qualifies for Iditarod

Local Competes in the Yukon Quest

"Nicky? What are you doing here tonight?" A woman who had to be Nick's mother with the same bright blue eyes and dark brown hair wiped her hands on a towel as she approached the table. She bent over and kissed his cheek.

"Hey, Ma."

"And who do we have here?" His mother beamed brightly at Jae.

"This is Jae Washington. She's new to town, working as the helicopter pilot with the CRT. Jae, this is my mom, Trudy."

"Nice to meet ya, Jae." Her Minnesotan accent was strong. "What can we get you tonight?"

Nick nodded to an older woman with spiky blonde hair filling coffee at a booth along the side wall. "Mom, you don't have to serve us. Dina can take our orders. Or better yet"—he stood up—"I can."

"Oh no you don't, mister." Nick's mom pushed him back down. "You stay here and enjoy your company. What about the Tuesday night special? It's your favorite. You want some Swedish meatballs?"

"We came for pie and coffee." A cute blush stained Nick's cheeks.

His mom turned to Jae. "How hungry are you, sweetie? Would you like to try the Tuesday special?"

"The meatballs sound intriguing. What makes them Swedish?"

"You've never had Swedish meatballs?" Nick and his mom spoke simultaneously.

Jae shook her head. "Noooo."

"Well, then it's settled." Trudy tossed the towel onto her shoulder. "We'll get you a plate of the Swedish meatballs out here in a jiffy." She left for the kitchen just as Dina set glasses of water in front of them.

Once they were alone again, Jae took a sip of her water. But as she looked into Nick's eyes, it was hard to swallow. His baby blues really did sparkle. It wasn't a trick of the screen or the sunlight. The fine lines at the corners of them fanned out, giving him a playful and mischievous smirk. As handsome as he was, she was surprised Nick didn't have more fans-turned-stalker stories. She finally managed to swallow her sip. "Your mom seems nice. Is she the owner you said you knew?"

"Yup. She and my dad run the bistro. It's part of the Dahlquist empire. My dad and his siblings each own a Deep Haven restaurant."

"How many restaurants is that?"

"Five. Well, one burned down and we're still trying to find a place to rebuild it, so four."

"Your whole family is in the restaurant business? You must be a great cook then."

The server came back to the table with silverware wrapped in napkins at that moment. "Nick? Cook?" She laughed so hard she leaned on the table for a second to catch her balance. "That's a good one. Not Smoky, here. We don't let him near the kitchen." She left as quickly as she'd come to seat another couple who walked in the door.

"What was that about?" Jae asked.

Nick's cheeks turned an even brighter red this time. Not that it detracted from his looks at all. It only made his eyes bluer. "I, uh, tried to help man the grill once when I was twelve. Let's just say it didn't go well."

"You can't get off the hook that easily. I need to hear this."

"Don't you think I've embarrassed myself enough today?"

Jae laughed. "You are supposed to be making up for this morning. I think it's completely fair. So spit it out. What did you do?"

He huffed, blowing a strand of his dark hair off his forehead, which made him look sheepish and charming all at the same time. "I had this great idea to make a Swedish meatball hamburger, but the grill was too hot when I added the cream sauce, and somehow I caught the whole stove on fire. Then I threw a pitcher of water on it."

"Oh no!"

"Oh yes. Which of course, only made it worse. And then, I panicked. It was like my feet were frozen to the spot. I couldn't move. I tried to yell for help but I couldn't make a sound."

"Then what?"

"Thankfully Antonio came back, grabbed the extinguisher, and put out the fire before it got too far out of control. But there was a lot of smoke and fire damage in the kitchen and we had to shut down for a few weeks to remodel. And now you can see why I don't cook anymore."

"Not at all?"

"Not for humans." He tried to laugh it off, but it obviously bothered him to some degree. "And now my poor parents are left without anyone to pass the bistro on to since it's our family legacy, but I can't be trusted in the kitchen."

"Oh, because you're an only child."

He cocked his head to the side. "Yeah. How did you know that?"

Jae's mind blanked. She couldn't very well say because they'd talked about it in their online chats. It was one of the things they had bonded on. She even called him Han Solo because of it. She fiddled with the napkin in her lap. "Uh, I must've heard Ronnie or Peter say something like that."

"Sure. So, now you've heard all about my embarrassing childhood and why I eat here a lot. What about you? Do you cook?"

"Yeah, I love to cook. My mom taught me a lot of traditional Korean recipes. And everywhere we traveled as I was growing up, we tried to learn some of the local cuisine."

"You moved around a lot?"

"All over the place."

"Do you have brothers and sisters?"

She shook her head. "No. My parents weren't ever able to have more kids. But I always used to imagine I had a bunch of siblings. I want to have a huge family someday."

Nick opened his mouth to respond, but his mother approached with two steaming plates. She set them down in front of them. "Now you two enjoy your dinner, but save room for dessert. I have fresh apple and pumpkin pie today—and I know apple is your favorite, Nicky." She looked down at her son with a mix of motherly love and pride that shot a pang of homesickness through Jae.

Nick didn't know how lucky he was to have a sweet hometown like Deep Haven, surrounded by family and friends. A place where he truly belonged. The kind of place she was still looking for. Yeah, she had a big passel of cousins, but they'd never hit it off. Jae was always an outsider.

But before she started crying into her meatballs, she breathed deep and looked down at her plate. A fluffy mound of mashed potatoes and five huge meatballs next to it were smothered in a creamy white sauce. Next to that were green beans with a pat of butter on top melting, a dinner roll, and a small, lumpy pile of a red jelly-like substance.

She whispered across the table, "What is this red stuff?"

"That's lingonberry jelly. Mom has it brought in from Sweden. She sells it here too. It's kind of like cranberry or a red currant jelly. The tartness pairs well with the meat and cream sauce. Try it."

Jae cut into one of the meatballs, dragged it through the potatoes and sauce and added a little dollop of the bright red jelly. The flavors burst on her tongue at first bite. Nick was right. The sweet-tart jelly cut through the smooth cream and buttery meat. "Mmm. If this is how Swedes do meatballs, I need to try more Swedish cooking. But with all this butter and cream, how are you so fit?"

And man alive, he was fit. His tight Henley accented well-formed biceps and a chiseled torso and shoulders. It was hard to look away.

He laughed. "I'm a musher. I run with my dogs while we sled. Otherwise, believe me, as often as I eat here, I would be in big trouble."

"How did you get into dogsledding?"

"I've always loved being outside, especially in winter. But after a really bad snowmobile accident when I was in high school, I wasn't sure I ever wanted to be out in the woods again. And this guy Ed—he's a neighbor of mine—had sled dogs and he said he needed help at a local race, someone to stay with any dogs that were injured, to prep for the trail, and keep track of supplies. I wanted to help. He taught me all about the sport and I fell in love with it. Being out in the woods with the pack helped me find some peace again, helped me heal. There's nothing like it. Pristine white snow, crisp air. Just man and nature. And the dogs of course."

Passion lit in his eyes and Jae fell for him a little bit more. As much as she'd thought she knew Nick, there was more to discover. And seeing him face-to-face only enhanced her feelings for the man. "And what do you do when you're not mushing?"

"Training for sledding, posting vlogs about sledding, or breeding dogs for sledding. Pretty much, my life revolves around it. It's a full-time job if you want to make a living at the sport."

"And you do? Make a living from it?"

Nick's smile fell. "Well, for the most part. I have some sponsors but lost a big one last year. So, it's been a little rough going, but I'm sure I'll get back on my feet."

"Rough?"

"Let's just say I eat here a lot because the price is right." He winked.

Oh yeah. He was worried about a debt collector coming around. "Does dogsledding cost a lot?"

"It's not a cheap sport. The equipment is very specialized and spendy. The races that are out of state mean travel expenses. And boarding and feeding a team of dogs takes a lot. But I've found some ways to cut costs."

"Like what?"

"I make my own dog food for one. I'll use fresh vegetables and meat that are fine for consumption but don't look pretty enough for the restaurants to use, so I get it at a discount. Dogs don't care what it looks like. And some of the hunters will bring me wild game if they don't need it. I even use fish from the lake out there if there's a surplus."

"So you *do* cook."

"Only for the dogs. There's no way you want me cooking for people. For now I need to watch every penny, so cooking for the pack helps. But it won't be so tight for long. I'll do short dogsled rides for tourists once we get snow. And I'm sure I'll get some more sponsors. Especially after the Mush Puppies race in a few weeks."

"Is that a big race?"

"It's only a hundred miles from Silver Bay to Deep Haven and then back again. Nothing like the Yukon Quest or Iditarod in Alaska. Those races are a thousand miles long. But at the Mush Puppies race, there will be a lot of potential sponsors watching because it's the first race of the season. It's local so it won't cost much to run. And if I can get a few companies on board with my team and win a little prize money, I'll be set to make up for that big dog food company sponsor I lost."

"So it's not a long race, but it is important."

"It is. I...I really need this one."

There was no mistaking the drive and maybe a hint of desperation in his voice.

"I'm sure you'll do great."

"Thanks. I think we'll do fine." He looked out the window where the fading sunlight had disappeared. "I could really use some snow, though."

A tall man with dark blond hair and a serious visage came to the table with slices of pie. "Your mom sent some pie out for you." His deep voice was a little gruff, but he seemed more awkward than aggressive.

Nick turned. "Dad. Thanks. Uh, you should meet Jae. She's new to Deep Haven. Jae, this is my dad, Greg."

Greg Dahlquist didn't have the warm vivaciousness Nick and his mother shared, but he had kind eyes. He gave her a curt nod with a shy smile. "Nice to meet you. Hope you enjoy the pie. My Trudy makes the best."

"Nice to meet you too."

He scurried once again to the kitchen.

Nick focused back on her, his gaze capturing her attention once more. "Now, enough about me. What do you think of Deep Haven so far?"

Jae took a bite of the pumpkin pie. The flaky crust crumbled in her mouth. The perfect balance of pumpkin, nutmeg, and cinnamon tasted even better than Mimi's Thanksgiving classic. "Mmm. This is good." She took another bite and sipped the coffee that had appeared at some point. "And Deep Haven so far, has been…interesting. I think I'm gonna like it here."

And, at this rate, it wouldn't be long until she could tell him the truth. And then she'd really be living happily ever after.

❄

Nick couldn't articulate what it was about Jae, but she seemed so familiar as she sat across from him in the bistro while they finished their pie and coffee. Not her face or mannerisms so much. He definitely would've remembered meeting a gorgeous woman like her. Maybe it was just that he couldn't understand how, in such a short time, she fit into the familiar surroundings like she'd always been here. The soft lights of the restaurant reflected in her intelligent brown eyes. The smell of cinnamon, apple, and pumpkin lured him into a cozy contentment he couldn't remember experiencing in a long time.

He was reluctant for the night to end as she stood to burrow back into her long black parka.

He jumped out of his chair to help her with her coat. "Let me give you a ride to the headquarters."

"It's not far. I can walk from here."

"Yeah, but it's cold. Let me drive you the whopping three blocks to see you back safely."

She plopped the glow-in-the-dark hat on her head. It was so big that it fell down over her forehead at an angle, almost covering her right eye. "You don't think I can handle the three blocks in the dark on my own?"

Nick held up his hands in surrender. "Oh, I know you can. You could light the way with that hat from here. They can probably see it from space."

She laughed.

And like a new favorite song, he couldn't get enough.

Seriously, how was this happening so fast? He didn't remember feeling like this ever. Even with Vivie.

"I'm just trying to be a gentleman. My mom will be watching as we go, so if you let me drive you, you will save me so much grief."

"All right, you can drive me. I'm sure Seymour will be missing me anyway, so the faster I get back, the better."

"Seymour?" Who was Seymour? And what was this swift sensation rising up inside? It was as bitter as the last cooled sip of coffee he'd swallowed.

"Seymour is my dog. The one I mentioned before."

Right. A dog. The sensation quickly dissipated. She was a dog person. Even better. "You should probably introduce me to him then. I'm a little bit of a dog fanatic."

She met his grin with a shy one of her own and the most delicious-looking hint of pink stealing over her cheeks. "All right."

After a goodbye to Dina and his parents, they walked out to his truck parked on the street. When he opened the passenger door for Jae, she paused. "What should I do with that?"

A tinfoil-wrapped dish and a quart jar of soup lay in the seat. Good grief. It was like people couldn't let him forget. Nick tried to laugh it off. "Oh, that. I think my mom is afraid I'll starve to the point of trying to cook again, so she and her friends always leave food for me if they see my truck. I should start locking it when I'm in town. I'll just set it down by your feet if that's okay."

"If I keep *my* door unlocked, will I get casseroles too?"

"Casserole? You mean hot dish."

"Huh? What is a hot dish?"

"That's what we Minnesotans call casseroles. There's a million variations of hot dish. My favorite is the Tater Tot Hot

Dish. My Aunt Barb, Peter's mom, makes a great one. She always gives me a whole pan on the last Monday of the month."

"That sounds like a pretty sweet deal. You'll have to let me try a bite. I've never had a hot dish."

Another meal shared with Jae Washington? He liked the sound of that.

Within minutes, they were parked again and Jae was unlocking the side door to the Crisis Response Team HQ. "Seymour? Did you miss me?"

A bark echoed in the cavernous bay.

"Hey, boy. Come meet Nick." Jae unlocked the indoor kennel and a beautiful dark brown and black Belgian Malinois licked her face.

He trotted over to Nick, sniffed his outstretched hand, and made a few turns before okaying him to come any closer to his owner. He was protective. Attentive.

Good. A beautiful woman like Jae should be protected. Once Seymour had accepted him, Nick knelt and scratched under the camouflage collar. "Nice to meet ya, Seymour. You look like you take good care of Jae." He held up a hand in oath. "I promise, my intentions are honorable."

She laughed again.

Mission accomplished.

"He does take care of me, just as much as I take care of him. And he probably needs a walk too."

"Let's give him one. Does he need a leash?"

Jae shook her head. "No, he's very well trained. He won't stray far." She pointed to the door they'd just walked through. "Seymour, let's go for a walk." The dog's ears perked and he ran to the door and sat at rigid attention, waiting for them to join him. Jae ordered him to stay even when she opened the door. She beckoned Nick to join her. They walked out a few steps and though Seymour whined a little, he stayed still where she left him. Eventually she relented. "Come."

At the simple command, he leapt to his feet and stayed on her heels as they walked toward the bay.

"Wow. If my dogs get loose, they'll run for miles." He knelt and gave Seymour another pat. "Someone spent a lot of time training you."

A sad sort of smile crossed Jae's face as she looked down at her dog. "Yes. My boyfriend was an Army Ranger and Seymour's handler."

"Boyfriend?" The icy bitter feeling rose up again. She was taken too? How had he missed that? They stepped outside of the shelter of the building and back into the brutal November wind.

Jae gave Seymour another command. He stayed right by her side as they walked to the shoreline. Then he waited until she nodded. "Go ahead." It was like she cut the imaginary leash. He rushed into the water and barked at the waves. He found a stick and happily picked it up and chewed on it. Nick buried his fists in his vest pockets and waited for Jae to answer his barely spoken question. Her whole body had gone stiff as she watched Seymour play.

Eventually she let out a long sigh and kept her eyes fixed on the dog and the water. "Matteo and I met while I was in the Army. Dated for three years. He was KIA." They walked a little farther. "Seymour was wounded too and, after he healed physically, he wasn't taking to any other handler so the Army retired him. Matt had earlier asked for permission to adopt Seymour when his career was done and I was listed as a next of kin. So they offered to let me adopt him instead. I was already done with my time in the Army by then, so Seymour came to me and we both adjusted to civilian life in Texas and a year in Northern California flying choppers for SAR teams."

Nick's clenched fists released. "Jae, I'm so sorry."

She shrugged. "It's been a couple years. We're okay...and ready for a new life. I really think this will be a good place for us."

Nick gestured to the CRT building. "Yeah, I mean who wouldn't want to live there? It has cozy written all over it."

Jae laughed. "Okay, so maybe not the CRT headquarters itself, but Deep Haven. It seems like a great town. And it will be even better when we find our own place."

"It *is* a great town. I think you'll fit in just fine."

Sleet started falling from the sky. Jae threw the stick to Seymour a couple of times for him to fetch. But as the cold, wet precipitation intensified, they walked back into the building. Nick wandered over to the two-story climbing wall installed at the back.

"Now that looks like fun."

Jae joined him. "Do you climb?"

"Oh yeah. Once it gets a little colder, I like to ice climb. Cascade Falls will be frozen soon. And the Nightfall ice is spectacular. You should try it."

"With all your wilderness expertise, why aren't you on the CRT?"

A humorless laugh escaped. "Nah. You don't want me trying to rescue anyone. I do not think well in a crisis."

"What do you mean?"

"Like that kitchen fire. I just freeze up. My mind goes blank." He nudged her arm and smirked. "So I let the real heroes like you do the dangerous stuff."

"I don't know. Ice climbing up frozen waterfalls sounds dangerous."

He discarded his playful tone. "It can be if you don't have the right equipment or training. There are no second chances in nature, so I'm always very particular about those things when I climb or when I'm teaching others. I do wilderness survival training too. So I'm kinda like preventative care. If I do my job right, you won't have to rescue people."

"Nice." She looked up at him with something resembling admiration.

And, yeah, it was nice. He'd never before felt such an instant connection with someone.

Seymour came and sat at Jae's feet as if to say it was time for Nick to leave so he could have all her attention again.

Nick bent down to pet him. "I should head home and let you sleep."

"Thanks for dinner and pie. It hit the spot."

"Yeah, we should do it again sometime."

What was he saying? This was sounding a lot like a date. Not that he minded. But he'd just met the woman. He didn't need to scare her—

"I'd like that."

Okay, then. Maybe he wasn't the only one feeling the connection. "Good to know. I'll see you around."

Nick let himself out into the cold, dark night. The frost and sleet had accumulated on his windshield and stung his ears and neck, but he didn't mind. His feet felt lighter than they had in a long time as he took care of the dogs for the night. With the sleet turning to snow, they were ready to get into their dog shelters. It would be a nice night for a fire.

Nick stoked the fire in the fireplace and settled onto his couch with his laptop. He opened up his messaging app, eager to give LadyJHawk an update on his crazy day. She'd get a kick out of it. Plus he wanted to hear how her new job was going even if she wouldn't share the particulars of what she did. His night was always better after chatting with LadyJHawk.

NixDogQuest: *I did it. I actually ran into the tourist. I didn't have chocolate, but I think I did alright and made up for my blunder this morning.*

LadyJHawk: *Oh? How?*

NixDogQuest: *Seems like pumpkin pie works just as well. And I was completely wrong about her being a random tourist or bill collector. She's actually moving here. I'll probably see her around a lot. So*

I'm glad to make things right. How about you? How was your first day?

LadyJHawk: *You know, it turned out okay. Rocky start, but it's a great place.*

NixDogQuest: *So are you glad you went for it? The new adventure?*

LadyJHawk: *100% yes.*

LadyJHawk: *And glad you made things right with your new neighbor. Try not to scare her away again. ;)*

A gust of wind and snow rattled the windowpane, breaking Nick's concentration. Picturing Jae and Seymour in that cold cavernous headquarters building worried him.

NixDogQuest: *I promise I won't scare her away but I can't vouch for the winter. I hope she doesn't freeze to death.*

LadyJHawk: *Give her a chance. She might be tougher than you think.*

CHAPTER 5

*I*t has still been pretty early when Nick had dropped Jae off after dinner. But between the extreme emotions of the day and learning a new town, Jae was ready for an early bedtime. Not that it seemed early with the sun setting before five o'clock. After warming up with a hot shower and bundling back up in her warmest pajamas, she lay down and fell asleep.

Sleep that was interrupted a couple hours later by a loud alarm.

The emergency signal blared from her phone and out in the bay. Jae quickly dressed as the dispatcher called over the speaker for medical personnel to respond to an accident on some county road.

Jae threw her hair back in a bun and grabbed her brand new orange CRT coat with the pine and lake logo on the back that someone had left on her bunk earlier. She ran downstairs and settled Seymour into his temporary kennel in the bay. Wrapping him in his anti-anxiety vest, she secured it snuggly around him. Despite the rumble and noise of the trucks someone was starting, he lay down with his favorite stuffed Chewbacca toy and seemed to be handling it all like a champ.

Boone stood in the middle of the bay, marking things off on a clipboard.

"How did you get here so fast?" Jae asked, still blinking the sleep out of her eyes.

Boone looked up from his board. "I was already here, working in the office." He checked his watch. "It's not that late. You ready to jump in?"

She nodded, nerves tingling in her middle.

"Good, because this is a bad one. Sounds like a semi truck slid into a minivan and pushed it off the road. I want you to chopper in as many crew members as you can. We need to make sure you have Ronnie and Colleen and Jack for sure. The ambulance and fire trucks will take longer to get there. Go ahead and start the helo."

Before Jae moved, Ronnie, Peter, and another guy resembling Ryan Gosling with blond curly hair and blue eyes rushed in. Peter shook the snow from his head. "Boone, these roads are glare ice under snow."

Ronnie pointed to the nearest rig. "I should get going with an ambulance. It's going to take us awhile to get to the scene."

Boone shook his head. "Let Peter and Jensen drive it. You and Colleen and any other support crew that come in the next few minutes can fly with Jae. She'll get there quickest. I'll need you to report back as soon as you reach the scene." He turned to Jae. "Go get the chopper ready and stand by."

Jae and Ronnie ran to the helicopter bay. Ronnie smashed the button to raise the big bay doors. Outside, snow came down. Not in the pretty fat snowflakes that swirled around like a dance but in hard, driving sheets taking on the red and blue glow of the ambulance's and fire truck's flashing lights in the next building.

Ronnie grabbed a shovel and started creating a path while

Jae concentrated on checking wind and weather stats and lifting the Bell 429 with the wheeled tug that rested under the helicopter's belly. Once the skids were off the ground, she used the motorized controller to roll the chopper out of the hangar and onto the landing pad outside the bay doors. When it was set, she lowered the helicopter back to the ground, maneuvered the tug out from under it, and stashed it back in the building.

Sirens screamed and lights flashed as one of the ambulances slid out onto the icy roads. Colleen, Cole, Jack, and Darek—all carrying gear—jumped into the helicopter. Jae did her inspection, hopped up into the cockpit, and said a prayer. She slipped on her helmet with the built in com-links.

Ronnie sat next to her. "We have four in the back. Let's go."

Jae nodded and started her preflight check while Ronnie called everything in to Boone. According to the weather tracker, the snow was easing up. The cloud ceiling wasn't great, but she'd flown in worse. Jae blocked all other voices and doubts running through her mind and focused only on flying. The nerves were silenced. The questions muted. With her feet on the antitorque pedals and hands on the cyclic and the collective, she knew what to do.

She fought the wind as they flew to the accident site. From up in the air, with the help of the spotlight, Jae could see a semi truck jackknifed and blocking the road. It was impossible to see much through the branches of the trees below, but there were glimpses of the minivan. As Jae lowered the helicopter onto the rural two-lane highway, the only clearing in the heavily forested area for miles around, the same adrenaline rush spiked. As soon as she touched down, Colleen hopped out, slipping and sliding around the jackknifed truck toward the minivan hanging over the edge of the gully.

Jae called into the coms. "Boone, we're on site."

His voice came through with static. "Give me a sit rep."

"I'm shutting down the helo and I'll let you know ASAP what we're looking at. How far out is the ambulance?"

Peter's voice answered back. "We're still a ways out. With all this ice, the rig is all over the place."

"Stay safe, Peter. Jae, go see what we're working with and report back," Boone said.

"Yes, sir." She went through the shutdown procedures, but the way the snow was accumulating and the temps were dropping, she needed to keep the engines running. Jae ran out into the blinding snow and slid over to the side of the road where Ronnie, Colleen, and the others gathered.

"—gotta get them out of there," Cole finished saying. He wrapped a tow rope around a tree trunk while Jack helped Ronnie and Colleen strap into their harnesses. Through the eerie sound of the wind, Jae could hear a cry. A child's cry.

"What's going on? What can I do?" Jae looked over the edge of the road. The silver minivan balanced at the brink of a gully, back wheels hanging over thin air. The front wheels caught on tree roots lining the lip of the ravine. Barely. The van teetered. The cry from inside intensified. From where she stood on the road, with airbags filling the windshield, Jae couldn't see inside the van. The sliding door behind the driver was crushed inward.

Ronnie was now strapped and her harness clipped to the rope. "Belay on."

Cole called out, though. "Ronnie, don't touch the van until I can secure it."

"Then hurry up!" She lowered herself next to the van without touching it.

Colleen turned to Jae as she finished strapping her harness. "Jae, check out the truck driver. Any word on when the others will get here?"

"Peter said they're moving as fast as they can but it's slow going. They're still pretty far out."

Colleen gave a curt nod and clipped into a line. Like a well-oiled machine, Colleen, Jack, and Darek worked silently in the driving snow, getting ready to rappel down to the van. Cole looped the tow strap around the front axle and strapped it back to the thick tree trunk next to the road.

"Hey, lady, can you help me?" A big man with a canvas jacket held his hand up to his bleeding forehead.

Jae tore her attention away from the side of the road and slid over to him, the snow pelting her face. "Come over to the chopper and we'll get you looked at."

In the back of the helo, Jae took the man's vitals. A big guy with a full beard and bald head, he was a little pale. "What's your name?"

"Bob Olson," he said, his voice shaky. Hard saying if it was the cold or the adrenaline.

"Okay, Bob, looks like you've got a cut on your forehead there. Can you tell me what happened? Does anything else hurt?"

"I...couldn't stop. I mean, I came as slow as I could, but the downward grade and the ice—I just couldn't stop in time."

"Did you hit your head?"

He nodded and raised a hand to the blood dripping down the side of his face. Jae pressed a piece of gauze to it and had him hold it there while she checked his pupil dilation, pulse, and breathing. Everything normal.

"Did you black out at all?"

A pained look flashed across Bob's face. "No. I remember everything."

Poor guy. She quickly bandaged up the cut. "Stay in the helicopter for now. Here's some water. Sip it slowly. I'll be back, Bob."

"Jae, I need an update. What's going on?" Boone's voice called over the coms.

Jae grabbed the radio, pressed the button to talk. "The minivan had to be secured first. Unknown number of patients.

The truck driver has minor injuries. I'll go see if they know more." Jae jumped out and slipped and slid over to the others through the snow that was quickly piling onto the road. Jack and Darek held lines for Colleen and Ronnie, while Cole kept an eye on the tow strap.

"What's the report?" Jae asked as the wind did its best to steal her breath away.

Darek's voice strained as he held tightly to Ronnie's belay rope. "Ronnie got the passenger-side door open. Looks like two adults in front—both unconscious—and three kids in back. One of the kids is unconscious too. We need more guys to get them out in order to treat them."

Jae relayed the information to Boone. Peter called in too. He and Jensen were turning onto Moose Valley Road. Only five minutes out now.

Soon the ambulance pulled up. It fishtailed and slid across the road, landing in a snowdrift. Jae ran over. The tires spun, kicking up snow, but not moving the vehicle. The Ryan Gosling look-alike—who must be Jensen Atwood—jumped out the passenger side. He and Jae tried pushing from the one back corner not blocked by tree trunks, but the ambulance was lodged tight in the snowbank.

"We'll have to deal with this later. What's going on here?" Jensen yelled over the wind. Peter slammed the door and joined them as they moved toward the others.

"They've got the van stabilized," Jae said, "but there are five passengers, three unconscious, that we need to get out. It's steep and super slippery, though."

"Finally," Cole said when they reached him. "Come on, you two, we need help. Grab a harness."

Jae spoke up. "Maybe I should go down. I'll fit in the van."

Cole shook his head. "It's not getting into the van that's the problem. It's getting the patients out and up here. We need more brawn."

Which clearly wasn't her. Jae grunted, but nodded her understanding.

Peter prowled the edge of the road, studying the van below. He turned to her. "Call Boone and tell him we'll need more help. Ask him to call the Silver Bay first responders and firefighters. A few of my firefighters will be coming up any minute. Have them bring me ropes and straps. We'll need a couple more strong backs and the basket stretcher to get these people out."

A child's scream rent the air.

"We need help. Now!" Ronnie yelled up to them.

Jensen and Peter scrambled to pull their harnesses on. Jae tried to update Boone as she watched, but the wind swallowed her words. She ran back to the chopper. By this time, she couldn't feel her frozen feet as she stepped into the shelter of the helicopter and reported to Boone over the coms.

"Silver Bay? I'll have them dispatched, but it'll take hours. Once you get the patients out of the van, is there anywhere you can keep them out of the cold? The back of the ambulance?"

"The ambulance is stuck in the snow and the rear doors are blocked by trees. We have the two cots in the chopper. We'll treat the most critical here."

Boone growled. "The ambulance is stuck too? Okay...I'm sending out a tow truck. Anybody not actively helping on scene should start making some kind of shelter. It sounds like a couple of the kids aren't critical but we'll need to keep them warm. And I can't hear anything you guys are saying out in the wind. You might need to keep running back and forth to the chopper or jump in the cab of the ambulance to keep me updated."

"Will do." Jae checked on Bob, who sat in the jump chair where she'd left him. "You doing okay?"

He nodded. "Those folks. They're gonna be all right, aren't they?"

"We're doing our best to make sure they will be."

"I should help. I caused all this. I should be out there—"

"Bob, right now, I need you to stay here and stay calm. I promise I'll come tell you if there's anything you can do."

It seemed to appease him for the moment, and Jae went back out into the storm. More flashing red lights approached the scene. The firetruck. Seth Turnquist, John Christiansen, and a couple of other men jumped out. Jae directed them around the truck and to the others.

Two of the older firemen started on a temporary shelter close to the ambulance. Peter, Seth, Jensen, and Darek together brought up the unconscious woman and ten-year-old boy in basket stretchers.

Jae followed them as Colleen and Jensen set up in the chopper. Colleen turned to her. "Get us up in the air ASAP. This woman has internal bleeding and I'm on the verge of losing her."

"What about the others?"

"The father is lucid now and other children aren't as critical. Jack and Ronnie can treat them. Jensen will help me here." She turned back to her patients. "We need to go. Now."

Right. Jae leaped into the cockpit and again ran through her preflight checklist. According to the weather tracking system, the storm had lessened, but another band was coming right behind it. The Bell 429 lifted off the ground and cleared the trees. The flight was bumpier than Jae liked as the wind fought them, but she kept the Bell as steady as possible. Colleen's and Jensen's voices carried over from the back.

"I need more..." A pause. "Hurry, Jensen."

"I've got it. Keep him still while I get this line in."

Their stress was palpable even through the wall dividing them. Jae clenched her jaw. Depending on how long it took in Duluth, maybe she could fly back and help on the ground with the others.

But once she landed on the helipad at the Duluth hospital, Jae knew—she would not be taking the Bell home tonight.

Once the skids touched down, a crew from the hospital ran out to assist Jensen with the boy on one cot, and Colleen stood by the mother on the other, calling out stats. "BP 80 over 40. She crashed once. Pulmonary hemorrhage evident…" The rest of Colleen's words were snatched by the wind.

Jae shut down the engines and went inside.

In the building, out of the wind and snow, Jae could finally think. Colleen and Jensen must've gone through the double doors labeled Staff Only. She paced, waiting for them. Sometimes—and she hated this—she felt like being the taxi driver wasn't enough.

Colleen came back through the doors.

Jae couldn't read her face. "Are they going to be okay?"

"I don't know. But they've got top-notch surgeons prepping for surgery now. There's nothing more to do but pray. Did you hear back from Boone?"

"No. I forgot to call him."

Colleen pulled out her phone, put it on speaker, and called Boone.

Jensen joined them, and relayed to Boone the status of the two patients. "They're readying the OR for both of the patients now. How are things at the scene? Did they get the other kids and the father to the Deep Haven ER?" Jensen asked, the worry evident on his face.

"No. The Silver Bay crew isn't there yet. All the tow trucks in the area are busy and won't get out there to help clear the scene until tomorrow."

Jae spoke up. "We could go back and help—"

"Jae, no. I'm not a chopper pilot, but even I know you can't fly in that." Colleen pointed at the window half-covered with snow. It was a complete whiteout now.

"She's right," Boone said. "We can't risk you guys driving or flying and getting stuck. Or worse, crashing. We have enough people there. Find a place to stay and check in tomorrow when you can."

Colleen ended the call. "There's a hotel across the street that we use. Come on."

"So we just do nothing?" Jae asked.

"We're not doing nothing. And, Jae, we couldn't have done this without you. At least now that mother and son have a fighting chance."

"Yeah. We're trusting the rest of the team to do their jobs. We did ours. You were amazing." Jensen stuck out a hand. "I'm Jensen Atwood, by the way. EMT. Nice to meet you."

Jae shook his hand and bit down on her cheek to keep the frustration at bay. Yes, she'd gotten them all here safely, but it still didn't feel like enough. She should be doing more. But she swallowed down the sour taste of her own shortcomings and managed something other than a grimace. "I'm Jae. Chopper pilot."

❄

While animals were burying themselves in burrows to hibernate and find shelter from the storm raging outside, Nick was finally waking up, feeling more like himself. Sure, it was the middle of the night, and he should be sleeping, but he relished the energy pulsing through him. It had been too long. And getting by on less sleep would help him prep for the long stretches of running the Iditarod.

He'd finished chatting with LadyJHawk hours ago. She was so easy to talk with. He wondered what she was like in person. All he knew was, she was the kind of girl that made him laugh. And as he'd figured out when he'd briefly considered dating Lena, he needed a woman who made him laugh.

Not that he and LadyJHawk were more than friends. Probably what they had online was special *because* they didn't complicate it with romance and such. Although that hadn't stopped him from wondering on occasion...

Nick shook his head and focused back on editing the video of the puppies. His followers would love it. Not that he had a million like Darek and others razzed him about, but those who did follow along on his adventures liked to hear about the different personalities and antics of the dogs. And he could use the same video on his dog breeder website to attract good potential buyers. Hopefully he could get the rest of the litter sold to finish paying his vet bill and make some progress on the balloon payment. He looked out the window.

Finally, some snow. Once the wind settled down and the sun came up, there would be plenty to start training with the sled. It was about time.

His phone buzzed with an incoming call. "Peter? What's going on?" It was late. Too late for a friendly chat.

"I need your help." Peter's voice broke up in static and wind. With sirens screeching in the background, he was obviously out in this storm.

Nick leaped out of his chair. "Where are you?"

"Out on Moose Valley Road. Bring any tow straps you can find. I need your help getting the ambulance unstuck. But be careful. The roads are bad. Really bad, man."

"Are you okay?" He stepped into his boots by the door.

"Yeah. I'm fine." Peter's reassurance quieted the panic that had started to flame.

"Okay, I'll be there as soon as I can." Nick grabbed his coat, gloves, and an extra strap on the way out. Thankfully he had four-wheel drive on his truck and didn't live too far from where Peter was. Between the snow blinding him, and the slick roads, he could go barely over twenty miles an hour. The usual five-minute drive took close to twenty by the time the ambulance lights glowed in the distance.

When Nick got out into the howling wind, snow slapped at his face and the drifts covered his boot tops. Once he slid over to the ambulance, he studied the wheels lodged into a drift on the side of the road.

Peter got out of the driver's seat. "Think you can help?"

"Dude, you got it stuck good. But yeah, I can pull you out."

The cousins worked quickly and quietly to strap the ambulance and hook up the tow rope to the truck. They both jumped into the separate vehicles. Nick feathered the gas and slowly pulled forward until the strap was taut. Then he pressed down harder. "Come on!"

Nick gave it more gas but his truck was starting to slip, and the ambulance didn't budge.

Peter knocked on Nick's window. "I'll go push from behind. We almost have it. Give it another go."

Nick waited a minute for Peter to get in place, then again pressed on the gas pedal. After straining, the truck lurched forward and finally the ambulance was free.

Nick looked around. It was eerily quiet except for the wind. "What happened out here?" He spotted a group of long, skinny branches leaning against a tree branch with a yellow tarp bellowing out around it. "And what is that?"

"That was our shelter. There was a bad accident. A semi truck and that minivan over there. The van with a family of five almost fell into the ravine. Once we got them out, they all needed to be treated. Jae flew the mom and oldest kid to Duluth, but I rendered this ambulance useless. We needed a place to keep everyone sheltered while we waited for the Silver Bay crew to come up and assist."

"So where is everyone?"

"Once I knew you were on your way to help me, I had the rest of the team head back."

Nick looked again at the flimsy sticks and tarp. "You were out here alone? Peter, that was a dumb move. What if

I got stuck and couldn't make it? And you call that a shelter?"

Peter rolled his eyes. "Can we discuss this back at HQ? I'm tired and cold."

Nick was ready to get out of the wind too, but he would be picking the subject up again. Winter was a beast. Peter needed to be more careful. "Yeah. I'll follow you." He wouldn't let his cousin get stuck alone.

The drive was again excruciatingly slow, but they finally pulled into Deep Haven and Peter parked the ambulance in the bay of the headquarters. There was enough room for Nick to pull in out of the snow too.

Boone and Cole walked into the bay from the offices and handed them steaming mugs of coffee. "It's fresh and hot."

Nick gladly accepted it. Heat seeped back into his fingers. In the warmth and safety of the building, the stark reality of what Peter and the team had done hit. As much as he respected these guys, they couldn't take stupid risks like that.

"I saw the shelter you guys built up at the accident site. Your team needs better wilderness skills. If you'd had to spend the night out in this for some reason, you wouldn't have made it." Nick should know. He'd already lost one friend like that. He wouldn't lose any more.

Boone mulled over his words. "We made it work, but I'm willing to admit it could've gone a lot better."

Peter slapped Nick on the back. "Are you offering to teach us? There's nobody better at winter survival than you."

That was intentional. When there were no second chances, Nick had to be prepared for the worst. But he wasn't looking for a spot on the team.

Had word gotten around that his bank account was in dire straits? He tried to laugh it off. "Nah, you guys couldn't afford me. I'm just saying, you gotta be careful out there."

Boone stared and Nick fought the urge to squirm.

"No, I think you're on to something, Dahlquist. We cover a lot of wilderness, and it's winter half the year here. We could use winter survival skills. What do you say, Nick?"

Peter agreed. "And whatever your price is, it'd be worth it. Everybody knows you're the expert. You survived the Yukon Quest. Went to the North Pole."

"You went to the North Pole?" Cole asked.

Nick didn't hate the astonishment on Cole's and Boone's faces. So he didn't correct Peter by telling them he'd only made it within a mile of the North Pole before having to head back when one of his teammates was injured. "It was a few years ago."

Boone nodded slowly. "Peter's right. You should train us. And we'll find whatever amount we need to pay you. We have grants for that kind of thing."

Nick shook his head. "I couldn't charge you guys." But the idea took root. Peter had always been on his case to join the CRT. Nick could never do that. Not the way he panicked in an actual crisis. But he could equip them, make sure they all had the skills to survive. It would be worth it to know that his friends would be safer out in the wilderness. "I'll do it."

A dog's bark pulled Nick's attention away from the conversation. "Who's that?"

"Jae's dog," Cole said.

"She's not here?"

Boone took a sip before answering. "No. She couldn't fly back in the storm so she's in Duluth with Colleen and Jensen. Probably sound asleep like we should be."

Seymour would be frantic in a few hours if she wasn't here to take him out. Nick followed the barking. Tucked back behind one of the fire trucks was Seymour's kennel.

Nick released the latch. "Hey, boy. Jae's going to be gone for a bit. Maybe you should come home with me." Next to the kennel was a dish and container of food. A row of stickers on the side of the crate caught his eye as he reached for the food.

Star Wars stickers. And the bowl was the shape of the Millennium Falcon.

Huh. She was a sci-fi fan and a dog lover too. Something niggled in the back of his mind, but he couldn't sort it out. He must be getting tired.

Seymour followed Nick and had no problem hopping into his truck when he opened the passenger door for him. "I'm going to take Seymour, but I don't have Jae's number." Something he should remedy. "Can you let her know?"

Peter nodded. "Of course. And you're sure about training the team?"

Oh yeah. Because if people he cared about were going to be out in the wild in the middle of winter, he would make darn sure they were safe. "I'm sure. We'll talk logistics after you get some sleep. You're lookin' a little rough there, Cuz."

"Get out of here." Peter waved him away with mock annoyance. "But shoot me a text when you get home."

Yeah, Peter had his back too. "Will do."

Looking at Seymour in his seat, Nick found excitement stirring inside for another reason. He had an excuse to see more of Jae Washington.

Yes, things were definitely turning a corner.

CHAPTER 6

*N*ow this was snow.

There was something almost holy about the forest blanketed in pure white that gave Nick space to think. Despite only getting a few hours of sleep, his brain and body buzzed with energy. The dogs were fed. He'd started a new batch of dog food for the evening meal, and he was almost done clearing the driveway.

With each pass of the skid loader clearing paths through the heavy, white snow, new ideas for training the CRT bounced through his mind. He could teach them how to make different types of shelters, build fires, where to find dry kindling and wood, how to filter water. He wanted them well equipped for any survival scenario.

And today he could finally start training with Kasha on fresh snow. As Nick drove past the enclosure in the skid loader, Kasha barked and pawed at the fence.

"It won't be long, girl. Let me get everything set up."

Nick parked the skid loader in the shed and grabbed the lines and his sled. He flipped the sled upside down to add new plastic to the runners and wiped out all the dust and dirt that had settled in it over the last seven months it had sat vacant. He carried everything outside to the stake lines where he would line up the dogs when it was time to go.

"So you finally got some snow, huh?"

Nick turned to find Jae walking toward him in her penguin parka and bright hat. Last night over their Swedish meatballs, they'd joked about her winter gear. She'd claimed she didn't mind sticking out if it meant she could stay warm. He liked that confidence and spunk, which seemed to be missing today.

"No ski goggles?"

"Not today." She smiled, but it wasn't her full grin. Her eyes looked tired with dark circles framing them. Her usual vibrancy and light were absent.

"I bet you're anxious to see your dog. I hope it was okay that I brought Seymour out here."

"I'm glad you did. I'm not sure I should have him at the headquarters when I'm going to be out for so long."

"He did great. He seems to love the snow." They walked over to the open enclosure where the dogs played.

Jae watched Seymour chase Mischa around a pine tree. They jumped into a drift and came out with powdery white piles on their snouts.

The creases in between Jae's eyebrows relaxed as she watched them. But she still didn't say anything. She looked like she could use a friend.

"Must've been a bad accident, huh?"

"Yeah. As of this morning, they still aren't sure about the mom, if she'll make it. And the boy is showing some improvement but isn't out of the woods either."

And people wondered why he didn't want to join the team.

But he hated seeing Jae so weighed down.

"Peter said you flew through the storm to get them to Duluth."

She shrugged. "Looks like it might not have been enough."

"Jae, you maneuvered a helicopter through a snowstorm. You gave those patients a fighting chance. It's more than enough."

"Is it? I mean, yeah, I flew the chopper. But I hardly helped on the scene." She dropped her head, her hand fisted around one of the chain links of the fence. "I just wanted to help—really help."

"You did help! According to Boone and Peter and Cole, you were vital to the team. No one else can fly that chopper."

When she looked back up at him, the blank stare was gone and passion burned in her eyes. "I move people. And yeah, that's important. But I want to do more than stay in the cockpit. I came to this job because I wanted to do hands-on emergency medical work. I want to save lives. I have to."

"Have to?" Nick was oblivious to a lot, but there was something more to the words Jae spoke. Something haunting. "What makes you say that?"

"I...I love flying. I do. And I fought hard for the chance to learn. In the Army, I flew troops and equipment, and I'm proud of the time I served. But after Matteo was killed, I needed a change. He sacrificed so much. He put his life on the line. I needed to do more too. I wanted to be more active in saving those in danger. I left the Army and got into flying for SAR groups and emergency medical flights. But even then...it wasn't enough."

"Wasn't enough? For who?"

"Roberto Torres."

"Who's he?"

"I was working during the floods last year trying to get people to safety. We picked up this family off a bridge, but the dad, he started having issues. He just collapsed in the back of the chopper and I didn't know how to help him. He died in my care. I can't—I can't have that happen again."

Her experience mirrored his own. Nick still remembered the

sick realization that someone in his arms was dying and the overwhelming sense of being powerless to stop it. He understood her drive to help and save so much more now.

But she couldn't see how vital she already was.

"Jae, I know it might not sound like much, but no one else on the team could've flown that chopper. In a storm, no less. The last guy who tried crashed. We're so far away from any trauma care. Colleen and the team know their stuff. And because you did your job well, she could focus all her energy on helping that woman and her son. They couldn't have done that without *you*. I know it doesn't feel like enough, but it is. Some things are simply out of our hands."

"I hate that too."

"So do I."

She was quiet for a while. Nick's dog River came over to them. Jae squatted down and scratched him through the fence. "That was my one chance for a good first impression too. When I come into a new situation, I *know* I have to prove myself. That was my first call with the CRT and I hated standing on the sidelines, not being strong enough to help carry those stretchers up the side of the gully. I want to do my share. I want them to know that I'm capable. That I can be a valuable part of the team."

Nick held out a hand and pulled Jae up to standing. "Believe me, you made a great first impression. I saw Peter, Cole, and Boone after the accident. There were things that everyone could've done better. But not once did they express that you weren't doing enough. If anything, they were grateful for your steady hand in the storm."

"You don't think they're sitting there wondering why they hired me?"

"No way. And I'm sure you'll have plenty of times when you can show them all the things you're capable of doing. But you should realize flying a helicopter is a pretty big deal. It is an important part of the team too."

"Maybe."

Mischa and Seymour joined River at the fence.

"Hey, boy. Did you miss me?" The light in Jae's eyes started to spark again, the corners of her mouth lifting. Her slim shoulders eased a bit. "I think he likes it here." She looked around the yard. "I know I was here yesterday, but I didn't notice your place."

"Yeah, weird, considering how welcoming I was."

She laughed. "Good thing your mom makes a mean pumpkin pie."

"We should start over." He held out a hand. "I'm Nick."

Jae's dainty hand might be small, but her handshake had strength and grit. "I'm Jae. Nice to meet you." Her eyes scanned the yard. "Wow. This is really something as far as kennels go."

Nick soaked in her admiration. "It's how I make a living. These dogs work hard, and I wanted to give them the best. Would you like a tour? I have puppies inside."

"Puppies?" Jae finally let loose a full-blown grin. "I'd love that."

"As you can see here, this is an open area the dogs can roam and play in. There's plenty of trees and ground for them to run, but the fence is high enough to keep them safe and stop them from escaping. At night, they go into their individual kennels. I have two dogs per kennel and each has a doghouse."

Jae ran a finger along the fence as they walked toward the Quonset shed, their boots crunching on snow. "Don't they get cold? I'm freezing."

"No. These dogs are bred for cold weather. But I have straw in their houses to help them stay warm too. I kept Seymour inside since I wasn't sure how he would do."

He opened the door to the indoor kennel. "Aww!" Jae rushed

over to the puppy area where Tilly and her remaining puppies woke up and started barking.

"They're so cute!" Jae scooped up the all-tan male Nick had named Mack. She giggled as he licked her chin. "Talk about a mood changer. This is great therapy."

"You can come visit them any time."

Jae carried Mack in her arms and slowly turned around. "What's this for?" She walked over to the tiled corner where there was a drain in the floor and a long hose hung with a showerhead attached.

"That's my dog washing station. It's a lot easier to clean them off in this instead of trying to give them a bath."

"And you have a stove in here too?" She wandered to the kitchen area with the extra fridge, multiple chest freezers, and some repurposed cabinets Nick had installed.

"I make dog food out here. Don't want fish guts and deer bones stinking up the house when I do."

"I don't know what you mean by stinking up the house. Whatever you're cooking now smells amazing. But it's gotta be convenient to cook a lot of food out here. This must've cost a fortune."

"I built it. That's why it *didn't* cost a fortune. Plus I used a lot of repurposed materials."

She stared openmouthed. "You did this?"

He leaned against one of the freezers and blew out an exaggerated huff. "Well, don't act so surprised. I'm more than just a handsome face."

She laughed. "I can't believe you run this operation, raise and train the dogs, *and* build incredible kennels. Did you build your cabin yourself too?"

He nodded. "Yeah. Again, it was the only way I could afford it."

"How did you learn all this?"

"YouTube."

"YouTube?"

"Yup. And I had help. Peter and some of my other cousins all pitched in when they could. My dad and uncles too. But most of it I learned by watching YouTube videos."

She spun around slowly, taking it all in. "It's amazing, Nick."

A warmth spread through him. To have a woman praise his efforts, to look at him like that? It wasn't something that happened every day. "Thanks."

"I wish I had a fraction of your skill and talent. Then I wouldn't be at the mercy of the rental market. I could build my own house."

"What would you build?"

She was quiet for a moment. Mack's little black nose nuzzled into her neck. She giggled. She was more than just really cute, like he'd told LadyJHawk. She was downright gorgeous. Something stirred deep inside as he watched her cuddle the puppy.

Yes, come over anytime. He could get used to seeing Jae here and bonding over dogs and puppies.

"I never really thought about it," she finally said. "I've never stuck around anywhere long enough to make the investment of building a house worth it."

"Why do you move so much?"

"I never found the right place to settle down. My mother is Korean, and my dad is from Texas. I've lived my whole childhood on military bases all over the world. And once I was on my own, I guess I just kept the nomadic lifestyle I was used to."

"Do you want to settle down?"

"I still love to travel, but I do long for a place to be my home base."

He knew what that was like. That was why he'd built this place. Somewhere to launch from and a steady mark he could always come back to after his adventures.

Jae continued. "My parents always find that grounding in each other no matter where they are. They stay at Daddy's family ranch when he's not overseas. I'd like to find my own home. And as much as I love my family, Texas is not it and neither is Korea. So I'm still looking."

Jae returned Mack to the puppy kennel.

"You should consider Deep Haven. This is a great place to call home."

"So far I'm really liking it. But I've only been here a day." She wandered back to the kitchen area and sniffed. "What smells so good?"

"I'm making dog food."

"With all the ugly vegetables from the restaurants and meat scraps?"

"You remembered."

"Of course." She pointed to the lid. "May I?"

"Go right ahead. That's for the evening meal. I've got a venison and brown rice stew with sweet potatoes and broccoli."

"Can I try some? Maybe it's just 'cause I skipped breakfast, but it smells amazing."

"Here, allow me." Nick opened the drawer for a small spoon and also pulled out a little saltshaker. He dipped the spoon in the stew and added a dash of salt. "The dogs don't need any salt in their diet, but we're so used to it in people food that it will taste really bland if I don't add some."

Jae took the bite. Her eyes widened. "Mmm. That's incredible. You make this for your dogs? You could serve this at your parents' restaurant."

"No way. It's just for the pack. But I'm glad you like it."

"You make dog treats too, right?"

"Yeah." Nick didn't remember saying that at the bistro, but he must've mentioned it somewhere along the way. "Now is a good time to make the pumpkin spice ones since pumpkins are cheap. I use pumpkin puree, oatmeal, and a little cinnamon."

"You'll have to tell me when you make the next batch. I'd love to learn and I bet Seymour would love to taste test."

"Okay then. It's a date." The words escaped his mouth before their implication sank in. "I...I mean, I'll let you know the date I'm baking the next batch." He pushed back the hair off his forehead and cleared his throat.

She glanced up shyly through thick lashes. "I know what you meant." She tilted her chin up farther and looked him in the eye. "I'll be ready when you are."

And somehow, the words fell through him and sat on his heart.

Almost like new fallen snow.

❄

Nick's words settled on Jae's soul. Maybe her first impression for the team wasn't as bad as she thought. Flying the Bell was still critical. She'd gotten that woman and her son to the trauma center where the right people and equipment could help. And maybe Jae could make a place for herself here. A place for her and Seymour. She'd have to find her own home, of course, but she couldn't deny how well Nick's cabin in the woods felt like a comfortable landing place after the stressful night.

That had to be the draw—the peace and calm he'd established out here. She shouldn't read anything more into his handsome eyes locked on hers. Or the way it made her whole arm tingle when his hand bumped into hers as they walked along the fence line. At least not until she had the chance for Nick to get to know her and she could tell him she was Lady-JHawk. She needed to slow things down.

"I was going to take my first sled ride of the season—just a short one through the woods to my friend's house. Remind the dogs what snow feels like again. Do you want to ride?" Nick asked.

She should say no. She had plenty of training still to do. But the truth was she'd wanted to go on one of Nick's sled rides since the first time she'd watched his videos. "Sure."

Besides, a sled ride would be a good test. She needed to establish a steady friendship before she could reveal her online identity. Prove she wasn't a desperate stalker.

"Great!" His cheek dimpled as he took her hand.

And shoot, her pulse surged.

Nick led her to lines laid out in the snow behind a blue sled and showed her how to put the harness and booties on the dogs. After hooking up Mischa and Kasha in the lead and getting all the dogs into the lines, Jae looked up at Nick. "So what do I do?"

"You get to sit and enjoy the ride. I have a down blanket and a snow proof covering, so hopefully you'll stay nice and cozy."

She sat down in the basket. "Is this where you want me?"

As the words tumbled out of her mouth, Nick bent over to tuck in the cover around her. He froze inches away from her face.

Wow. His sky-blue eyes were flecked with darker blue starbursts. They reflected the sparkle of the snow. His minty breath puffed around her, and the smirk in his half smile captured all rational thought and rendered her speechless for a moment.

"You're exactly where I want you." His deep voice sent a humming through her whole body.

Yup. Daddy was right.

Nick Dahlquist was a dangerous man. Dangerous to her heart.

Once again, she may have gotten in over her head.

But as she basked in his gaze, it was hard to care.

He stood up and moved behind Jae. His voice carried over the wind. "Let's go on an adventure! Hike! Hike!"

The dogs leaped to action. The sled glided over the snow-covered trail between the cabin and the kennels and out into the woods.

"Hold on tight. We've got a bit of a hill here and the dogs like to go fast." They hit the crest of the hill and flew down the other side, tree trunks all a blur as they flashed past. Nick howled at the sky like one of his dogs. "Whoooeee!"

His scent, a hint of manly spice and musk, wafted up from the blanket wrapped around her.

This was amazing. The fresh air, the snow. Everything before she had watched on a computer screen of Nick's rides now seemed flat and lifeless.

This was real. The glint off the ice crystals and snow was more brilliant. The fresh green of pine and evergreens more verdant. The blue of the sky was deeper than any blue she'd ever known.

She leaned against the back of the sled basket, Nick's legs right behind her. She looked up. "Where are we going?"

"To Ed's," he shouted, the wind scooping up his voice. "He's the one I was talking about last night. The guy who taught me all about sledding."

"Does he race too?"

"Not professionally anymore. He just keeps a few dogs now, takes trips on his own. But he used to run the Iditarod every year. Even lived in Alaska for a while."

The dogs pulled the sled around a thick copse of spruce. Before them was a small clearing with a timber frame house situated in the middle of it. It was a small ranch-style home with a front porch running the whole length of it. "That's Ed's place."

Shoot. The ride was over already?

A pack of dogs—most of them huskies—rose from the yard and began to bark. A few ran off the porch as a lanky older gentleman with a salt-and-pepper beard and a wide smile stood up. "C'mon back, boys! It's just Nick!"

He raised a hand in greeting. His wool plaid jacket had seen better days, frayed at the cuffs, his boots scuffed and scratched, but his deep voice had a jolliness to it as he came off the porch.

"Hullo!" The dogs ignored him and came to sniff and bark at them as they stopped the sled.

Nick jumped down and helped Jae stand before petting each dog. "Hey, Ed. I just came to pick up those dog tags."

"Sure. They're in my workshop." He walked over to them. "And who did you bring with you?"

"This is Jae. She's the new chopper pilot for the CRT."

Ed shook her hand. "Glad to meet you, young lady. And welcome to Deep Haven. How are you finding it so far?"

"It's a beautiful community."

"That it is." He led them around the side of the porch to a small workshop behind the house. A sharp smell of turpentine and wood dust tickled Jae's nose when she walked inside.

"Ed, what are you working on?" Nick pointed to a wooden frame that looked like a large basket on runners.

"Oh, that? I'm designing a custom ash wood sled. It would be more flexible than the aluminum ones you youngsters are running these days."

"I didn't know you built your own sleds." Nick ran his fingers along the curve of the back.

"It's been a long time, but I learned out in Alaska from a native there. He made the best sleds. They flew over the snow and ice. Haven't quite got his touch, but this one is shaping up better than I'd hoped for."

Alaska was one of the places on Jae's bucket list to visit. "So how long were you out in Alaska?"

"Oh, about fifteen years. I went out there for college and ended up staying."

The way his eyes lit, it was obvious he loved the place. "Did you get homesick? Is that why you came back?"

"Not exactly. If I had my way, I would've lived out there until my dying day."

"Really?"

"Oh yes. I love the ruggedness, the sheer grit it takes to make it out there, and oh, the glory. The most amazing sunrises over those mountains. The sunsets on the ocean. There's nothing like it." Ed swept stray wood shavings off the counter and into his hands.

"So why did you come back to Deep Haven?" Nick asked.

The older man's hands stilled. A sad look dimmed his eyes. "Guess I needed a change of scenery. Some might say I came back to lick my wounds. But after my dad passed away, I wanted to make sure my mother was taken care of. She wouldn't dream of leaving Deep Haven."

There had to be more. Jae sensed a tragic romance at the heart of this story. And nothing intrigued her more than a romantic tale. "There was a woman," Jae whispered reverently.

Ed gave a sad chuckle. "Very perceptive, young lady." He moved to the garbage and brushed the sawdust off his hands. "Yes. There was a woman."

"What happened?"

"I was the world's biggest fool for not telling her I loved her when I had the chance. She chose someone else and I couldn't bear to watch them live their lives together knowing it could've been me. So I moved back here. She was happy. That's all that mattered. And my mother needed someone close by. It's all worked out in the end."

Jae wasn't sure as she looked around the bachelor's work-shop—all neat and tidy, everything in its place. But it seemed lonely too.

Nick looked eager to change the subject. "I was telling Jae how you used to run the Iditarod."

"If you really want to know Alaska—as much as you can know such a savage land—there's nothing like a thousand-mile race through the wilderness."

Jae could see the wanderlust, the longing in Nick's whole face. He lit up like a little boy sitting at a grandfather's feet waiting to hear a beloved tale.

"Tell us about it, Ed. What was it like?" he asked.

"You've heard me tell it a thousand times, Nicholas. It was miserable." He gave a snarl and snort of disgust, but the twinkle in his eyes betrayed the old man's true feelings on the subject. "And I loved every minute of it."

Something about Ed reminded Jae of her own grandfather in Texas. Riding in the saddle with him as a little girl, Pap would tell her stories about cattle drives and hunting down rustlers and predators. It was all such a foreign world for a little girl who'd grown up in Korea and on military bases. But she loved the timbre of his voice as they rode, his strong arms around her, the sweet smell of his tobacco, and the root beer candies in his pocket.

Ed should have his own passel of grandkids surrounding him, begging for stories. How sad it would never come to be.

They joined Ed for a cup of coffee while he told them more of his Iditarod adventures, like the time his dogs were attacked by moose and once when he was chased by a bear. After the stories, Jae was back on the sled with Nick. When they reached his cabin, she checked on Seymour while Nick pulled the sled into his shed.

Seymour snoozed, snuggled up to Mischa at the base of a towering white pine tree. He didn't seem to be missing her at all.

Maybe it was Ed's tragic romance still swirling through Jae's mind, or the sweet pups together that nudged the desire, but suddenly she wanted to know Nick's story. Why was he alone out here in the woods? As soon as he walked up to join her at the fence, she brought up the subject.

"Thanks for introducing me to Ed. He seems like a character. But how sad for him to have lost out on the love of his life."

Nick's grin died. "Some of us aren't meant for love like that."

"You sound like you know from experience." A pause. "Who was she?"

"Hey, do you play board games? We could see if Peter and Ronnie are up for an evening of Catan. Tiago loves that game." He led her over to the indoor kennel and held the door.

Nice try, but she wouldn't be swayed. "Nick, you're not avoiding the question, are you?" she asked with a playful smile as they walked in together.

"I don't know what you're talking about." He stirred the doggy stew in one of his pots on the stove and scooped it into a five-gallon bucket.

"Come on. It's not like I'll tell anyone. What are you afraid of? I told you my tragic story." She stilled his hand and took the ladle from him.

"I'm not afraid of anything." He finished by lifting the pot and dumping the rest of the stew into the bucket. "It's just—I don't know. But yeah, maybe there was someone. I really thought we'd end up together. But we're not. I don't know that it was love."

"What happened?"

He carried the pot to the industrial sink and started rinsing it. "I finally got up the nerve to ask her to prom our senior year. I went all out. Got the flowers. Showed up on her doorstep and told her how I felt."

"I take it she didn't feel the same?"

Nick shook his head slowly and kept washing the pot. "Nope. She let me down easy, said she didn't want to be tied down at that point in her life and she had already agreed to go with someone else. But later I overheard her friends laughing about it. She must've told them."

"Ouch."

"Yeah. She left Deep Haven right after high school. I knew she was made for bigger and better things. But I still hoped when she was ready, she'd come back. So I worked on getting this place together."

"Did she ever come back?" Jae rinsed off the ladle she'd carried over.

"Yes. But she found someone else." He set the pot down and watched the puppies scamper in their corner before lifting up the second pot and carrying it to the sink too. "She'd never like living out here anyway, so it's all for the best. Maybe, like Ed, I'm not made for relationships like that."

"I don't think that's true. But I'm sorry it didn't work out with her."

"No biggie. I've got a lot of other things going on."

"Like your millions of adoring fans online?"

He balked. "It's not millions."

"Okay, so it's only a hundred and twenty-five thousand, give or take a hundred."

He stopped scrubbing the pot, stared at her. "And how do you know that?"

Oh shoot. If she told him she was LadyJHawk, he'd probably run her off, thinking she was another stalker.

Did he know her well enough?

Not really. For all he knew, they met yesterday. It was too soon. "I, uh, might've looked you up."

"Really? You looked me up, huh?" He gave her a slow devastating smile with an added quirk of his eyebrow.

His flirty look did a number on her, making her lose some of her resolve to slow things down. She could feel the burn of a blush stealing up from her neck. "Well, it's not like you're that hard to find online. And you have quite the following. I'm surprised you don't have the paparazzi out here watching your every move."

"Nah." Nick dropped the flirty act and Jae got the impression she was seeing the real guy underneath all the party-boy persona when he gave a humble shrug. "Everything you see online is just that. I want to encourage people to experience the outdoors. It's not like I mean anything to those people."

"You're kidding, right?"

He frowned.

"Nick, I watched some of your videos. You're an inspiration. I looked at those chats and vlogs. You have a loyal following. You've made an impact on them. And by the way, why haven't you monetized that? You could probably make a living off of advertising on your own YouTube channel and Instagram account."

He turned back to the sink and finished rinsing the pot. "I just want a way to share my love of outdoor adventure. Encourage people to get outside. And, yeah, it's a way to get the word out to sponsors and generate interest in the sport. But who's gonna actually buy advertising on it? I know this life...it's not for everyone."

And the way he said it made her wonder what girl it was who turned her nose up at Nick Dahlquist's life. Because this life...this was exactly what she had always dreamed of.

The only thing standing in her way was the truth.

CHAPTER 7

*N*ick piled the bags of marshmallows next to the ferro rods on a lightweight plastic table he'd set up behind his shed. The clear skies let sunshine filter through the forest canopy and reach the frozen white ground in patches. He was looking forward to teaching winter survival skills today. No more flimsy shelters. No more bumbling around in a blizzard unprepared.

People died that way.

But not anymore. Not if Nick had anything to say about it.

And he didn't mind at all that it would be a chance to see Jae again after their sled ride a few days ago. Not that he would admit that to his cousin, who set a box of World's Best donuts and Fika coffee thermoses onto the other end of the table.

"Marshmallows, huh?" Peter picked up a bag. "What's this have to do with survival?"

"The ferro rods and magnesium can sometimes be tricky to learn, so I want to give them an incentive. Once they get their fire going, they can roast a few marshmallows to celebrate."

"Great idea. See, this is why you should join the team."

Nick glared at his cousin. "You know that's not gonna

happen. Now make yourself useful and tell me if everyone is here. We should get started soon."

Peter went to count those mingling around the dog enclosure watching Nick's Alaskan huskies. Most of the faces he knew well: Seb Brewster, Jensen Atwood, Ronnie Morales, Cole Barrett, Kyle Hueston and his brother Kirby, Colleen Decker, Jack Stewart, Seth Turnquist, and Darek, Casper, and John Christiansen. It was a good mix of sheriff's office, fire department, and emergency medical professionals—all people who went most often on the calls.

True rescuers.

Although, they were missing a certain chopper pilot in the group.

Nick busied himself getting his own tinder and kindling ready for the demonstration but kept an eye out for Jae. They'd had a blast on that sled ride to Ed's. He had hoped to see her the last couple of days, but he'd had to get the training time in with Kasha before the race. It was only three weeks away. Still, he missed the enthusiasm and light Jae brought with her. She was fun to be around.

And pretty. Really pretty. The kind of pretty that stirred things inside him. Things he probably shouldn't feel so soon after meeting her.

But something also had seemed to shift in his chats with LadyJHawk too. He was tempted more and more to see if she'd be willing to do a video call and maybe put aside some of the boundaries they'd set early on in their chats. She didn't want to talk about her job and that had been fine with him at the time because then he could keep his family off limits. Ever since his stalker issue, he did more to protect their privacy.

But they were beyond that now. Right? Although, he hated the thought of losing that special connection they shared. Maybe taking things up a notch would destroy it.

Ugh. Why were women so confusing?

Peter whistled and called the others. "Help yourselves to some donuts and coffee and we'll start in five." He grabbed a maple bacon long john and sauntered over to the firepit. "You ready?"

"Yeah. But where's Jae?"

"Why? You worried about her?" Peter bit into his donut and studied Nick like he was a specimen in a science experiment.

"No, not worried." Nick rearranged his pile of twigs.

"You sure? You look a little worried."

Was his cousin always this annoying? Nick stood up to meet Peter's teasing glare. "I'm just sayin' she's probably the one that needs this most since she didn't grow up in this kind of climate."

"Hmm." Peter narrowed his eyes. "You sure that's it?"

"Never mind." Nick sidestepped Peter and went to the table to grab his own donut, but he could still hear Peter's rumbling laugh behind him. Nick stuffed half a glazed cake donut in his mouth and gulped down some coffee while the rest of the team chatted.

Nick glanced at his watch. As much as he wanted to, he couldn't stall for Jae any longer. If they were going to get through everything, they needed to get started. "All right, everyone, we've got a lot to cover, so grab another donut and let's go."

After Peter gathered them all and gave a brief welcome, Nick brought everyone to a makeshift firepit he'd prepped earlier. "One of your biggest dangers in winter wilderness will be hypothermia. So today we're going to focus on fire starting and building a shelter."

He walked to a nearby spruce tree. "Under these low-lying green branches, you will often find dry, dead branches on spruces. When the ground is covered in snow, this is the place to find dry kindling." He tore twigs and branches off with his gloved hand and carried them to his firepit. He moved to a slim, white tree trunk and picked at the curling bark. "Anywhere around here you can probably find a birch tree. Peel off a small piece of bark or two and you've got nature's perfect fire starter."

Nick stuffed the bark in his pocket and showed them how to scavenge for dry wood, teaching them which would burn fast and slow. He found a few dead logs and brought everything to the firepit, where he showed them how to use the magnesium shavings and ferro rods to start a fire.

They were taking turns using the rods when Jae walked up in her long black parka. She had the fur-lined bright green hat on her head and purple mittens. "Sorry I'm late. I couldn't get my car started."

Boone approached her. "That's okay. Why don't you come over here and I'll show you what we've gone over so far."

No way. Nick stepped over. "I'll show her." Boone might be the CRT manager, but Nick was the instructor here. If anyone was going to equip Jae with winter survival skills, it would be him. "The rest of you can work on constructing your own firepit and collecting wood."

"Sure thing." Boone trotted off and, like the others, started clearing snow for a firepit.

"So, what are we doing?" Jae asked.

Right. Nick moved his focus back to the woman in front of him. "Your car didn't start? You should've called me. I would've come to get you. Or anyone on the team could've helped. Most of them are in town, so you could've ridden with them."

She waved his concerns away. "It wasn't a big deal. I got it going again. I'm just sorry I'm late. What did I miss?"

"First off, it *is* a big deal. We help each other out around here. Next time you have trouble like that, call me."

"Nick, I'm capable. I really didn't need the help." The irritation in her voice was unmistakable.

He lifted his hands in surrender. "Hey, no biggie. I know you're capable. I just want you to know that even though you're new, you've got people here that you can call on now. That's all."

"And thanks for that. If I ever do need help, I'll call you. I promise." Her voice was back to its normal tone.

"Okay then. Now, let me show you how to start a fire." He went over all the points again with Jae. "I'll give you some time to practice this after we do the next part." Maybe even after all the others left.

Jae, a cozy fire, and a starry night backdrop wouldn't be a bad way to end the day.

After gathering the others, Nick showed them how to make a simple shelter structure. "Once you find a good strong limb for a ridgepole, set one end of it on a thick tree in the V where two branches veer off and the other end on the ground or on another tree if you need a bigger shelter. You can then gather branches and logs to lean against the ridgepole and create a wall. This is a lean-to shelter. If you put branches on both sides of your ridgepole, it makes a tent-like or A-frame shelter. Then cover your frame here with green branches—or, if there's no snow cover, you can use moss."

Nick demonstrated each step. "Use the resources around you. If you're going to be sleeping in your shelter for any length of time, you'll also want to line the floor of it. Leaves, pine branches, and things like that can help insulate the shelter so you're not lying directly on the frozen ground. You want to conserve your heat and energy as much as possible."

Seth stuck his head inside the shelter. "Not bad, Dahlquist." He came back out and nodded toward the structure. "How's that for a honeymoon suite, Boone? Think Vivie will like it?"

Boone rolled his eyes but chuckled. "I think she'll prefer the log house you're building for me instead."

Vivie.

Funny. For once, the thought of her and Boone together didn't tear through him like it had for the last months. Nick studied the man. He had to admit, Boone was one of the good ones. He led the team well. He was fair, hardworking, and had done a lot for the town and for Vivien. Peter and the others only had good things to say about him. If he made Vivie happy, he must not be too awful.

"Now it's your turn, everyone. Right, Nick? We make our own shelters?" Peter's voice cut through Nick's thoughts.

"Shelters. Yeah." Nick moved over to the table. "Partner up and come get your marshmallows and flint. Then you can spread out and work in pairs making a shelter and starting a fire. And to make it interesting, there's a prize. First ones done with their shelter and to have a fire going get a gift certificate to the Trailside Bistro."

With a buzz of excitement, everyone grabbed their supplies and moved out into various directions. Except Jae. She stood alone by Nick's firepit, her lower lip caught in her teeth.

"Need a partner?" Nick walked over to her.

"I guess I do. Do you mind?"

"Of course not. Stick with me and I'll warm you right up."

She raised an eyebrow.

Oh boy. That hadn't come out right at all. "I mean, we'll start fires. You know, make sure you're set for any winter wilderness challenge."

"Lead on." Her wide smile and bright eyes set off a different kind of fire inside him.

Sheesh, they'd just met, and here he was bumbling around and acting like a boy with his first crush. Peter's teasing repeated in his mind.

Maybe he should make sure everyone else was set first so he could focus on Jae. Er, on Jae's training. Not on Jae herself.

Nick snatched the beanie off his head to cool off. "Why don't you head down that trail? I'll meet you behind the big shed. Gather material for a shelter, pick out a ridgepole, and I'll be there after I do a quick check on the other teams."

Her hat bobbed on her head as she waddled down the frozen trail looking very much like a penguin in her shiny black parka.

The neon green hat stood out among the drab November landscape like a glow stick in a dark room. She tripped over a root and caught herself before she could fall, but the hat fell over her face.

Nick couldn't help but grin as she pushed the hat back on her head. He would have no problem finding her.

Most of the people, being native to the area, were already well underway with their shelters by the time Nick checked them. The Christiansen brothers were over halfway done. Peter and Ronnie were laughing as they dragged branches and limbs over to their site. At least they weren't making puppy eyes at each other or kissing like the last time Nick went hiking with them. Brothers Kyle and Kirby were naturals, and the other pairs were making good progress.

By the time he found Jae, her scarf and parka were piled on the ground. Dragging a dead pine branch behind her, she stumbled over a log and fell. She stood and gave the offending log a good kick. The sag to her shoulders and the way her head drooped screamed defeat.

Nick jogged the rest of the way to her. "Sorry, I got caught up helping one of the other groups. How are you doing here?"

Her pink lips turned down into a frown. "Fine." She shivered. Grabbing her middle, she rubbed her arms and stamped her feet. "I mean, I'm freezing, but my coat kept getting caught on the branches, so I took it off." She reached down for the log again and grunted as she dragged it a few inches. "These things are heavier than they look." Her voice trembled through the chattering of her teeth.

Nick looked closer at her clothing. The fleece pullover wouldn't be so bad, but with sleeves that thick she must have a bunch of layers under there. Her thin skinny jeans were wet and streaked with mud where she'd fallen. "Well, there's your problem. You're not dressed for the cold."

"Not dressed for it? I have three long-sleeved T-shirts and a sweater under this fleece. How many more layers do I need before I can feel my feet again?" She yanked the log a little farther, determination and misery fighting in her eyes.

"Come on. First we'll get you dressed for the weather, then we'll work on your shelter and fire."

She threw down the log. "Um, in case you haven't noticed, I'm already dressed. I mean, I look like Jabba the Hutt right now, but I'm not this thick. It's all layers."

Nick almost laughed at the thought of petite Jae Washington being mistaken for Jabba, but the look on her face told him it wouldn't be appreciated. He grabbed her hand. "Believe me, no one would mistake you for a Hutt. And you may have more layers than Shrek, but they aren't the right layers. You're wearing cotton."

"So?" She stubbornly planted her feet, pulled her hand free, and crossed her arms.

He took a step closer and kept his voice calm. "When you work up a sweat, like when dragging dead branches or hauling logs, the cotton absorbs the moisture and it has nowhere to go, so it stays wet against your skin. You need a good base layer to wick that moisture away."

She didn't respond. Just stood there staring. And shivering.

As much as he wanted to reach for her hand again, he didn't. He nodded toward the cabin. "I've got some clothes, base layers, that my cousin Abby left here. She's a little taller than you, but they should fit."

"You really think it will make a difference?" Her tone was thawing.

"I know it will. I'm the expert, remember?" He puffed out his chest and wagged his eyebrows.

She rolled her eyes and shook her head. "All right, Obi-Wan Kenobi. I'll try these fancy clothes you speak of." She picked up her hat and mittens. "But mostly I want to get warm. You have heat inside, right?"

This time, she took the hand he offered, even if it was only to step over a big log. They followed the trail around the shed to the back deck of the cabin. Nick led Jae inside.

She stood inside his dining area and studied the small kitchen to the right with its butcher block counters and shaker oak cabinets, the living room straight ahead with log walls, a desk with his computer tucked in one corner, and the fireplace on the end wall.

What did she think of his modest little cabin? It was no grand house on the hill like Seth was building for Boone and Vivien.

"Wow. It's even better from the inside. I can't believe you built all this."

Guess she didn't mind at all.

As she continued to look around, Nick watched her. She fit nicely in the scene and added an element of sweetness that was typically absent in his bachelor pad. She laughed when she found an old picture of Nick and Peter in their peewee football uniforms. Her laughter filled the empty places inside him with warmth and light.

"I suppose I should try these special base layer things and get back to the shelter."

Clothes. Right. Nick found the stash Abby had left and brought them to Jae. "Take this base layer—it's a merino wool blend. There's pants and a shirt. Both should be tight to your skin. Then these snow pants. And here's some wool blend socks that should keep your feet warmer. You can change in the bathroom right there." He pointed to the first door on the left side of the hallway.

Nick busied himself while she changed—straightening up the coffee table, clearing away the random coffee mugs and papers he had scattered all over it. He snatched the pair of socks on the rug he had left by the couch last night.

Jae came out. With the fitted shirt, he noticed her petite and graceful frame as she walked toward him. Her long hair hung in loose strands, framing her face, and her dark brown eyes probably didn't miss much. They were inquisitive and sharp, balanced out by out a wide, sweet mouth.

A mouth with very appealing full lips.

"Are you going to say something?" she asked. "Am I not wearing it correctly?"

"No!" Nick shook himself and cleared his throat. "No, you look great. Uh, let's go make a shelter."

This time, she slipped just the thick fleece over the wool shirt and they went back to her chosen shelter site. Nick offered her a pair of work gloves that her dainty hands swam in, but it helped as they dragged dead branches and logs. He showed her how to break off longer limbs by using standing trees as levers and her body strength to snap them off at the right length.

Darek and Casper finished first and won the prize. No surprise there. The others all left long before Nick and Jae finished their shelter, but Jae didn't want to give up. She was determined to finish. She had a perseverance he could appreciate.

And she looked downright adorable when she did a victory dance after setting the last branch in place. She glowed with the accomplishment. "I have to admit, that was a lot harder than I thought it would be. You make it seem easy."

"It's not a lot of talent or smarts. Just practice."

"But it does take skill. Skill I obviously don't have."

"You just built a decent shelter without the use of a saw or any other tools. You should be proud of yourself."

"Thanks." Her cheeks glowed a rosy pink and her smile warmed him inside. "Now should we move on to the fire?"

"Everyone else is gone for the day and the sun is setting. We can do it some other time, if you want."

She shook her head. "No way. You're not gonna gyp me out of my toasted marshmallow."

All righty, then. He'd give her this: she was a determined woman. She insisted on doing everything herself. First, she collected birch bark as he suggested and then was on the hunt for a spruce tree. She carefully gathered a pile of dry sticks and twigs and then a few small logs. He hated to watch her do it all, but she refused any help beyond verbal instruction and letting him hold the flashlight as the darkness of night crept in.

It took multiple tries with the ferro rod and magnesium shavings to spark the birch bark and get it to catch, but finally she had a blazing fire. Nick used his jackknife to carve some green roasting sticks and she added a marshmallow to each one.

While she carefully toasted hers over the flames to a nice golden brown, Nick's caught fire right away.

They laughed as he blew it out. He stuffed the black and white gooey mass in his mouth and savored every last bit of it.

Yes. This was exactly how a guy survived in the woods.

❄

After a full day of training videos and the new-carpet fumes of the headquarters classroom, Jae needed some heavy-duty painkillers. The pounding in her head had her begging for mercy. But Ronnie was relentless.

"Keep going, Jae."

Jae continued her compressions on the CPR dummy.

Ronnie moved around the dummy to the other side. "Great form. Your shoulders are directly over your wrists and your elbows locked."

Jae blew her bangs out of her eyes for the millionth time and held back a grunt. She knew CPR. She'd made sure she learned it and learned it well after the disaster with Mr. Torres. But convincing Ronnie was another story. "How much longer?"

"You wimping out on me here?"

"Come—" Jae pressed down on the dummy's chest. "On."

Another push. "I know we have machines for CPR compressions. I saw the LUCAS in the chopper."

"We do, but we have to be prepared for worst-case scenario. Especially in the wilderness." Ronnie watched more compressions. "There you go. That's how it should be done."

Jae slumped down. "Done. I heard you say it." She reached for her water on the table and chugged it down.

"Done for now." Ronnie took a sip from her own bottle. "I'm impressed with your skills, Jae. I think you'll pass the Minnesota First Responder requirements, no problem. Go ahead and study for your written test while I put this away."

Jae managed to climb up to the nearest chair and plop her bottom down in it. Ronnie's training was no joke. And that was good. Jae wanted to be ready for any scenario. Plus, in order to keep this job, she needed to pass her Minnesota boards, so she downed a couple of Excedrin and opened up her book.

Ronnie left the room to put away the practice dummy, leaving Jae to study in quiet. But more voices out in the bay broke her concentration. Deeper voices. Jae's ears perked at the sound of Nick's baritone.

Nick was here.

Which was fine. Totally fine. And didn't interest her one bit.

Not when she needed to remember the points about how to approach a scene and check for safety.

She flipped another page and read the first line.

Were those footsteps?

It doesn't matter. This is more important.

She reread the line.

Nick popped his head in the room, a boyish grin and that mischievous twinkle in his eyes. "Whatcha doin'?"

"Studying." She held up the book. "What does it look like?"

His lip curled in disgust. "Boring. Come on. It's Trivia Night."

She wanted to jump up and follow without another thought.

But she should buckle down and read the next chapter. Besides, as much as she thought she could be around Nick and keep things on the D-L until she'd proven herself and could tell him who she was, her time with him sledding and eating marshmallows around the campfire had been its own kind of test—and she wasn't sure she'd passed it.

Her heart was definitely *not* safe if Nick Dahlquist was on the scene.

She'd spent the last few nights night reliving the sensation of flying through the woods on the sled with him. She couldn't trust herself around this guy. "I have to study. Ronnie's going to test me tomorrow."

"You fly helicopters, which are complicated machines. I'm sure you'll pass a measly CPR test."

"I really shouldn't. Ronnie—"

Nick closed the book, grabbed her hand, and tugged her up to stand. "Leave Ronnie to me."

"Why should I do that?" Oh man, he smelled good. And he was clean shaven again like he usually was in his videos. That fresh and spicy-scented aftershave he wore lured her closer. And when his hand moved from her palm to her back as he guided her out the classroom door, she forgot all her good intentions and fatigue.

"Like I said—because it's Trivia Night. We're young. We should be out having fun. And this is what we do for fun in Deep Haven on a Monday night."

He looked at her so earnestly. How could she resist eyes that blue? "How are you going to convince Ronnie?"

"I know her weakness." His smirk just about undid her. He was too cute for his own good.

Talk about weakness.

Jae narrowed her eyes. "You're going to appeal to her competitiveness, aren't you?"

"See? You're smart. This is why we need you on the team.

They've lost the last three weeks. They need us." He slung an arm around her shoulders and steered her toward the bay.

Well, she did want to bond more with the team. Maybe a little trivia fun would be the thing. "All right, all right. I'll come. But for the record, everyone told me you are just as bad as Ronnie when it comes to competition."

"I just want to have fun. And admit it, winning is a lot more fun than losing."

Oh, she could admit it. She just wasn't sure if her heart could take another loss. And she would definitely lose Nick Dahlquist if she didn't time things right. She couldn't get ahead of herself until she told him the truth.

Then again, she should be safe tonight. They'd be in the crowded VFW. And she could use some sustenance.

She went to the bunk room to grab her parka. Since she was there, a little lip gloss and a fresh coat of mascara wouldn't hurt either.

At the VFW, they squished eleven people around a table for six. The place was packed. Jae could hardly hear over the music and chatter, but her headache was gone and she didn't mind close quarters. Tiago and Josh ran for the ancient arcade games in the corner while the server passed out menus.

"Nick! It's about time. I thought you'd abandoned us." Seth Turnquist pounded Nick's fist in welcome.

"Yeah, it's been a while. Glad you're back." Ree offered a sweet smile as she sat down in the chair Seth pulled out for her. "And that you brought Jae along."

"I hear you guys have done dismally the last few weeks, so I brought reinforcements." Everyone laughed as Nick helped Jae out of her coat and draped it over the back of her chair. The smell of burgers on the grill made her mouth water.

"Last time I was here, I just got a drink. But I'm hungry tonight. What's good?" Jae asked.

"No question about it. The burgers. They're famous here,

especially if Jack is behind the grill. But it's the sides we always debate. Tots, fries, or onion rings. And I should warn you, it gets a little heated."

Vivien leaned over from across the table where she sat next to Ree Zimmerman. "The onion rings are the way to go. They're hand-made, beer-battered, and delicious."

Nick leaned back in his chair, his arm brushing Jae's. "I'm more of a tot guy myself."

"Really? Tots? I thought you liked onion rings too. You always order them." Vivien looked confused.

Nick shrugged. "They're okay."

She studied him a second longer and then turned back to her conversation with Ree, comparing their engagement rings and talking wedding plans.

Interesting.

Nick nudged Jae. "So what will it be? Team Fries, Tots, or Rings?"

"I like all three, but the question is do they serve fry sauce here?"

"Fry sauce? If you mean ketchup, of course. What self-respecting burger joint wouldn't?" Nick pointed at the red plastic container in the middle of the table.

"Not ketchup. Fry sauce. I can't have fries or tots without it. It's a mixture of mayonnaise and ketchup."

"You're making that up. I was raised in a family of restaurateurs. Fry sauce is not a thing."

"I assure you, it is. One of my friends from Idaho taught me this. And I will prove to you just how amazing it is. You've been missing out."

The server came around to Jae. She ordered a side of mayo with her burger and fries. When the food arrived, Jae mixed up her fry sauce on a small plate and pushed it toward Nick. "Try it."

He eyed the plate with skepticism. "I don't know about this."

"Come on. You're an adventurer. Food is supposed to be adventurous. Try it."

Nick dipped his tot in the sauce and took a tentative bite. He made a big deal of chewing it, humming, acting like he was analyzing it. He finally swallowed. "Not bad. Where'd you learn this sauce wizardry again?"

"I'm the Yoda of condiments and sauces. Stick with me, S-s-s-kywalker and I'll have you expanding your flavor horizons in no time." Jae stuffed another fry in her mouth and looked away. She'd almost called him Solo like she did online. Whew, that was close.

Nick didn't seem to notice. Instead, he laughed. It was a deep baritone rumble that spilled out of him and made her want to lean in closer. But a seed of unease broke through. Did he know Jae Washington enough to know she wasn't a stalker? She needed to tell him soon that she was LadyJHawk. Not here in a crowded bar, but the way he looked at her...yeah, the next time they were alone, she needed to say something. Surely she'd proven herself by now.

The rest of the chatter at the table stopped, and everyone's attention zoomed in on them.

Peter tilted his head. "What's so funny, Nick? Haven't heard you laugh like that for quite a while."

"You guys gotta try Jae's fry sauce. It's"—he looked at Jae and winked—"out of this world." He pushed the small appetizer plate of sauce to the middle of the table and told everyone to try it.

Tiago was the first to give it a try. "Ronnie, try it. It's good."

Ronnie didn't seem convinced. "I don't know—"

"Come on, Babe. You try and I will too." Peter took one of his fries and one of her tots and dipped them both. They took a bite at the same time.

Ronnie nodded slowly as she chewed. "Not too shabby."

Vivien shuddered. "There's no way it's good. I hate mayo."

"And yet you'll put ranch on anything you eat." Ree gave Vivie a pointed look.

"So?"

Nick laughed. "Ranch is pretty much glorified mayo."

He started chanting and pounding on the table and the rest of the group chimed in. "Try it! Try it!"

"Fine." Vivien huffed with a dramatic sigh, but she looked like she enjoyed the attention. She snatched a fry from Ree's plate. "But I'm not going to taint my onion rings." She dipped the stolen fry in the sauce and slowly moved it to her mouth. She paused for theatrical effect, took a bite and quickly spit it out in a napkin. "Ew. No thanks." She reached for her pop and gulped it down. Everyone laughed again.

Nick leaned toward Jae. "Don't worry about her. I've always questioned her taste. The woman likes cauliflower crust pizza."

Before the group could debate pizza crust options, Ed Draper rang a bell up on the stage and announced the beginning of the trivia contest.

Jae dunked another french fry in her sauce and ate it. She could really get used to this. The team, the fun, the trivia.

Nick.

Especially Nick.

She still needed to keep her imagination in check. Those dimpled grins, flirty winks, and strong arms around the back of her chair were not things she could give in to right now. Not while there were secrets between them.

But they could be friends. Friends online. Friends in person too.

Nick leaned over and whispered something in her ear. His warm breath tickled her neck, setting off a flush that swept her cheeks and ears.

Just. Friends.

❄

NixDogQuest: *Hey, you're a girl, right?*

LadyJHawk: *Duh.*

NixDogQuest: *Have you ever fallen for someone...like really fast? I mean, I've dated some, but I spent a lot of time waiting on one woman and that didn't work out, so I'm a little out of the game. But I've met someone new. And we have this instant connection. Do you think that's crazy?*

Jae's breath caught in her throat as she read the message in the break room later that night. He had to be talking about her, right? She fought the urge to squeal and pump her fist. But she had to handle this carefully. Dropping the popcorn she'd been snacking on back into the bowl, she responded.

LadyJHawk: *I don't think it's crazy. Sometimes you just know. My parents claim they were a love-at-first-sight couple. They met and were married within a couple of months.*

NixDogQuest: *So do you think I should make a move? Ask this girl out?*

Nick liked her. So much of her wanted to type out the word in all capital letters—YES! But the guilt slicing through her stayed her fingers. She had to tell him first. Here he was baring his heart online. He deserved to know.

Before she could begin to type a response, a new message popped up.

NixDogQuest: *I know it's fast, but last time I hesitated, another guy swooped in. And now they're engaged. I don't want to miss my chance.*

The other woman. He was talking about the woman he'd loved, had waited for. Someone recently engaged.

Ree and Vivien's conversation about rings and weddings rushed back. They were both engaged and ran in Nick's circle of friends. Could Nick have been in love with one of them?

Really? Tots? I thought you liked onion rings too. You always order them.

Vivien.

Someone said she'd recently moved back from New York.

Nick had said he'd waited for a woman who had moved away to come back to Deep Haven. But she didn't want his life.

Oh no. Jae slapped a hand over her mouth. Her insides twisted. He'd been in love with Vivien.

Vivien Calhoun was a picture-perfect theater star. Of course Nick would fall for her.

Peter's words suddenly made a lot more sense.

What's so funny, Nick? Haven't heard you laugh like that for quite a while.

And hadn't Seth said something about Nick being gone for some time?

The truth settled heavy into the pit of her stomach. Nick was nursing a broken heart. This whole flirting with her was merely him on the rebound.

She'd almost thought this was real. And yeah, maybe she wanted it to be real. But she should've known. She wasn't the girl guys committed to. She and Matt had dated for years and he'd never proposed. The same with Shawn before him.

Nick was a good guy, but he was just lonely and looking for a distraction. She, on the other hand, wanted so much more.

LadyJHawk: *It's probably better to take your time. Maybe it is a little fast.*

Jae closed the app and tossed the phone on the table. Her headache came back full force.

But no amount of Excedrin would fix the ache in her heart.

CHAPTER 8

$\mathcal{N}$ ick drove to Evergreen Resort a few days later and walked into the lobby with a stack of flyers. The room smelled like it was freshly cleaned, probably with some of Ella Bradley's organic soaps that the resort used and his mom was always raving about. Sunshine spilled in through the big window. John Christiansen stood behind the pine-wrapped welcome desk and looked up from the light fixture he was fiddling with at the counter. "Good to see you, Nick. What can I do for you?"

"Just came out to leave these flyers and then Peter is bringing Tiago out here to meet me. We're gonna cut a trail and get it ready to go for your guests."

"Good. Leave the flyers here for Darek. He ran the snowmobile over the trails to give you a bit of a path." John laid his screwdriver down. "While you're waiting, any chance you know about light fixtures? This one keeps flickering even with a brand-new bulb."

"I'll take a look."

A laughing trio outside walked past the lobby window, breaking Nick's concentration before he could study the light.

He watched Ree Zimmerman, Amelia Christiansen, and Vivien Calhoun all bundled up in bold colored parkas and scarves, talking over each other and laughing like a flock of brightly colored birds. Some things never changed.

"Amelia is home, as you can see. She's taking a long furlough to be here for the holidays and to stand up in Ree's wedding. Who knows, maybe she'll finally set a date for her own wedding while she's at it." John let out a little sigh. "But I still remember when you and Peter and Seth all used to hang out with those three. I kinda miss those days."

"Yeah, me too."

John studied Nick a second and then went back to his fixture. "I hear Vivien's engaged now too."

"Apparently."

"I know there was a time you were hoping to have a future with her. It's got to be hard to see her with someone else."

Nick shrugged. John Christiansen was one of the guys who Nick had always looked up to. He and Ingrid were at every game for their kids. They were involved. Easy to talk to. Nick didn't mind admitting the truth. "Yeah, it was rough."

"You know, as long I've known and cared about you two, I never really thought you would be a good couple. It might be hard to see now, Nick, but I think it's for the best."

"Why do you say that?" Because he wasn't good enough?

"You should be with someone who makes you stronger, someone who brings out the best in you. Can you really say that's true of you and Vivien?"

Nick thought back to their high school years when they had spent the most time together. Vivien was flirty, vivacious, and always ready for fun. She was the perfect girl. "When things were hard, Vivien was there for me, willing to go for a ride, find a party, or hang out."

"If I'm remembering correctly, you also ditched class together. A lot."

Nick's neck grew warm. "I didn't have an easy time at school after the...accident. I just wanted to blow off steam sometimes. Vivie would come with me."

"So she helped you avoid your problems is what you're saying."

"Well, no. I mean, we were good friends too. We could always count on each other." Even after she'd turned him down, she went out of her way to make sure they were still friends. Ree and Amelia thought the whole prom-posal was hilarious, but he'd never heard Vivien laughing at him.

"And being there for each other is important, but what was your friendship based on? Did you talk about those things you were struggling with? Did you keep in touch when she was in New York?"

The more Nick thought about it, the more he didn't like the answer. He might know Vivien's favorite perfume and her food preferences, but he'd never really asked about her dreams, her struggles, her fears. And they would touch base every now and then when she was in New York, but mostly he followed her career at a distance. That wasn't making someone a better person, was it?

Nick picked up one of the screws lying on the countertop and twisted it between his fingers. "Not really."

Last night in their tots versus onion rings debate, Vivie had no clue what his true preference was. And why should she? He had always ordered *her* preference, trying to impress her, to be the guy he'd thought she would want to be with. But he'd never let her see who he really was.

It stung to admit. She had been a beautiful and alluring distraction for him.

John removed another screw from the fixture. "I think Vivie is with the right guy. And I think there's someone better for you too, Nick."

"Maybe there is." Nick shrugged and pointed to the light

fixture. "If you tighten the post screws in the socket, it will probably stop the flickering."

"I'll give that a try. Thanks."

Nick waved and walked back out into the brisk air. He mulled over John's words as he set up the dogs and waited for Tiago.

Someone else for him? He'd been stuck on the thought of Vivien so long, he'd never had room to think of anyone else. He'd had other girlfriends, but he'd never been really serious about them. They were more of a placeholder until Vivie came back.

Nick thought about Peter and Ronnie. Yeah, he joked about Ronnie being pushy, but she brought out a side of Peter, a confidence Nick hadn't seen before. And Peter was a calming influence on Ronnie, who tended to get a little hotheaded and passionate. Together they had worked through that big youth center and Westerman disaster. Together they *were* stronger.

You should be with someone who makes you stronger, someone who brings out the best in you.

John was right. Maybe Vivien hadn't been right for him. He just hadn't been able to see past the fantasy he'd built up around her. So what—he'd been in love with the idea of Vivien Calhoun and not the woman herself?

Oh, wow. It was like someone took off the blinders and he could see Vivien for who she really was and always had been—a good childhood friend.

And, if he were honest, he wasn't the kind of guy Vivien needed either. From everything he saw, Boone was an upstanding guy. Boone did bring out the best in Vivie.

Nick could finally say he was happy for her.

And maybe deep down, he knew he wasn't the one. If he had been, he would've made a move long ago. Vivien was always an escape. An illusion. A fun distraction. And they had a blast together.

But it wasn't enough to build a life, a future on.

Now, he wanted more. He wanted someone who wanted to be with him, who wasn't afraid of facing the hard times by his side. That would never be Vivien.

But could it be Jae? Last night, they'd had a real connection. He didn't feel the need to impress her. She wasn't the vivacious center of attention Vivien was, but she had a great sense of humor. Plus, she was passionate and smart—and she had about the creamiest skin he'd ever seen. He was constantly having to hold himself back from brushing her long bangs out of her eyes just for a chance to see if her cheeks were as soft as they looked. At one point, he'd whispered in her ear and was so tempted to kiss her neck he had to pretend to take a call outside to cool off.

But that was just physical attraction. He barely knew Jae. If he wanted a romantic relationship—and okay, yeah, he did—it needed more substance. No more illusions like Vivien.

LadyJHawk might be right. There wasn't a need to rush with Jae. He could take some time and get to know her.

Then again, maybe he'd be better off pursuing things *with* LadyJHawk. He had no clue what she looked like, yet they had this relationship that had started with fun banter and grown into something...real over the last two years. Because he *did* share his true desires and fears with her.

But it wasn't like she was really in his life. They were online friends, nothing more. Still...maybe it could be more.

Nick cinched the strap on his pack with a little more oomph than necessary. Grr. Maybe he was destined to be alone.

Seemed less complicated.

Peter and Tiago pulled up as Nick finished hooking the last two dogs into the lines. The ten-year-old kid hopped out of the truck with his own dog, Blue, on his heels. They ran off to explore the trail while Peter walked over. "Thanks for inviting him out here. He's super excited."

"Good. So am I." He couldn't figure out his love life but

teaching a ten-year old boy how to dog sled was totally within his skill set. "What are you going to do?"

"Ronnie and I are going out." Nick doubted his cousin could hold back the sappy look if he tried. He was totally in love with Veronica Morales. And why not? They made a good couple. And Nick was glad Peter had found a woman who wouldn't take advantage of his easy-going nature.

An easy-going nature that Nick enjoyed ruffling whenever he could. "So, when are you going to ask Ronnie to marry you? Seems like there's a growing trend in our crowd."

Peter just smiled and rolled his eyes. "As annoying as you can be, it's nice to see you back to normal."

"Normal? Don't know what you're talking about. I've never been normal, but if you'll excuse me, I've got a boy waiting for a ride." Nick whistled for Tiago and Blue to join him. He pulled his gloves on and got his phone out and ready to go live.

Peter yelled goodbye to Tiago. "I'll be back later this evening for T. Have fun."

He intended to.

Tiago ran up. "I can't wait to hit the trail. Where are we going to hook up Blue? Are you really going to let me live stream today?"

Nick laughed. "Hold on. One thing at a time. Let's hook Blue up behind the sled."

Soon Blue was set and Nick settled Tiago into the basket. "All right, when I tap you on the shoulder you hit this button and start recording. You'll need to tell the audience what everything feels like, what we're doing. It will make them feel like they're on the trail too."

"Got it!" Tiago gave him a thumbs-up.

Nick stepped onto the foot boards of the sled, right behind Tiago. As soon as the dogs knew what was happening, they jumped and howled, eager to run. The boy sat bundled in the sled and looked up with a huge grin on his face. Nick tapped him on the shoulder to start livestreaming. Then he let off the brake and shouted, "Hike! Hike!" And the team was off.

Tiago whooped in delight. Fresh snow flew up behind the dogs' paws. They bounded down the white trail through the woods. Since this was more about a ride for Tiago, Nick let the dogs run faster than he usually would for the first mile. Eventually he slowed them down to the pace they'd need to keep for the race, which was just over two weeks away. Tiago did some great narration as they loped up the trail. Kasha was doing great, and Blue had no problem keeping up with the team.

Nick took them on the short loop since it would be dark soon and it was a school night for Tiago. The sun broke through the clouds on their way back to the resort and capped off their run with a brilliant display. Fiery colors reflected off the snow, washing everything in a rosy light.

The sled zipped through the forest.

"You ready to guide the team?" he yelled over the wind to Tiago.

"Me? How am I supposed to do that?"

He pointed ahead. "See the fork in the trail up there? You pick where we go. Say 'Gee' if you want the dogs to go right and say 'Haw' if you want them to go left."

"Gee!"

The dogs veered to the right. Nick had hoped Tiago would pick this trail. It had a little incline to it and he would love the downhill portion.

Sure enough, he laughed and shouted the whole way down the hill. Followers online would eat it up.

They made the last fork. The dogs could take it from here. They were almost back to the resort. As they rounded a bend in the road, Kasha and Mischa jerked right to miss a fallen branch in the path. Kasha fell to the ground, her yelp of pain echoing through the trees.

"Whoa!" The line lurched to a stop before the word was even

out of Nick's mouth. He threw down the brake and ran to Kasha, who was sprawled in the snow. Mischa whined and nudged Kasha's neck. Nick pushed her away and scanned Kasha's body. Her eyes were open, her breathing shallow, and—oh no. Her back leg was tilted at an unnatural angle.

"What's wrong?" Tiago stood over them.

"Her leg." Nick ran his hands down Kasha's leg. Even in the brace he could tell it was worse than before. "She reinjured her leg." His mouth went dry. He shook off his coat and handed it to T. He released Kasha's neckline and tugline, slipped his arms under her trembling body, and lifted her carefully. She was still. Too still. "Come on, girl. You'll be okay. Stay with me." She had to be okay.

If she wasn't—oh no. The possibility didn't even compute. His mind went blank.

Tiago must have Ronnie's nerves of steel. His voice cut through the panic seeping in. "Kasha needs help. We need to get her to the vet."

Right. The vet.

"And we should keep her warm. That's what Ronnie always says. To keep hurt people warm and as comfortable as possible."

He could do that. Keep her warm and move her toward the vet. Nick looked around.

"We can use your parka," Tiago suggested. "And take her in the sled."

"Yeah."

Without asking, Tiago ran and spread Nick's coat in the sled basket. Nick laid Kasha on top of his coat and wrapped it around her. Her whine about broke his heart. He swiped at the moisture in his eye. "Come on, T. We're close to the resort. We'll take it really easy. I want you on the foot hold. Grab on to the bar and ride. Keep an eye on Kasha. I'm going to lead the team."

Nick led them back the last bit down the trail. The cold air seeped into his bones as they pulled onto the main Evergreen trail. Peter was walking out of the lobby, the smile on his face fading as he watched them come to a stop.

Nick didn't have to say a word as he scooped up Kasha. Tiago jumped off the sled and told Peter everything.

"What can I do, bro?" Peter asked.

"I…I gotta go." Nick lost the words. What would he do with the other dogs?

Peter clapped a hand on Tiago's shoulder. "T and I will load up the dogs in your truck and take them back to the kennel. You take Kasha in mine. I'll call Lena and tell her you're on your way."

And that was why Peter was a hero and Nick was not. Peter could think in a situation like this. Sheesh, even Tiago could.

Nick couldn't.

He had only one thought. Kasha had to be okay. He adjusted his grip on her and carried her over to Peter's truck. He drove on autopilot into town and crashed through the doors of the vet clinic with Kasha in his arms.

Lord, please let her be okay.

Lena came from the back room in scrubs, her brown hair pulled back. "Peter called me. Bring her here to the surgical room."

Good, because Nick still didn't have words. He followed Lena to the surgical room with harsh lights bouncing off all the stainless-steel surfaces. One of her assistants helped as he laid Kasha on a table, her tan and gray body still. Eyes closed.

Lena slipped on a fresh pair of gloves and removed the brace and gently felt the length of Kasha's leg. Her lips pursed.

"It's broken, isn't it?" Nick asked.

Lena nodded. "She'll need surgery this time, Nick. It's the same leg."

"Did I run her too hard? I swear, we took it easy all week. I let them run for a little bit, but the rest of the time was their normal pace, and it was only a short jog tonight."

"Something's not right. I have a hunch, but I'll know more once I get her into surgery."

"Please, Lena—" His voice caught.

"I'll do everything I can. Go wait in the lobby and I can get started."

With one last stroke along Kasha's head, Nick left. He had no concept of time. No conscious thought. A glance at the clock showed it had only been half an hour when Lena came out to the sitting area. And the look on her face was not encouraging—even for stoic Lena.

"She's still under. But we need to talk."

"It's my fault, isn't it? I ran her too hard."

Lena shook her head. "It wasn't you, Nick. It was only a matter of time before the bone was injured again."

"Why?"

"She has cancer."

The word didn't land—he couldn't put his mind around it. *Cancer?*

"Bone cancer. I've seen it before. So far, I'm guessing it's localized to just the injured leg, but it's only a matter of time before it spreads. She'll never be able to run on it. I need to know what you want me to do."

Nick tried to swallow, but his mouth was bone dry. What he wanted her to *do*? For once, blunt Lena wasn't really saying what she meant directly, but he'd heard her just fine. Many mushers would put a dog down that couldn't run. They were work dogs.

But he was not like those mushers.

And Kasha wasn't just any dog.

"Lena, I don't care how much it costs—what can you do to save her?"

"If we want to make sure we get it all, I would have to amputate."

"Amputate?"

She gave him a grim look. "I can do it right now. She's already sedated. We would amputate here, under the shoulder." She drew a line with her finger between the shoulder and elbow on a framed poster of a dog on the wall.

A fist was closing around his chest. "And the odds?"

Lena gentled her voice. "In most cases, that extends a dog's life by many years."

"But she'll only have three legs."

"True."

And maybe he should ask about the cost, but really, did it matter? It was Kasha.

He couldn't lose her. "Do it."

Lena nodded. "I thought that's what you would say. I interned in a dogsled race once and well, I know not every musher would make that decision, but I know what she—all your dogs—means to you."

Nick's swollen throat choked off all words.

Lena put her hand on his shoulder. "You're welcome to wait. Or you can go home. I can call you as soon as she's out of surgery. But it will take a while."

Go home? No. "I'm not going anywhere."

Lena left. After pacing a while, Nick stopped and sank into a chair. Glanced at the clock. Hated the visuals that played in his head. Kasha, barking and running as she led the team. Kasha, running in circles as he set down her food. Kasha, the first dog that had seemed to read his mind.

He sank his head into his hands.

What would he do without her?

He was done racing. The Mush Puppies race was only a couple weeks away now. Without that race, there were no more sponsors. And without the sponsors, he would lose the cabin, the kennels.

Everything.

❄

Jae rushed through the front door of Pet Haven Veterinary Clinic with her bag of donuts, letting in a blast of arctic air. But Nick didn't bother to look up. He sat on a lime-green vinyl bench. His body leaned forward, his head hanging down and hair fisted in his hands. She had been watching the livestreaming of Nick and Tiago's dogsled ride when it cut out with that awful yelp that kept repeating in her head. Maybe it was a little desperate, but after waiting, messaging NixDog-Quest, and hearing nothing, she finally broke down and called Ronnie, who didn't need any prompting to spill what she knew.

Kasha was hurt. Nick was with her while Ronnie, Peter, and Tiago were at Nick's taking care of the other dogs. She practically begged Jae to check on Nick.

Jae pushed aside her own bruised feelings and need for self-preservation and rushed over.

She sat next to Nick who finally lifted his head. "Jae? What are you doing here?"

"I saw—I mean Ronnie told me something was wrong with Kasha. We didn't want you to be alone. What happened?"

"She was running and reinjured her leg. Not only that...she has bone cancer. Lena is..." He winced and looked away. "Amputating her leg as we speak."

"Oh, Nick." Her voice caught at seeing his misery firsthand. She laid her fingers on his arm. "I'm so sorry."

"What is she going to do?" he said softly. "I mean, that dog loves to run, loves to race. How is she going to do that now?" He rubbed his forehead, a slight tremor in his hand.

The worry and concern for his dog made Jae fall even harder for Nick Dahlquist. He might still be brokenhearted over Vivie, but right now he needed a friend, and Jae could at least be that for him. She settled into the seat. "She'll adapt. And dogs are probably better at that than people. You'll see."

"Adapt." He shook his head.

"Yeah. Haven't you seen three-legged dogs before? Kasha will learn how to use her other three legs and she'll be running again before you know it."

"I don't know…"

"Listen. I don't know about being an amputee, but I do know what it's like to have life change in the blink of an eye. I grew up in the military, remember?"

He looked at her, understanding pouring forth from the depths of his blue eyes. "That was hard, huh? Moving all the time?"

She wanted to reassure Nick, but the simple question took her by surprise and hit deep. "Yeah. It was."

It was hard to always be the new girl. Hard to see everyone else fitting in perfectly and never quite finding that for herself. It was hard to pick up and leave again when the newness wore off and the place started becoming comfortable.

Then again, her daddy's words whispered to her heart.

It hurts to say goodbye, Jae Lynn, but it gives you the opportunity to say hello to a whole new place. Think of the opportunities and the new friends you're gonna make. A new place to explore. New skills to learn. You get to keep all that wherever you go.

Daddy's words gave her the hope she could share with Nick. "It was hard. But it also made me resilient. And now I have friends all over the world. Each place taught me new things, and all of these experiences helped shape me into the person I am today. Kasha will adapt to her new circumstances. You'll see. The pain of this surgery will last for a moment, but she will heal and acclimate and have a great doggy life. Even if she doesn't race again."

He studied her face, those beautiful eyes locking in on hers. The lines across his forehead relaxed a bit.

"I'm glad you're here," he admitted.

"You shouldn't be alone when you're hurting. This is what friends do."

Friends. Even though she didn't think of him as merely a friend. She couldn't deny the pull he had on her, how much she admired him. Liked him. Not just as NixDogQuest but as Nick Dahlquist. The guy who drove through a snowstorm to help his cousin. The man who spent time with young kids like Tiago. The man who had this special touch with animals was quickly boring his way past her defenses and into her heart.

But *his* heart could very easily be tied up with the memory of someone else. A heaviness suddenly weighted her down. Regardless, she needed to tell him the truth about being Lady-JHawk. Not that this was a good time, while he was worried about Kasha. But soon. For now, she would sit here as long as it took and offer whatever comfort she could.

A high-pitched whine of an engine outside drew Jae's attention to the window. Darkness had descended on Deep Haven, and with the lights reflecting off the window, she couldn't see anything outside. "What is that?"

Nick's brows took on a distinct V shape. "A snowmobile."

"I didn't realize they were so loud. But they always look like fun. I bet you've ridden one, huh?"

"Not in a long time. And I never will again." His voice went dark. He walked over to the lobby Keurig machine and pressed the button to heat the water. His shoulders were taut, and his jaw pulsed as he clenched and unclenched his teeth.

It was completely unexpected. She would've thought Nick would relish being outside rushing over the hills on a—oh wait. Jae moved to stand next to him. "The snowmobile accident."

"Right. A snowmobile accident killed my friend." Forgetting the coffee, Nick spun around and sat again on the bench.

"Nick. I'm so sorry. I didn't know." She sat beside him.

He glanced at the door to the back surgery area. "It was a long time ago."

"What happened?"

"I was snowmobiling with my friend Grady. We were sixteen and thought we knew it all. We didn't think we needed to stick to groomed trails or tell anyone where we were going."

Jae leaned forward to hear his somber words.

"I can still see it all in my head. It was dark. We were out in the middle of nowhere. Started snowing pretty hard. I was following Grady but his ski hit something under the snow and the next thing I knew, he was airborne. My snowmobile crashed into his and I was knocked off too. I broke my leg. I crawled over to Grady. He was just lying there in the snow, not moving. I didn't know what to do. I panicked. Again. Just like the fire. All I could do was try and keep him warm and pray for someone to find us."

"How long were you out there?" Jae swallowed through the emotion clogging her throat and reached for Nick's hand. It was calloused. Big. Cold. She wrapped both of her hands around it to warm it up, but it still seemed so meager compared to the trauma he had gone through.

"I don't know. My leg was busted up pretty bad. I might've blacked out a bit. Eventually Ed Draper and one of his dogs with a search team found us. But it was dark, freezing, and I couldn't save Grady. He died. And I did nothing to stop it."

She drew in a breath. "Nick. Seriously, that's not your fault. You were a kid. Accidents happen."

"Maybe. But to this day, I've never been back on a snowmobile."

"I know I wasn't there, but I still say you did the best thing for Grady that you could. You were with him and you prayed."

"Not like it did much good." The last words were a mere whisper. He sounded so hopeless.

It tore at her.

"Don't you see? Grady wasn't alone when he died because you were with him." She found his gaze, and held it. "And you aren't alone either, Nick. Not then and not now. I'm going to sit here with you until we know how Kasha's doing. And whatever happens, we're going to face it together."

It was the least she could do after he'd rescued *her*.

Nick had brought her back to life after her soul had fallen into a never-ending state of winter. He'd helped her find the sunshine again after Matt died.

So she would not abandon him in his hour of need.

They sat together and waited. Jae persuaded him to eat a little from the sack of donuts she'd brought. They drank coffee and did a magazine quiz matching the best dog breed for each personality type to pass the time.

The tightness in his jaw and shoulders subsided a little until Lena finally came out.

"All right, Nick. Surgery is done. Her vitals are good. Go get some rest now and we'll call you if anything changes. But she looks like she's going to be fine."

Nick nodded, relief in his eyes. "Thanks, Lena. Can I see her?"

"Of course."

❄

Nick came back out to the lobby where Jae waited a different guy. He walked with more ease. He even gave her a small smile. Not the full-blown dimpled grin, but he didn't look hopeless anymore.

And call her a glutton for punishment, but Jae wasn't ready to say goodnight to him yet.

Maybe she could help him, feed him, and bring back that carefree twinkle he usually carried. "Why don't you come to the headquarters with me, and I'll make you some dinner. I've got all the ingredients for ramen."

He chuckled as he held her coat for her. "Ramen? What more

do you need than a package of ramen and water? Even I can make that."

She slipped her arms in the sleeves and turned to face him, resting a hand on his chest. "Oh, Nick, please tell me you haven't been eating ramen made according to the directions on the package. It can be so much more than that."

"Really?" He looked down at her hand and covered it with his own, causing a sweet swirling sensation in Jae's middle. "I didn't know there was any other way. Better show me."

There was the old Nick. The twinkle was back in his eyes and oh so alluring.

She'd better be careful. Her heart was already way too invested and his might not be free from Vivien's hold.

But the warning faded away as he held the door for her and they walked out into the starlit night. He held out his arm. As slippery as the sidewalk was, she'd be a fool not to accept it.

Back in the HQ kitchen, Jae put Nick to work slicing green onions while she pulled her hair back and tried to get a hold of her runaway heart. She blamed her flushed cheeks on the water she heated on the stove in a shallow pan. It had nothing to do with the earlier glance of Nick's bare skin and chiseled muscles she'd caught as he pulled his sweatshirt off over his head, his T-shirt riding up. And it certainly wasn't the way he'd gently swept her bangs back and wiped the snow off her cheek before they walked in the door.

She went up to her tiptoes to grab the packages of ramen from the cupboard. Who had moved them to a higher shelf? She reached again. Hello! She'd had it on the bottom shelf for a reason.

A reason that she completely forgot when Nick stepped up and wrapped one arm around her so she wouldn't lose her balance while he reached up to get the ramen himself.

"This what you're looking for?" He still had her in his hold.

Was his voice always so dreamy? Eyes so smoldering? "Yes, that's it."

He grinned. A full grin, dimple and all. "I like that Texas twang. It's cute."

Goodness gracious biscuits and gravy. She needed to get a hold of herself. She cleared her throat and scampered away.

"Oh, look. The water is boiling." Jae took care to pronounce each word carefully without a hint of her drawl. She dropped the blocks of noodles and sauce packets in and stirred until they were almost cooked. Then she added two slices of American cheese, broke two eggs on top of the noodles, and covered the pan with the lid.

Nick leaned over the counter and sniffed. "Cheese and eggs, huh? That's your secret?"

"Well, that and the brand of ramen. This is the good stuff. Wait until you try it."

Soon the eggs were cooked. Jae added a splash of soy sauce and toasted sesame seed oil and split the food into two bowls. She topped everything with the green onions and handed Nick chopsticks and a spoon. "Go for it."

Nick's face lost the uncertain expression after the first bite. "You're right. It's great. But doesn't seem very authentic. Is this really how they would eat ramen in Korea?"

"I ate it this way in Korea all the time. Except I always add kimchi to mine."

"Do you have any?"

"Yeah, but most people aren't crazy about the smell of it so—"

"No, get it out. I want to try the kimchi."

"Are you sure?"

He leaned in with his dangerous smolder once more. "Oh, yeah. I want the authentic ramen experience. Don't sell out on me."

When he looked at her like that, she was tempted to give him anything he asked for. "If you insist." She grabbed the jar of kimchi she'd brought from home and kept in the fridge. She braced herself as she opened it.

Maybe the kimchi was a good thing. This would kill any of the romantic mood lingering in the air. The potent smell of fermented vegetables was one she'd grown up with and enjoyed, but she knew many Americans didn't.

Nick sniffed the open jar. "That smells good."

"Really?"

"Yeah, how much do you put on?"

She added a dollop of the kimchi to her noodles and passed the jar to Nick. "About this much."

Nick took the same amount and added it to his dish. He stirred it and took another bite. "That's some good ramen. Now it has some real flavor."

She waited for a grimace or gag. He was probably holding back simply to be Minnesota-nice.

But he only took a bigger bite.

"You really like it? The kimchi?"

"This is amazing. Who wouldn't like it?"

A bitter memory stung despite the many years that had since passed. "Plenty of people. Believe me."

Nick laid his chopsticks down. "Why did you say it like that?"

Jae tried to shrug it off, but with Nick watching her all concerned, like he really cared, she couldn't help but open up to him. "In Korea, it's a badge of honor to be known for making good kimchi and my mother was one of the best. Daddy and I were always proud of her. So when I was young and moved to the States, my daddy's family had a big potluck family reunion to welcome us. Of course, mom made her specialty and she let me help."

Jae breathed in the familiar scent and remembered. "I was so proud as Omma, my mom, took the time to explain how to soak and salt the napa cabbage, how to slather the paste of spices and sauce evenly, how to bundle the portions together and stuff them in the onggi crock that was passed down from my grandmother. We covered it and set it aside for a day or two. Then it finished fermenting in the fridge. Daddy made a big deal of it too as I helped. It was practically a rite of passage."

Nick ignored the food in front of him and watched her with a warm gaze. "How old were you?"

Jae stirred her ramen with the chopsticks.

"I was eleven. And not only was I old enough to learn the art of making kimchi, we'd just moved back to the States and Mom and I were going to stay for the next school year while my father was going to be in Afghanistan. This was my chance to really get to know my cousins and extended family. I was nervous and excited all at the same time. I knew Mimi and Pap, but not the aunts and uncles and cousins as much. But I wanted to. We were going to be close enough to visit often, and I really wanted to feel like I was one of the Lavaca County Washingtons Daddy would tell me about. I wanted to show them all who we were at the big potluck."

"They almost sound like the equivalent of the Cook County Dahlquists. We have some big potlucks too. And it's always a competition over who brings the best dish."

"I bet the Washingtons could give you Dahlquists a run for your money. I grew up hearing all about these famous potlucks. I was so excited to add my kimchi to that long table of food. But I'll never forget the faces of all my cousins when I opened that onggi up in front of them."

"Something tells me they didn't enjoy it." Nick's baritone soothed, but it couldn't quite reach the jagged edges of the memory.

"My cousins gagged and pretended to barf and said horrible things. That was their first impression of me and it didn't get any better. They called me Baby Jae to differentiate me from my cousin Jason who went by Big Jay."

"So, you showed up at the potluck wanting to belong and left with a broken heart instead."

"And a broken arm."

"How did that happen?"

"If the kimchi wasn't bad enough to make me stick out, you should've seen their reaction when they realized I had never ridden a horse by myself before. They seriously looked at me like I was from outer space. So I lied and told them I could ride."

"You did?"

"Well, I grew up thinking this was my family. Daddy said, 'Family is always there for you. They're the ones you can depend on.' Even though they made fun of the kimchi, I still thought I could trust them. Or maybe I was desperate to belong. So Big Jay saddled up this huge stallion and said it was a gentle old horse. I believed him. Then he told me to prove I was really a Washington and could ride."

"So you rode him?"

"Not for long. I fell off and broke my arm. Right outside the barn." Jae rubbed the spot that had long since healed but always brought a twinge of pain with storms and the memory resurfacing.

"Wow, and I thought growing up with my cousins was harsh."

"Yeah, I'm not as eager to go horseback riding or share my love of ethnic food as I used to be. And maybe that's why Texas never quite felt like home."

"The strongest flavor anyone ever serves around here is sauerkraut. But this"—he picked up his chopsticks once more —"is great. Your cousins are the ones missing out." He took another big bite. "And for the record, I think you fit in here just fine. Maybe you belong in Minnesota more than Texas."

"It hasn't always been easy, but I have learned to embrace both my American and Korean heritages."

"Well, you for sure have the cooking part down." And he slurped another noodle off his chopsticks. "Now we just need to find you a place in Deep Haven that's all your own. You've talked with Nathan Decker, right?"

He really seemed like he wanted her to stay. "Yup. He's on the lookout for a rental. He showed me one today, but it was too much."

"I'm sure he'll find you something soon. I don't know when Ree's and Vivien's weddings will be, but I wonder when their rental will be available." Nick grabbed a donut from the bag sitting on the middle of the table.

Right. Vivien. Reality came crashing down. Here Jae had been playing house, making supper for him, but she was only a stand-in for the woman he couldn't be with. Jae turned away from him, took her own dishes to the sink, and started filling it with hot water.

"Hey, did I say something?" Nick hopped up to sit on the counter with the donut bag in his hand. He stuffed the last bite of his chocolate cake donut in his mouth.

She tried to shrug away his concern and kept her eyes on the dishes. "I'm not sure if Vivien and Ree's place is right for me. The rent is probably more than I can handle alone. I think I heard Ree's wedding is coming up soon, but who knows how long Vivien will stay there."

Nick chuckled. "Knowing Vivie, she won't want to wait too long. I bet she and Boone will have a short engagement."

The lid of the pan slipped out of Jae's hand and into the soapy water. She studied Nick. He didn't seem too upset. In fact, he poked around in the bag and grabbed another donut, took a big bite, and grinned at her.

"Is that a good thing? Vivien's engagement?"

He nodded and swallowed his bite. "I think so. Had you

asked me a month ago, I probably would've answered differently, but...Vivie is with a good guy."

"She was the one, wasn't she? The one you were waiting for?"

Nick hopped off the counter, grabbed a towel, and dried the lid. "Yeah. She was. For a long time I thought she was 'the one.' But...I've realized lately that we weren't really a good fit. She belongs with Boone and I'm okay with that."

Oh. She slid her gaze over to him. He hummed as he dried the spoons. He certainly didn't act brokenhearted. Was he truly over her? She tried to stop her heart from hoping too much as they finished the dishes and put everything away.

Seymour gave a big yawn and stretched.

"I hear ya, boy. It's my bedtime too." Nick scratched the dog behind his ears. "I should head home. But I gotta say, that was the best meal I've had in a long time." He pulled his sweatshirt and coat on.

Jae walked him to the side door with Seymour following close behind. Nick looked down at her, and she was caught in his gaze—suddenly more awake, more aware than she'd ever been.

"Thanks for the ramen." His voice was a little husky, his lips curled up on one side in a boyish smirk.

Was it bad that she didn't want him to go? She could stand here all night, soaking in his presence, that blue-eyed gaze, the spicy, musky Nick scent.

Seymour knocked into the back of her legs, catching her off guard and pushing her into Nick who once again wrapped an arm around her and pulled her against him. "Whoa, there."

Her palms, now both against his chest, could feel his thudding heartbeat. She met his gaze, the look of surprise in his eyes melting into unmistakable desire, and Jae was powerless to look away. Heat shot through her from his embrace, and her own pulse spiked as he dropped his chin and their lips met.

Her fingers curled themselves into his sweatshirt and Nick's arms drew her tighter, closer as their kiss went from gentle and sweet to one filled with the same passion that this man brought to everything he did. His hands cupped her face, one thumb tracing her jawline.

With a moan that sounded a little like regret, he pulled away. He rested his forehead against hers. "Jae."

They stood there for a moment longer in the dark hallway, their breaths mingling, the air between them hot. She couldn't move. Couldn't speak. Nick was so much more than she'd ever imagined. So much more in flesh and blood than he had ever been on a screen. But he seemed troubled by something.

"It's Vivien, isn't it?"

He recoiled. "No! No, it's not Vivie. I promise." He looked her straight in the eye, his gaze not wavering at all. "I just didn't mean for things to happen so fast. I'd...better go." He slipped out the door before she could say anything else.

As she heard his truck drive away, the heaviness on her shoulders grew unbearable. She leaned against the door and closed her eyes. She had to tell Nick the truth.

Because she couldn't deny it any longer. His kiss had brought it front and center. She was in love with him. And she wasn't sure what his hang up was tonight, but she believed him when he said it wasn't Vivien Calhoun's memory.

And if they were going to figure anything out, she couldn't do that without telling him that she was LadyJHawk.

He'd known LadyJHawk first. He needed to hear it from her. Jae ran up to the bunk room and flopped down on her bed. She opened up the messaging app and typed.

LadyJHawk: *Hey, Solo, are you there? I need to talk to you. I need to tell you something.*

Nick wasn't even home yet, but this was the time of night they usually started chatting. He'd probably check his messages soon after he arrived.

Jae took Seymour for a walk, but her hand stayed in her pocket next to her phone, waiting. It didn't buzz with any incoming message. After brushing her teeth, she bundled into her pajamas and bathrobe. Still no response.

She stared at the screen and its blinking cursor, waiting for an answer.

CHAPTER 9

$\mathcal{N}$ick sat at his dining room table and stared once more at the message on his laptop. What did Lady-JHawk want to tell him? It was weird. Ominous. And he didn't like it.

Maybe it was the off day he was having.

He'd had such a great time with Jae last night. He'd never felt so comfortable with someone. The way she sat with him, cooked for him, looked at him with those fathomless brown eyes like he could do anything. He hated to leave but he barely knew her. Right? He had promised himself he'd take things slow.

And yet, he'd dreamed about her all night. Dreamed about their kiss.

With a haunting voice that sounded a lot like what he imagined LadyJHawk to sound like accusing him in the background. How could he be falling for two women at the same time? And one he'd never met? Was he going crazy?

He groaned. His body was sore, like it had been dragged behind the sled for miles. It took three cups of coffee before he could go out and make a batch of food for the dogs. And even then, the dogs were more restless than normal. He spent the morning restocking the dog food and treats, the old standby recipes, but they didn't make him feel any better.

The walk to the mailbox didn't help either. The envelope from the bank held only more bad news. A second notice. He'd have to sell a lot more puppies to keep the cabin. And now another vet bill to pay for Kasha's surgery.

And after all that, he'd opened up his app to this message. How was he supposed to respond?

A knock on the door interrupted his thoughts. Before he could get up from the table, Peter's voice and the aroma of marinara and Italian sausage permeated the room. "Hope you're hungry." Peter walked into the dining room and set down a pizza box from the Trailside Bistro and a huge bag. He pulled out plastic containers and baggies of food and set them on the table.

"Dude, I thought you were just picking up pizza." Nick closed his laptop and set it over on the counter.

"Yeah, but when I called in the order at the Bistro, Grandma Doris was there, and she told me to swing by Aunt Connie's because she had food for you. It would save her a trip and she wouldn't have to come all the way out here to the boonies to make sure you weren't starving to death. And then Dina said she had cookies to add, and my mom wanted you to have a couple of freezer meals."

Nick rolled his eyes. "When will they believe me that I'm capable of feeding myself?"

"Did you forget the family motto?"

"What? 'Don't go to bed hungry'?"

"No, that's their how-to-have-a-happy-marriage advice to engaged couples. I was talking about the motto, 'Food fixes everything.'"

Nick grabbed two of the frozen meals. "How could I forget? I've got it stitched on a pillow and it's Grandpa's email signature." He sighed and stuffed the meals in the freezer, next to all the other frozen offerings he lived off of. "I suppose it's what I get for being the only Dahlquist that can't cook."

Peter dropped the smart alecky smirk and was serious for a moment. "They want you to know they care. They heard about Kasha. Besides, this is the Minnesota way. We demonstrate affection through hot dish."

There were worse ways to show support.

Once the food was put away, Peter and Nick dug into the pizza. Nick chugged down one of his cousin's Mountain Dews.

Peter grabbed a slice of sausage and pepperoni pizza and covered it in Parmesan cheese. "Oh yeah, last night when we fed the dogs, I moved a bale of straw that was too close to the furnace in the big shed. Might wanna be careful of that."

"Okay, Fire Chief Dahlquist. Now, can we get down to business and figure out the next wilderness training course session?"

"You're bucky today. What's the deal?"

"Nothing."

"Come on. It's me. I know something is up."

Nick picked the olives off his pizza. "Isn't it enough that my lead dog is never going to race again? I've got a major race in two weeks and if I don't do well in it, my career is over." Nick could only imagine the stockpiling of freezer meals he'd have if his family knew how dire his financial situation was. He'd have plenty of food, but no place to live. At least he'd never have to worry about starving to death.

Peter sprinkled pepper flakes on his pizza. "I suppose you have a point. I thought it was maybe something to do with Jae."

Nick's olive-free slice hung in the air halfway to his mouth. "Jae? Why would you think that?"

"Um, because you couldn't take your eyes off her at trivia the other day. The way your voice got all squeaky when you said her name just now. Or because you were there at headquarters with her until pretty late last night. Take your pick."

Nick dropped his pizza onto his plate. "Now how'd you know that? Do you have cameras at the HQ?"

"Maybe." Peter smirked and took a bite.

Great. What all had he seen on that camera?

"Chill, dude. I'm just kidding. I happened to drive past HQ after I dropped Ronnie and Tiago off and saw your truck parked outside."

"Oh."

"Oh? That's all you have to say? What's got you so uptight?"

"Nothing."

"Really? So what was going on at HQ with Jae?"

"She made me dinner." Okay, even to his ears it sounded defensive. Nick chugged more Mountain Dew.

Peter laughed. "She may not be full-blooded Minnesotan yet, but she'll fit right in."

"What are you talking about?"

"She made sure you didn't go hungry. Grandma Doris will love her."

"Shut up. It was just dinner." And maybe a goodnight kiss. But Peter didn't need to know that. And Nick should maybe make sure it wasn't caught on camera for real.

Peter stopped eating and stared him down. "Why don't you make it more? Ask her out."

"It's not that easy."

"Because of Vivie?"

"No. I'm over Vivien." Nick picked off a stray olive on his slice. "It's not that."

"You sure you're over Vivie? You've loved her since second grade."

"I didn't love her. Not really. It might've taken me awhile to realize it, but she is better with Boone. I'm happy for her."

"Then what's the hang up with Jae?"

Nick stood up and brought his laptop back to the table. Releasing a sigh, he opened it up and showed Peter the screen with the messaging app. "This is the problem."

Peter scrolled through the messages watching the ongoing conversation roll down the screen. "Wow. How long has this been going on?"

"Over a year. Maybe two."

"So this is a fan? This LadyJHawk?"

"Not a fan. A friend." Nick cupped the back of his neck with his hand. "Maybe more than a friend. I dunno. I mean, we've shared a lot. Personal stuff. Stuff I've never dreamed of sharing with Vivie."

But some things he had told Jae.

Huh. Maybe that was his hang up in answering the last message. He'd shared so much with LadyJHawk. He didn't realize how much he'd come to depend on her until he was standing there in the hallway with Jae in his arms. Kissing Jae was...amazing. But it also felt like betrayal. He didn't know what LadyJHawk wanted to tell him, but he didn't deserve her confidence. And something told him whatever it was would change the course of their relationship.

Peter pointed to the screen. "This LadyJHawk could be anyone. She could be some granny with permed white hair and a million cats. Or a thirteen-year-old girl with a major crush on you. LadyJHawk might not even be a 'she.'"

"No, LadyJHawk is definitely a she. I asked."

"Oh, right. And everyone on the Internet is a hundred percent honest."

"Look, I know it's a woman." Nick sat back in his chair and folded his arms.

"Regardless, LadyJHawk is an online avatar. Jae Washington is a real live human being. An attractive, intelligent, real woman. What are you waiting for? Forget the screen fling. Ask Jae out. I know you like her." He narrowed his eyes, almost daring Nick to deny it.

But he couldn't. Yeah. He did like Jae. And it didn't seem right to be kissing her and yet messaging LadyJHawk on the side. It was like he was cheating on one of them with the other. But how did he simply end a two-year online friendship like that? Should he?

How did he go from pining over one woman for over a decade to now being caught between two women at the same time in a matter of weeks?

Peter clapped a hand on his shoulder. "Bro, you were the one who encouraged me to make a go of it with Ronnie when I wasn't sure. Now it's my turn. Jae is the real deal. Do what you want with this Hawk Lady, but don't overlook the gift right in front of you."

Nick stared at LadyJHawk's message. His cursor blinking, waiting for a response. "Maybe you're right." He closed the laptop and pushed it aside. No more illusions like he'd had with Vivien for so long. It was time to live in the real world and have a relationship with a real woman.

"Good call," Peter said.

"So you ready to talk wilderness survival?" Nick picked up another piece of pizza and took a bite.

"Let's do this."

❄

Jae parked her Subaru behind an old Chevy truck along with other CRT vehicles at Nick's place. Even with her engine off, a buzz of anticipation lingered in the afternoon air and it wasn't for the upcoming training session.

She hadn't seen Nick since their kiss under the exit sign of the HQ hallway two days ago. Two long days to relive that kiss over and over in her mind as she was busy on calls and training and Nick was busy with his team. Two days to torture herself waiting for a chance to unburden the secret she held inside. But she'd never heard a peep from NixDogQuest.

She turned to Seymour in the passenger seat.

"All right, boy. This is it. I'm going to tell Nick. I'm gonna tell him in person. It will be better that way, right?"

Seymour barked.

"I just need to get him alone."

She grabbed her parka and gloves from the back seat and started down the path that led from Nick's driveway to the kennels and sheds behind the cabin. Seymour followed her. Since whatever they were doing for their survival training was going to be overnight, Seymour would stay with Nick's dogs. Surely there would be plenty of time to find Nick alone at some point if they were going to be here all night.

By now Nick knew her, knew she wasn't a crazy stalker. It would be fine. All she had to do was say the words.

I'm LadyJHawk.

How hard could it be?

Jae pushed aside the hint of unease and approached the group gathered at Nick's firepit. The clear blue afternoon sky sported a few thin wisps of clouds. The sunshine was deceiving though. The brutal wind almost knocked Jae over with its arctic chill.

But the yeasty smell of freshly baked bread and a dark roast coffee promised some comfort and warmth. Her stomach grumbled, reminding her that she hadn't eaten breakfast or lunch.

Ronnie waved her over to join her and Colleen, who stood by a table. "Jae, have you tried the Flashy Fox Bakery rolls or Peter's mini-quiches? They are amazing."

Bite-sized quiches filled a crockpot. Another basket of soft, cloud-like rolls and carafes of coffee covered the table. Jae's mouth started watering. She grabbed a quiche and stuffed the whole thing into her mouth.

Mmm. Ronnie wasn't exaggerating.

Nick walked up to them while her mouth was still full. "Hey."

The sun caught his tousled hair, bringing out auburn highlights she'd never noticed before, and a fluttery sensation filled her. She tried to smile around the food in her mouth. She swallowed the too-big bite and started to speak, but a portion of it went down the wrong way. She coughed to dislodge it. It stuck fast to the back of her throat. She coughed again and again, but it wouldn't budge.

Nick's hand on her back only added to her embarrassment as he tried to calm her. Here she was trying to be as normal as possible, show him she wasn't a psycho stalker, and she couldn't even swallow food properly.

"Here. Drink this." Ronnie shoved a bottle of water in her face. Everyone's attention centered on Jae as she guzzled the water. Anything to calm the seizing in her throat. Water dribbled down her chin, but finally the piece of egg went down and she could breathe again. The way her cheeks and ears were burning, she could only imagine the shade of red that she glowed as she gulped in air.

"Are you okay?" Nick's blue eyes gazed with so much concern.

"I'm great. Just checking out everyone's emergency responses." She bent down and scratched Seymour, who hadn't moved from her side. She readjusted his harness. Anything to keep her hands busy while her cheeks cooled back down to a normal non-lobstery color.

Conversations around her resumed, and when she stood back up, only Nick still watched her. He leaned in close and whispered, "Are you sure you're okay?"

"Oh, yeah. All good." She couldn't quite look him in the eye. "So you have a place for Seymour tonight?"

"Yup. I'm hoping he and Mischa can be buddies. She's not

doing well without Kasha." They walked away from the others toward the kennels. "I've been thinking about you. It's been so crazy though." Nick shot her a shy smile. The light caught his baby blues, highlighting every speck of sapphire and aquamarine in them.

"I've been—"

"Yo, Nick!" Peter called from the other side of the yard. "I need your help."

"Be right there," Nick yelled back to his cousin. He turned to Jae. "Just go ahead and see how Seymour does with Mischa. I know they were fine before, but she hasn't been herself. I've gotta help Peter." He jogged away.

Okay, so getting Nick alone might be more of a challenge than she'd originally thought. And now her nerves were really buzzing. Or she was shivering from the cold. At this point, it was hard to say.

Seymour and Mischa sniffed each other through the fence. Jae opened up the gate and Seymour went right in. They sniffed some more and then ran off to the other end of the kennel.

"Looks like you two make a good pair." That was a positive sign, right? Their dogs got along. Now if she could just get Nick alone for two seconds to tell him that Seymour was C and she was Lady J, maybe they could get somewhere.

Jae stayed and watched the dogs until Boone called the group back to the firepit to start their wilderness training.

Nick went over all the fire-making skills again and then strapped on snowshoes and led them farther into the woods, where he showed them how to make a snow shelter. "If you find a big enough drift or have enough snow cover, you can dig a trench into it." He took off his snowshoes and used one to dig the trench, reminding them of using the resources they had around them. "Now you line this with green branches. After that, lay long, thin logs over the top of your trench and cover it with more branches. If you use full green branches and they're thick enough, pile snow on top of them, and you've got a cozy shelter for yourself. In a group setting, we could make a quinzee shelter, which is like a snow cave, but we'll work on that a different time."

He reminded them of the lean-to and A-frame log shelters. Then they spent the next hour reviewing basic mapping and orientation skills they'd learned earlier. After that, they formed an assembly line for putting together survival kits. Nick walked around and checked their packs. Everyone had a tiny propane burner, a small cooking and utensil set, flint, paracord, an all-purpose tool, solar blanket, and a small ax.

Jack Stewart finished fastening his pack. "So what are we doing with these packs now that we're done?"

Everyone stopped packing and looked to Nick.

"You're going camping."

That could be fun. Jae could see the whole group sitting around the—

"Alone."

Wait a minute. What?

Nick continued. "I've got a map and we have an area marked for each of you. Peter and I will take you each out to your spot on the four-wheeler or the side-by-side. You still have a few daylight hours to make a shelter of your own and start a fire. And this time you have the small ax to use."

"Are you sure we're ready for that? Staying out all night alone? The wind chill is supposed to drop below zero." Colleen didn't seem thrilled at the idea.

Jae didn't blame her.

Nick didn't seem worried though. "If you use the skills we've practiced, you'll be fine. It won't be like staying at the Grand Moose Resort or anything fancy like that. It will be a little uncomfortable, but you each have a radio and water. I've even included toilet paper and an MRE for you. This will give you a chance to use what you've learned and really experience a winter survival situation. However, do not hesitate to ask for help if you need it. You'll be spread out enough to be by your-selves, but no one is too far away. If you call, I can be there in a matter of minutes."

Jae held back the groan building inside. This time they wouldn't even be in pairs. She would be completely alone. In the woods. At night.

It might be too adventurous even for her.

But then again, maybe this would work in her favor. If Nick came to check on them—and knowing him, he totally would—she would have plenty of privacy to tell him the truth about their online relationship. Not only that, but she could also prove to him that despite her Texas twang, she could totally hack it here in the wilds of Minnesota. She could fit into his world.

The idea took root. Assurance grew. Like Nick said, they'd been trained. She could do this.

When Nick offered to take her out first, she jumped at the chance. She settled into the seat behind him on the four-wheeler and didn't mind at all when he told her to hang on to him tightly. She wrapped her arms around his middle.

Oh, he smelled like adventure and cozy nights around a fire. She breathed in deep.

"Ready?" he asked.

"Oh, yeah!"

He gunned the engine. She squeezed her arms tight as they lurched forward. The wind blew her hair back and took away any chance of conversing. For now, she soaked in Nick's pres-ence, the hard plane of muscles she held on to, his spicy after-shave, and the howl of sheer enjoyment he released as they flew past trees and branches.

Yeah, she could get used to this.

The ride was over too quickly. When they stopped, he hopped off and took her hand. "Here's your spot." It was in a bit of a dip in the landscape, surrounded by huge spruce and pine trees. The snow was up to her knees. "What do you think?"

What did she think?

She thought she wanted to hold on to Nick forever, just riding through life like an adventure in the woods. But she couldn't exactly say that out loud. Not until he knew who she was. "It's great."

"Just let me know if you need any—"

"Yup. I'll be fine. No babysitting necessary." She gave him a playful shove away. "I've got this."

"Whoa. Okay." Nick stared a moment and then went back to his four-wheeler. "I'll be back later."

But Jae didn't say anything else. Instead, she started scouting out good limbs for her shelter. Nick left and soon she was by herself in the forest.

This was her chance. She would prove to Nick and the others that she belonged on this team and she belonged in Deep Haven. Nick needed to see she wasn't like Vivien. Jae In Real Life was someone he could trust, who didn't turn her nose up at this lifestyle. She embraced it. She loved being outdoors, she loved the woods, the dogs, the whole package.

If he could see how well they fit together, then he could understand why she'd moved here. When she told him that she was LadyJHawk, he would know it wasn't because she was a crazed fanatic, but because they had real potential at something lasting. What had started as a simple online chat had grown to be so much more.

She just had to get over the cold. Getting out of the wind would help.

Jae grabbed a long, skinny branch that leaned against a birch tree. It would be a decent ridgepole for her shelter. She tugged and yanked until it was free from the snow and the big trunk it had been attached to. By the time she got it set in place, her bones felt like ice. But she was tough. She would ignore the chill and make sure she had a good shelter before Nick inevitably showed up to check on her.

However, after working on it for what felt like hours, Jae gave up on her A-frame shelter. The small ax from her pack was useless in her frozen hands. Her measly ridgepole had four thin logs leaning against it. Not nearly enough coverage for even a squirrel. She would get back to it later. For now, she needed a fire. If she could warm up to the point of being able to feel her hands again, she could finish her shelter. Besides, she would soon need the light as well as the heat. It was only four o'clock and the sky to the west was rosy gold.

But her fingers were so numb, she couldn't pull the knife blade out of her all-purpose tool.

She refused to let herself think of riding off into the sunset with Nick—preferably to a heated cabin or a warmer climate. Instead, she hacked off another branch and dragged it to the pit she'd dug in the snow for a fire. The green branches were supposed to line the bottom of it to keep the fire off the ground, but she couldn't wait that long.

How did people live out here? Jae stomped, trying to get feeling back in her feet. The core-deep shivering overtook her whole body as she tried to collect more branches.

She looked at her measly pile of pinecones and twigs. It would have to be enough. She ripped birch bark off and scraped the knife edge against the small block of magnesium to create a pile of shavings.

Heat. She needed heat.

Tears froze on her cheeks from the wind whipping her bangs into her eyes. She struck the ferro rod with the knife, trying to create a spark. Again and again, she tried.

She looked at her pack lying on the frozen ground against a tree trunk. The radio was there in the side pocket.

No. She had to show the team she could do this. She had to show Nick. Jae gulped in another breath and steeled herself. It was supposed to be uncomfortable. But it wasn't impossible.

She *could* survive a Minnesota winter.

Dropping the knife and ferro rod, Jae stomped again. She shoved her hands under her armpits, scrambling for any semblance of warmth. She sank down onto the fallen log by her pathetic excuse for a firepit.

The shivering stopped.

Maybe she just needed a rest. A little nap to regroup. She would wake up refreshed, could finish the shelter, get the fire going.

She would not give up.

But she would take a break. Her bottom slid off the log and Jae curled into a ball. Through the trees, the last bit of sunlight died as darkness swallowed it. Her lids grew heavy as she watched the sky.

Just a short rest and she would be fine.

If only she had a tauntaun right about now.

CHAPTER 10

*I*f there was a moon out tonight, Nick couldn't see it as he drove his ATV through the dark forest. The temperature had dropped with the sun and time was up. He was heading back to check on Jae. He had helped everyone else who'd called in. Now he could give her his undivided attention and make sure she was okay. He gave the four-wheeler more gas as he headed back in her direction.

There was no light from a campfire as he approached her site. With the temps dropping into single digits, she had to be cold. Hopefully she would be a little more accepting of assistance this time. She needed to have a fire going by now.

But where was she?

"Jae?"

No shadowy form of her puffy parka appeared. The spotlight on the four-wheeler caught the structure she had started as a shelter. A few measly branches leaning against a ridgepole.

Nick jumped off the ATV and clicked his flashlight on. "Jae?" He called her name louder this time. He swung the beam of light around the area. Had she decided to hike back to his cabin? The light caught on her backpack leaning against a tree.

No. She would've taken the pack with her.

A chill ran down his back. "Jae!" Maybe she'd wandered a little farther. He called again.

No response. Even though it was ludicrous, he checked her shelter. No Jae. Nick kneeled by her pack. The radio was still there.

Where was she? Gathering more wood? Maybe she'd started a snow trench. He ran his light along the ground, looking for a mound of snow she might've tunneled into.

A lump of rock he didn't recognize caught his eye. He shined his light in that direction and his breath caught.

Jae.

He ran over and shook her. "Jae, wake up."

She didn't stir. She was curled onto her side against a log. Her lips were blue, her eyes closed. He shook her harder and yelled her name. Her eyelids didn't even flutter.

His own hands shook as he grabbed his radio. "Peter! Jae's in trouble. She's unconscious."

Peter's voice crackled over the radio immediately. "I'll be right there."

Nick listened as Peter called all the others. Running on instinct alone, he scooped up Jae's cold body and started walking in the direction of his cabin. "Come on, Jae. Wake up!"

He couldn't think. His only thought was a prayer.

Save Jae.

Save Jae.

Save Jae.

He said it with each step he took.

It couldn't have been long, but it felt like an eternity until the CRT side-by-side engine sounded in the woods. Soon lights moved in his direction. Help.

Peter grabbed Jae from him and told Nick to sit in the back of the side-by-side. He laid Jae on his lap and they piled their

coats on her. Colleen hopped in next to him and felt for a pulse as Peter ran back to the driver's side.

"She's got a pulse. It's light, but it's there," Colleen said as she continued to check Jae's vitals with the kit they kept on the off-road vehicle.

Peter glanced back. "Boone already called the ambulance. It should be at the cabin by the time we get there."

Everything was a blur as they rushed down the forested trail and met the ambulance in Nick's driveway. Dean Wilson and Jensen Atwood were there with the cot waiting. Ronnie and Colleen were yelling out directions. When Peter pulled up, hands grabbed Jae and lifted her off Nick's lap. They surrounded her and Nick couldn't say or do anything. But when they loaded Jae into the back of the truck, he had enough wits to know he was not going to be left behind. He jumped in.

"Nick, you can't—" Dean Wilson started to say.

"I'm staying with her."

Dean looked to Peter, who stood ready to close the back door of the ambulance. "Let him ride along. He'll keep out of your way."

As long as they let him ride with her, he'd agree with anything. He sat on the bench and watched Ronnie and Dean.

"Temp is 88 degrees," Ronnie said. "BP is eighty-two over fifty-five."

It was the longest ride of Nick's life.

At the Deep Haven hospital, the emergency room nurses and doctors weren't as accommodating as Peter and Dean, and insisted Nick wait in the sitting area. But hours later, once Jae was settled in a private room with her temperature back to normal, Nick was right by her side again while the others stayed in the lobby.

The doctor said she would be fine, that she had woken up earlier with them once they'd brought her temperature back up from 88 degrees. But Nick would believe it when he saw it.

A steady beep from the monitor beside the hospital bed confirmed life. Pulse, oxygen stats, and other numbers that Nick didn't understand blinked on the screens. Jae's body looked tiny in the hospital bed. White cotton blankets covered her and were tucked up to her chin. Nick dragged the only chair in the room to her side. All he wanted was for her to open those beautiful eyes.

She stirred and moaned.

Nick brushed aside the bangs that swept down her forehead. "Jae?"

Her forehead creased and she slowly opened her eyes.

Nick released a long breath, and the tightness in his middle eased. "Hey. How are you feeling?"

Her gaze fixed on him for a second before dropping to the bed covers. "All right." She looked around the room and pulled her arms out from under the blankets. Her IV line tangled around her wrist.

"So that was some training session, huh?" Her weak smile wasn't at all convincing.

He could imagine her embarrassment, though. Maybe right now wasn't the best time to lay into the dangers of hypothermia. He pushed aside the urge to lecture and found her hand.

Her *warm* hand. It anchored him, and the storm inside calmed. "You had it all planned out, huh? Wanted to see how good our response time would be again? Is that what this is?" He twirled his finger around in a circle in the air.

"Nah, I wanted an insider's tour of the Deep Haven hospital." A little of that Texas accent tinted her words. She lifted her gaze and finally looked him in the eye, squeezed his hand. "Thank you."

For a moment everything stilled. "We were worried about you."

"We?"

"Yeah. The whole team. Everyone is in the waiting room, but I called dibs so, lucky you, I'm the first face you get to see."

"It's not such a bad face to wake up to." Her sleepy voice was music after all the harsh mechanical sounds of the hospital.

"I'm glad you think so, because you're gonna see a lot more of it."

She chuckled weakly and pushed herself up to a sitting position. Nick stood. "Here, let me help—"

He reached over to plump up the pillow but Jae pushed him gently away. "I've got it."

The storm that had been banked flashed back to life lightning fast. "Sheesh, Jae. Can't a guy be chivalrous now and then?" He worked really hard at keeping the words light and teasing.

"I simply don't need help sittin' up." Her lips thinned into a stubborn line.

Okay, forget the teasing. "Everyone can use some help now and then. What is your deal?"

"Calm down, Nick. I'm fine."

"You're not fine. You almost died out there!"

His words echoed in the room.

Her mouth stayed clamped shut.

"Why couldn't you just ask for help? We gave you a radio to call us. Why didn't you use it?" He raked his fingers through his hair and paced near the foot of the bed.

"I thought I could handle it."

He planted his hands on his hips and stared at her. "Obviously you couldn't. Look at where you are."

Maybe that lit a fire in her too because her back snapped straight up, she lifted her chin, and her eyes sparked. "My whole life, people have underestimated what I'm capable of. I just wanted to prove that I could do this."

"You're new. You haven't lived in this climate before. There's no shame in asking for help. When I say use all the resources around you, I mean the people too. If this had been a real rescue situation, you could've jeopardized the whole thing."

She said nothing. But her pursed lips and sparking eyes didn't back down one bit.

Nick looked at her. "How are you supposed to save lives if you're not honest about your own abilities? It literally almost killed you to ask for help. If we're a team, that means we need to be there for each other and we need to be honest with each other."

"What team are you talking about? Last I heard, you weren't part of the Crisis Response Team despite everyone asking you to join."

"I was there tonight. You should've asked me for help."

And then the excruciating reality hit him. How close he'd come to losing her.

And it wasn't entirely her fault.

He was her instructor. He knew better. He knew how lethal winter could be. That there were no second chances in nature. He hadn't prepared her. If he hadn't gone back to check on her—

The sharp medicinal smell of the room closed in on him. The present slipped away and the past took over. The wailing of Grady's mother haunted the halls. Same smells. Same gray walls. Same sounds. Nausea hit.

He had to get out of there.

The door opened and the shuffling of feet and voices invaded the room as the rest of the team came in. Nick backed away from the bed as the others surrounded Jae. Peter turned to him as Nick moved toward the door.

"You all right?"

Nick nodded and left without another word.

Maybe now Peter would understand. Nick had no place trying to be a part of the Crisis Response Team—not even as their survival instructor.

✳

Jae was tough. But sometimes a girl just needed a good cry—preferably without an audience. Yet here was she, on the verge of an emotional breakdown with the whole CRT team stuffed into her tiny hospital room. And to top it off, the sharp antiseptic smell of the room stung her nose and the adhesive holding down the IV line on her hand was starting to itch and burn. It was getting harder and harder to hold back the tears.

Jae should be grateful. And she was. This was what she wanted. To be one of the team. And here she was surrounded by Deep Haven's finest as they did their best to make her feel better by swapping stories about their own winter blunders, most of which involved tongues getting stuck to various metal objects.

But the only person she really wanted in the room had left. And it was all her fault. Here she was trying to prove she belonged, and she'd failed miserably.

Nope. She wouldn't be able to hold back much longer. She tried to clear her throat, but with so much emotion squeezing it, she ended up in a coughing fit.

"Here, Jae." Colleen handed her a glass of water. "Are you okay?"

She nodded but couldn't speak.

Colleen seemed to interpret because she stood up and clapped her hands. "All right, everyone, the patient needs some rest. Let's go."

The team trickled out with a chorus of "Get well soon" and "See you tomorrow, Snowflake." The new nickname caught on quickly.

At one point, Jae would've been thrilled to have a nickname, but Snowflake? Really? Then again, she didn't care what they called her at this moment as long as they left her alone to weep in peace.

Because the tears were already falling.

She laid her head back on the pillow as soon as the door closed, and curled onto her side.

Nick had left.

Not that she had given him a reason to stay, pushing him away like she had. As soon as he'd turned to the door, regret for her stubborn pride slammed into her. She'd wanted to call him back, but she didn't have a chance to say a word with everyone else flooding in at that exact moment.

And it wasn't just her big mouth betraying her—it was her body too. How was she supposed to make it here in his world when she couldn't handle a winter training session and needed to be hospitalized herself? She was supposed to be an asset to the CRT, not a liability.

A light knock on the door had Jae wiping her eyes quickly and sitting up.

Colleen peeked around the corner. "Hey, I just wanted to make sure you were okay."

Jae managed a nod and sniffed. "I'm all right."

"You gave us quite a scare." Colleen laid her coat over the arm of the chair and sat down. Something in her friendly, direct gaze loosened some of the emotion in Jae's chest. "Are you sure you're okay? You seem sad. Upset."

"Let's just say you're not the only one I scared today. I think...I think I scared Nick away too. Probably for good. Just when things were going so well." And the tears fell again, big fat drops rolling down her cheeks.

Colleen handed her tissues. "Yeah, I noticed you two have been getting close. Anything going on?"

"I thought so. He did kiss me. Not that it was a real kiss... more like an accident. But it's probably nothing now." Jae blew her nose. "I think I'm doomed in the romance arena."

"Like Romeo and Juliet?" Colleen's lighthearted tease was closer to the truth than she realized.

"You're not too far off. The last guy I dated, Matt, we were together for three years. I kept waiting for him to propose, to make a commitment, you know? But he never did. And then he was killed overseas."

"Oh. That is...tragic. I'm so sorry. He was military too?"

"Yeah. He was Seymour's handler." Matt's face came to mind. His bronzed skin, honey-brown eyes. His smile dazzled, his teeth always gleaming white against his dark skin. "As tough as he was, he was the most romantic guy I knew. It wasn't always easy to see each other when we were both deployed, but when we did, he made every moment special. Candlelight dinners, picnics. He even hired a mariachi band once to serenade us. We talked about the future together, having a family, and yet, he wouldn't take that final step. And neither did the guy before him. I just don't seem to have what it takes."

"Have what it takes?"

"Yeah, what it takes to find the place...and the person... where I belong. You know? The kind of place where I have a purpose and a home. A place where I fit. I really thought this was it."

"And now you don't? Because Nick left?"

"This is Nick's world. How can we have anything lasting if I can't work here? Or if I can't survive a Minnesota winter?"

"I don't think Nick left because you couldn't start a fire in subzero windchills. He's not that kind of guy. What did he actually say?"

Jae picked at the soggy tissue in her lap. She could still hear Nick's words.

It literally almost killed you to ask for help. If we're a team, that means we need to be there for each other and we need to be honest with each other.

"He thinks I wasn't honest." Jae huffed. "Honesty isn't the issue. I think I wounded his male ego by not letting him help me."

"He helped me a ton at my site. I couldn't get my fire going until Nick showed up. Why didn't you let him help you?"

"I didn't think I needed it. I'm used to everyone underestimating me. I know I have to work harder to prove myself. So I learned to push through difficulties. I really thought I could handle it."

"So maybe there *is* an honesty issue and the person you need to be honest with first is yourself."

"What do you mean?"

"You need to be realistic about things. I mean, I've lived here most of my life. We did camping trips, hikes, portages, all the wilderness things. But I still needed assistance. Everybody needs help sometimes. It's not a sign of weakness to ask for it."

"It sure feels like it, though," Jae whispered. There was something absolutely humiliating in having to ask for help, to admit she couldn't keep up. Asking for help only proved people's first impression of her—that she was different and didn't fit in.

"Home is where you make it. It's not some location you're going to stumble upon. And as far as finding that person to belong with, a big part of making this a home will mean relying on people. We're here for you, Jae. You don't have to prove anything to us."

"But it seems like everyone else just fits right in without a hitch and I'm the alien from Planet Hoth."

"That's not true. Have you heard some of the stories of the others when they first moved to town? Cole came to Deep Haven and tried to kick Megan out of her apartment. Adrian Vassos and Ella Bradley fell in love while doing community service sentences. In fact, I'm pretty sure Adrian spent his first night here in jail. And at some point, you should ask Ronnie about when she and Tiago first moved to town. Believe me, we're all just trying to do the best we can to fit in ourselves."

"Easy for you to say. You grew up in this town. Of course

this is your home. And you have Jack." Jae crumbled up her soggy tissue and reached for another.

"Yeah, but I still deal with people judging me for things I did back in high school. Sometimes, having my family close is great. And other times it's the worst. Like when I run into my parents while Jack and I are on a date. It's hard to keep the romance going when your dad is cracking lame jokes and trying to close a real estate deal at the next table and your mom is watching your every move."

Jae wasn't convinced.

Colleen got up and refilled Jae's water. "But in the end, it's up to me. I'm here because I'm deciding to make Deep Haven my home. Not just because this is the place I grew up. And yes, Jack is a big part of the home I'm building here. But it doesn't work if we're not honest with each other. Believe me. The secret he kept almost tore us apart."

Jae didn't want to talk about secrets. She knew she needed to tell Nick the truth about her identity. And she would. But now there were even more obstacles to deal with. And she needed some time and privacy to think through things.

Colleen came back to the bedside. "All I'm trying to say is don't wait for a home to find you, Jae. Decide and make a home for yourself where you are. Here. And that means letting others help you sometimes. That's what friends are for."

"I'll think about it."

"Good. Because we all want you to stay." She set the water on a rolling tray within Jae's reach. "Even Nick. I've never seen him so worried. He carried you almost all the way back to his cabin until the rest of us could get to you. Then he refused to leave your side, insisted on riding in the ambulance."

"I don't think he wants much to do with me right now." Jae took a sip of the water.

"He probably needs a little time to regroup. He was pretty shaken up."

Is that why he left in such a state? "I didn't help matters. I said some things I shouldn't have."

"I've worked in emergency situations for a while now. People deal with stress differently. And the more you care, the more deeply it affects you. Often we lash out at those closest to us. You might want to go easy on the guy and easy on yourself. He did save your life. And...Nick cares about you. A lot."

And maybe Jae was a little rattled too. If Daddy ever found out about this episode, he'd hog-tie her, throw her in the back of his truck, and drive her back down to Texas in a heartbeat. Maybe Nick was being protective and weird for the same reason. She was so busy trying to prove herself, she hadn't stopped to think that Nick never made her feel like she didn't belong here.

Talk about honesty. Once she let down her guard, she could see. It was her own frustration and sense of helplessness Jae was fighting. Not Nick.

Colleen pulled her coat on. "I'm going to let you rest for real now. Do you want me to pick you up tomorrow when they release you?"

"I'll let you know."

Colleen leaned over the bed and hugged her. "Talk to you in the morning." She left and closed the door behind her.

Jae sank back into the pillows, Colleen's words settling into her heart.

The more you care, the more deeply it affects you... You might want to go easy on the guy. He did save your life. And...Nick cares about you. A lot.

And she'd pushed him away because she was so worried he was looking down on her. Like she had a right to anything from Nick when she was hiding the truth about being LadyJHawk. The thought had her on the verge of weeping again.

And this time she didn't even attempt to hold the tears back.

CHAPTER 11

$\mathcal{N}$ ick strapped on his cross-country skis as soon as the sun was up. He had to do something with his restlessness and the reminder of another grand failure. Clearly he had a long way to go to prove himself as a wilderness instructor if one of his students had almost died from hypothermia. And he didn't even want to think about all the other mixed-up feelings about Jae. He might as well stick to the dogsledding and figuring out a way to prevent another accident like Kasha had had the first time she broke her leg.

His legs and arms fell into an easy rhythm. The swish of the skis against the snow helped bring order to his thoughts. He followed the trail through the quiet trees. There was no wind, only the sound of chickadees and woodpeckers to break the silence until Ed's dogs picked up his scent and started barking. It was early, but Ed would be awake. Hopefully he could help.

Nick found Ed back in his workshop putting the finishing touches on his wooden sled.

"Wow, Ed. Looks great! You ready to hit the trail with it?"

The older man put down his sandpaper and welcomed Nick inside. "Very soon. What brings you by?"

Nick pulled the harnesses and lines out of his backpack. "I wondered if you could help me figure out a different harness system, something to prevent what happened to Kasha. There wasn't even much slack in the line when it caught on her leg. Now she'll never race again."

"From what you said when it happened, it sounded like a freak accident. I'm not sure there's much we can do, but let's take a look." Ed spread out the lines on the workbench. "How is she doing since her amputation?"

"Better than I thought. She's been at the clinic, but she can come home on Monday. Lena said she's getting restless and wants to be with the other dogs."

"She's not meant to be alone. She's a pack animal." Ed tugged on the cords and tested their give.

"Yeah, but I need to keep her isolated until she heals. She might become an indoor dog."

Ed looked up. "What did Lena say?"

Nick avoided Ed's direct gaze and bent down to scratch Ed's favorite husky, Captain. "She said as long as the incision was kept clean and was healing over, she'd be okay in the indoor kennel with Tillie and the pups."

Ed studied him a little longer than Nick was comfortable with. "You like the idea of having her in the house though, huh?"

"I just want to keep her safe. You know dogs. They jump on each other, roll around. The puppies aren't so little anymore either. I don't want Kasha to get hurt again."

"Nick, you need to let her go back with the others when she's healed enough."

"How do I know she won't get hurt again?"

"You don't. But you're not doing her any favors by isolating her. Listen to a man who understands. I thought isolation would bring healing, prevent more pain. I was wrong."

"You mean when you left Alaska?"

Ed nodded. "I was hurting. And I thought holing up here in

the woods and keeping to myself would prevent my heart from breaking again. And it did."

"So what's wrong with that?" Nick picked up the sandpaper and rubbed it against the sled runner.

"It also kept me from *living* again. My mother was right. I could've put myself back out there. Found love with someone else. But I was convinced I was doing the right thing by avoiding it all. Now I'm left with nothing to keep me company except my dogs and my regrets."

"Aw, come on, Ed. You've got a great life. You do more for this community than anyone I know. Everyone loves you."

"I have good friends, my mother, people I care about, of course. But I still believe I've missed out on one of the richest blessings of all. Not because it was my calling, but for the sake of trying to keep my heart safe from breaking again. After I moved back here, there were a few women I could have seen myself building a life with. But I was too scared to try. Too scared to fail."

Ed laid a heavy hand on Nick's shoulder. "Take it from me, son. Give it a real shot with that sweet young lady you brought out here. Take a risk and let her in. Vivien was never the woman for you. But Jae? Now there's real potential with you two."

Yeah, potential for disaster. What would she want with him? He was a joke of a wilderness instructor, he was barely making it as a dogsledder, and he was on the verge of losing his cabin and kennels. Nick continued sanding. "I don't know, Ed. I really screwed up. I was supposed to teach her about how to survive the winter wilderness and she ended up in the ER."

"What happened?"

"Hypothermia. She got too cold. I should've known she wasn't cut out for this."

"Nicholas, life is full of risks. You're going to let one little hiccup get in your way?"

Nick tossed the sandpaper on the counter and spun around. "She almost died!"

"But she didn't." Ed paused. "Did you hear anything I said? Believe me, son, you don't want to live with regrets. If anything, this should show you how precious time is. Why are you here with an old bachelor in the middle of the woods when you could be with a beautiful, intelligent woman like Jae?"

Nick yanked the beanie off his head and pushed back his hair. "I don't know. I was kinda hard on her last night. She was so stubborn and she wouldn't ask for help. I got upset." He twisted the knitted hat in his hands. "But then I realized the person I should most be upset with is myself. What kind of instructor leaves a green student out in the middle of the woods overnight? If nothing else, I should've checked on her sooner. But I—never mind. It was dumb."

"Maybe not. What were you going to say?"

"I was busy helping the others, trying to prove that I'm not just the Dahlquist kid who can't cook and set his family's legacy on fire. We've got all these town heroes and I wanted to show them that I had skills too. And I was waiting. I wanted to wait until dark and join Jae by the campfire. I thought I would show up and be the hero for her, you know? But now, she probably doesn't even want to see me."

"Nick, do you like this woman? Could you see yourself with her?"

"Yes." The word spilled out without hesitation.

"Then go groveling like a good hero should. I've seen your stubborn side too. If you're persistent, I bet she'll forgive you. Eventually." Ed winked.

Maybe he had a point. Nick hoped so but at the moment it was hard to believe. And he hated to think of Ed and his regrets. "You know, you're not that old. Why don't you get back out there in the dating game? You still have a lot of life left to live."

Ed rolled his eyes. "Oh, believe me, my mother reminds me

of that all the time. And it's not that I've given up. Maybe there will be someone for me yet. But I don't want you to miss out, Nick." He nodded toward the door. "Now, get out of here and go get the girl."

This time, Nick was blind to the winter beauty around him as he rushed back on his skis to his own place, Ed's question repeating in his mind.

Nick, do you like this woman? Could you see yourself with her?

Of course he liked her. She intrigued him. She wasn't like anybody he'd known before. Her delight on their sled ride. The way she'd sat with him and held his hand during Kasha's surgery. In such a short amount of time, he'd come to like her. A lot.

And that kiss. Yeah, they had something special.

Had it really only been a couple of weeks that they'd known each other? It felt like longer.

John Christiansen's advice repeated too. They were good together.

Aw, man. What had he done walking out on Jae like that last night? He'd panicked. What would she think of him now?

Yes, she needed to learn her own limitations and ask for help. But it was the fact that she'd come to mean so much to him and he'd almost lost her that had him freaking out. And like a wuss, he'd gone off hiding in the woods.

But for the first time, he could see a future with this woman. Jae wasn't the center of attention, or the spotlight diva Vivie was. But she wasn't elusive either. He found himself letting down his guard with her. She was easy to talk to. Easy to be with. Jae was the kind of woman who made Nick feel more like himself—not like he should be someone else to impress her. She was comfortable and fun and...yes, sexy as all get out. He'd be honest. He was still a hot-blooded male and was dying to kiss her again.

The morning sun was still low in the sky by the time Nick

got to the hospital and rushed through the automatic doors. He didn't stop in the reception area, just waved to Shirley Dixon behind the desk. He strode down the hall and to Jae's room. Voices from inside drifted out of the wide open door.

"Yeah, my dad thinks this cabin will be perfect for you and it's in your budget. So he wants you to call him once we get you settled. But first, priorities. Coffee."

It sounded like Colleen. Nick knocked on the door and peeked in. Jae was fully dressed in street clothes sitting on the bed, her legs dangling off the side. She stopped mid-laugh when Nick came into the room. "Nick? What are you doing here?"

Colleen Decker stood with a Java Cup drink in her hand. "I'll go see if the nurse has those discharge papers ready." She winked at Jae and whispered to Nick as she passed by him. "Don't mess this up, Dahlquist."

The soft click of the door told him she'd left the room, but all his other senses homed in on Jae.

Her long hair was a little disheveled but still shiny, tempting him to touch it. Her bright eyes looked a little wary and her brow wrinkled a bit.

Two more steps and he faced her, close enough to reach for her hand. "Jae, I'm an idiot and I'm sorry."

Her eyebrows lifted in surprise. She opened her mouth, but nothing came out.

So he plunged on. "I walked out last night when I should've stayed. I shouldn't have flaked out on you like that. I was just so afraid of losing you."

She just looked at him.

And like a man with a second chance at life, Nick leaned in and kissed her. His fingers slid through her silky hair. She smelled sweet and fruity, like peaches or apples—or maybe that was the taste of her lips. It was hard to tell when all his senses were exploding.

All he knew was kissing Jae was an adventure he hoped

would never end.

❄

Jae couldn't get the lingering memory of Nick's kiss out of her head. And this time, there had been nothing accidental about it. That kiss was intentional. It was breathtaking. It had tugged at dreams she'd denied for so long. Dreams of home and family, laughter, and dancing in the falling snow. Dreams that had died with Matt. And now Nick's kiss had resuscitated them and brought them front and center once more.

Not only that, but after taking her home from the hospital yesterday, he'd asked if she would come to church with him.

Apparently it was a big deal, like a small town ritual. He explained that by sitting with him and his family, they would be declaring themselves a couple. Her mouth said yes before her brain could catch up and remind her of things that needed to be said. And she would've said them.

But Ronnie wasn't kidding when she said the CRT took care of their own. All day yesterday, team members had stopped by and checked in on her, brought her food, and insisted on "hanging out." It was probably more babysitting, but as much as it chafed, Jae tried to be gracious and accepting of it like Colleen had suggested she should. Unfortunately, it gave her no privacy to talk to Nick before he had to leave to do more training.

But now he held her hand as they walked into Deep Haven Community Church. He steered her toward the other Dahlquists, including his parents and Peter, who sat with an arm slung around Ronnie's shoulders on one side and Tiago on the other. She hadn't been here long, but she already knew the Dahlquist clan was one of the biggest in Deep Haven, and she would be sitting with them.

Almost like she really belonged.

But as Mimi used to say, there was a big ol' fly in the ointment. Not until she told Nick about her online identity would she be at peace.

Nick moved his hand to Jae's back. "Jae, you remember my parents from the bistro?"

Trudy ignored Jae's outstretched hand and went for a hug. "It's so nice to see you again, Jae." She beamed as she welcomed Jae into the family pew.

Greg, on the other hand, gave a quick nod. He must be a reserved, shy man. So different from Nick, who made everyone feel like his best friend, even when it was only on a screen.

But she was still waiting to see the Nick she knew from their chats online. He wasn't quite as open in person as NixDog-Quest. Not that she'd heard a peep back from NDQ since sending him the message that she needed to talk, which made her think that Nick in real life was distancing himself from the online relationship.

Dare she hope it was because of her? That their relationship in real life was taking precedence?

She hoped so.

Oh, how she hoped.

And it didn't seem too farfetched as Nick's arm rested on the back of the pew behind her and his thumb traced little circles on her shoulders, sending a tingling sensation up and down her arm.

Somehow she still managed to pay attention to Pastor Dan's sermon.

"Faith is not about being strong, having all the answers, or having our act together. Throughout the Bible, God chose unlikely heroes. He chose the younger son rather than the older. Uneducated fishermen instead of scholars. Despised tax collectors and prostitutes instead of revered rabbis. He often chose the weak, the despised, the needy. I wonder if that's because they were aware that they had little to offer while the strong and proud were busy trying to prove themselves worthy. When we are courageous enough to be honest about our weakness, to be vulnerable and yet willing to say, 'Here I am, Lord,' that's true faith. It's in our weakness that He shines through."

Courageous enough to be vulnerable? Obviously Pastor Dan had never been the new guy and the shortest guy, only coming up to everyone's shoulders. He probably was never the alien one, looking different, eating different food, wearing different clothes. Everything within Jae rebelled at the thought of showing weakness. She'd worked so hard in her life, in her career, to present herself as capable.

They stood for the last song, a familiar hymn and one of Pap's favorites that must've been chosen to go with the sermon. "I Need Thee Every Hour." Even though she knew the words by heart, Jae listened to the lyrics more than she sang.

I need Thee every hour,
In joy or pain;
Come quickly and abide,
Or life is vain.

And even though she'd been to church almost every Sunday of her life, it stung to admit, but she maybe could be better at trust—trusting God and trusting others. She could do better at being a team player.

Before the last note of the hymn finished, an older woman with soft white curls and sharp blue eyes grabbed Jae's arm. She had a firm grip too.

"Now, who is this, Nicholas?" Next to the woman was a lanky giant of a man with a head full of silver hair. They both looked to Nick expectantly.

"Grandma, Grandpa, this is Jae Washington. She's the new helicopter pilot with the CRT." Nick squeezed her hand. "Jae, this is Doris and George Dahlquist, my grandparents."

"Well, the more the merrier. We'll have Dina set two more places at brunch." Doris pulled a cell phone out of her purse.

Nick's eyes went wide even though he tried to smile.

"Brunch?"

"Of course, dear. You and Jae will be joining us, right?"

Nick looked at Jae, panic flashing across his features. "Uh, we haven't talked about—" Apparently, he was okay showing up at church together, but didn't want to have her interrogated by his family at brunch.

No better time to show that she could be a team player. She was all for Team Nick.

"Brunch sounds great."

"Wonderful. I'll call Dina and let her know. We'll see you at the bistro," Grandma Doris said.

George didn't smile. Just a nod to Jae and to Nick a reminder —"We'll eat at noon. Don't be late." And then they were gone, with Nick's parents following close behind.

Nick leaned close. "Are you sure that's okay? I didn't mean to put you in line for the firing squad so soon. I can come up with an excuse—"

"No, it's fine. They seem sweet. Besides, I'm hungry."

"You're always hungry." His gaze dropped down to her mouth and for a second she thought they might shock the whole church with a kiss right there in the aisle.

Instead, Tiago rushed over, oblivious to any romance, and tugged on Nick's arm. "Hey, when are we going to go for another dogsled ride, Nick? Will you let me film again? Is Kasha okay?"

Nick winked at her and turned his attention to Tiago. Peter and Ronnie stepped over too. While Nick answered Tiago, Peter and Ronnie asked Jae if she wanted to join them for lunch.

"Thanks, but we're going to the bistro for brunch. With your grandparents, actually, Peter."

Ronnie's and Peter's jaws dropped. "You're going out with Doris and George?" A bit of awe in Ronnie's voice surprised Jae. Ronnie didn't intimidate easily.

"Yeah, no biggie. They seem sweet."

"Don't underestimate them," Peter said. "They can be sweet. But they didn't build the Dahlquist restaurant empire out of nothing. I've seen my grandmother shove an apple pie in someone's face before."

Jae laughed—until she realized Peter was dead serious. Ronnie patted Peter's arm as if he were reliving a traumatic experience and needed comforting. If it wasn't so concerning, Jae would've laughed at that too, to see big brawny Peter worried about little old Grandma Doris.

But he'd already turned to Nick and slugged him on the shoulder. "Dude. You're taking her to brunch with the grandparents? Are you trying to scare her away?"

"You know how Grandma is. She swooped in and acted like brunch was part of the plan all along. What was I supposed to do?"

Ronnie elbowed Peter and shot a look over to Nick. "Settle down, you two. You'll spook Jae. I'm sure George and Doris will behave. It's in a public place, right?"

Okay, this was getting ridiculous. Jae stood tall. "First of all, I don't spook easily. Did you forget what I do for a living? And secondly, I'm great with grandparents. They love me. So if I can fly a helicopter in a snowstorm, I think I can handle brunch with a couple of senior citizens."

But later, sitting across the table from Nick's grandparents, Jae couldn't deny a sense of unease pooling inside. The initial third degree wasn't bad. The typical details were provided—jobs, family, former addresses. Trudy sat next to Jae, but was a lot more subdued and quieter than the first time they met. Nick, on the other side of Jae, talked more with the staff and the others in the buffet line than with his family.

It didn't take long to understand why. Everything in the restaurant was under Doris's scrutiny—from the water spot she rubbed off the butter knife, to a quick finger swipe across the chair rail and windowsill as they sat down. She didn't say it, but she gave the impression that every flaw was all Trudy's fault. Nick's father and grandfather said even less.

Until the discussion turned to business matters.

George buttered his dinner roll. "So what is this I hear about my cousin Floyd retiring?"

Greg set down his water glass. "He's been here since I was a kid. I think it's time to let him retire. Don't worry, though. We're already looking for another cook. I've got interviews tomorrow."

"Hmph. You should've told me. We could have one of the other grandkids come in to help. Not like Nick here could cook, but we could've made sure the recipes stay in the family." George bit into his roll.

"You know we would have to be pretty desperate indeed to have Nick attempt to cook." Doris laughed. George chuckled. Trudy glared at them both across the table.

Hello. The guy was sitting right here. Jae tossed down her napkin. "Nick can cook."

Everyone at the table froze and stared at her.

She didn't mean to blurt it out, but they talked over Nick like he wasn't even there and laughed at him. It was infuriating.

Nick released a nervous chuckle. "No, they're right. I'm a disaster in the kitchen."

"No, you're not. You cook for your dogs. It's practically gourmet."

Grandma D's shock turned to a patronizing smile. "That's sweet of you to stand up for Nicholas, but that's not the kind of cooking we're talking about. We need a real cook in the kitchen. We want to serve edible food. For humans. We have a business to run."

"So does Nick. He's running his own business. And he makes delicious food. I've tried it."

A blush started creeping over Nick's cheeks. "It's just dog food."

"You have a real talent, Nick. And they shouldn't discount you because of one mistake in the past."

George glowered. "One mistake? He almost burned this building down to the ground. It's been here for a hundred years, and we almost lost it. Smoky here doesn't have what it takes in the kitchen."

"Maybe not, Grandpa. Guess it's a good thing the dogs aren't too picky." Nick's laugh fell flat. He finished his last bite of roast beef and stood.

Trudy laid her napkin down. "You know, that's enough. Nick might not cook but he is still a member of this family. He's a good boy and his father and I are—"

"Mom, it's okay." Nick bent over and kissed her cheek. "Jae and I should get going. We need to check in on Seymour." Nick pulled on his coat and helped Jae into her own parka. "Great brunch, Mom and Dad. And we'll see you later, Grandma."

The fake smile he sent them almost broke Jae's heart. Here was this amazing guy and they held a simple accident over his head and treated him like he was still a child.

They walked out to the cold sidewalk. The clouds overhead blocked the sunlight, and Nick pulled the collar of his coat up around his ears. "A little nippy out, huh?"

So they were going to ignore everything and talk about the weather? Nuh uh.

"Nick, why didn't you speak up for yourself in there? You do cook. You run your own business. You're successful and—"

"It's just not worth the fight, Jae. This is how it is. Dahlquists don't do second chances. And the only business they see as valid is the restaurant business. So it's bad enough I'm the only child, but I'm an only child who can't cook. Who can't take over the family legacy."

"Yeah, but there're so many other things you do well. You've got the dogsledding, your social media following. A lot of people believe in you, Nick. Your family should too."

"Don't get me wrong. Mom and Dad...they try. I don't think they get the whole dogsledding thing. They don't come to any races, but that's because they have to run the restaurant. And they never pressured me to be involved. They support me in their own way. Still, you will never convince my grandparents that I run a legitimate business or am doing something with my life. I stopped trying long ago. I knew if I let Mom finish her tirade, she'd never hear the end of it from Grandma and Grandpa." He shrugged. "I don't need them to understand. I don't want to run the restaurant. And in some ways, maybe they're right."

Before Jae could object, he continued. "I hate to cut this short, but I need to do a long run for training today. Are you okay if I drop you off at the CRT headquarters?"

"Yeah, of course."

Nick dropped Jae off with a chaste kiss on the cheek, the kind he probably gave his grandma. But the way he then caressed that same cheek when he brushed her bangs out of her eyes, his fingers lingering on her skin, the desire evident in his gaze gave her hope. "I'll see you later."

Later couldn't come soon enough.

Because the afternoon loomed before her long and empty. She was distracted for a couple hours with a call to transport a critical patient to Duluth. But eventually she was landing back in Deep Haven with the burden of her secret weighing her down and the cold once again sinking in.

After waving off Jack who attended in the back of the chopper and cleaning the Bell herself, she settled in the bunk room with a cup of tea. Jae opened up her computer and saw a notification on her messaging app.

NixDogQuest: *Hey...sorry I've been MIA.*

He was back. Was that good? Jae nibbled on her fingernail and then typed out a response.

LadyJHawk: *Is everything okay?*

NixDogQuest: *I dunno. I thought so, but there's a lot going on.*

LadyJHawk: *Like what?*

NixDogQuest: *For one, my lead dog is out of racing forever. I really needed a win this season but it's looking less and less likely. I haven't told anyone this, but I'm on the verge of losing everything.*

What did he mean by that?

LadyJHawk: *Losing everything? I know winning is important, but it's not everything.*

NixDogQuest: *It is this time. When I lost that sponsor I told you about, it was right before the Iditarod last year. I took out a second mortgage to pay for the expenses, to pay the fine for breaking my contract, and to keep me afloat until I could find new sponsors. I really needed to do well in the Iditarod for that to happen. But I scratched. No prize money and no sponsors. Then I lost a litter of puppies. And I have huge vet bills to pay off. It's all added up to me not being able to make my bank payments. I have to pay off my loan by the end of the year or they take everything.*

NixDogQuest: *Oh, and if that wasn't enough, I'm teaching a class and one of my students was hurt too. She's fine now, but I failed her. It could've been bad. Real bad. Once again, I'm the town joke.*

Jae stared at the screen. Nick was about to go bankrupt, lose his home, lose his dogs, and nobody had a clue. He was fine baring his heart to Lady J but couldn't talk about this with her in person?

He didn't trust her. Not Jae in real life. She obviously wasn't the only one having a hard time trusting. Guess she still had a ways to go to prove herself as Jae Lynn Washington as far as Nick was concerned.

NixDogQuest: *Anyway...enough about me. What did you want to tell me earlier?*

The cursor blinked for a full minute before Jae quickly typed out one word and closed the app.

LadyJHawk: *Nothing.*

Maybe this really wasn't the best time.

In fact, maybe she didn't need to tell him at all.

187

CHAPTER 12

*N*ick stood in his kitchen at the counter and stared at the slip of paper in his hands. "Second Notice" was stamped in blood red at the top. The bank wanted that balloon payment or they were foreclosing.

He sank down to the barstool. Grandma and Grandpa were right. Three days later and he could still see Grandma's patronizing smile as she spoke.

We need a real cook in the kitchen. We want to serve edible food. For humans. We have a business to run.

And then to have Jae stand up for him like that. So indignant as she spoke up.

So does Nick. He's running his own business. And he makes delicious food. I've tried it.

Sure. Nick was running his own business. But Jae didn't know he was about to lose it all if he didn't come up with the payment. And without Kasha to lead them, the Mush Puppies could be a complete flop. He had yet to have a good run without her. Which would mean no sponsors. No income. *Dahlquist Kennels fails spectacularly.* It would be another newspaper headline for his parents to put on the wall.

But Jae was right. His dog food was top of the line. He did his research and wanted the best for his pack. And knowing they would never complain about what they were served made it easy to try different recipes.

So, maybe he *could* go back to the bistro kitchen. The way Mom stood up for him was a good sign. He could talk her and Dad into giving him a chance. Maybe he should forget dogsledding and join the typical Dahlquist legacy, contribute to the family business. If he got out now, he could take a little of the burden off his parents. Maybe they could even go to Florida like they'd always talked about this winter.

If he did work at the bistro, he probably couldn't afford to travel and race anymore, but he could keep a few dogs and continue to dogsled as a...hobby.

It might be enough. Maybe do a few tours on the side for kids.

Then again, he'd have to go by the restaurant schedule and work most weekends and evenings. There wouldn't be time for tours. Nick would be stuck indoors all day, which would take some getting used to.

A lot of getting used to.

But if he started now, in the next five weeks he could sell off equipment and dogs and earn enough to get the bank off his back. He could at least keep his home.

One glance out the french doors to the deck and Nick's heart plummeted. A fresh blanket of snow covered everything. He was dying to cut a new trail through it. To feel the rush of the sled, to experience God's creation. Where most people saw desolation, he found solace and awe.

Could he really give up the travel and competition? There were so many more places he wanted to see. No more Iditarod or Yukon Quest. No more North Pole explorations. He'd never even gotten over to Norway like he'd wanted. And the drive to race beat so powerfully inside him.

Nick looked up his last posted video. Already 100K views. And a private message?

He opened it up. It was the company he ordered his dog booties and jackets from. They were sending a rep out to the Mush Puppies race and wanted to talk to him. That could only mean one thing—sponsorship.

It had to be a sign. He didn't have to give it all up now and slave away in the stuffy Trailside Bistro. He just needed to do well in the race next week.

With renewed purpose, Nick threw on his winter gear and got the dogs ready for a long run.

He rubbed down Mischa. "I'm counting on you, girl. We've got a shot at this but we have to do well in this race. Anakin hasn't led before, so you show him how to do it? Ready?"

She licked his face.

He'd take it as a yes. "All right. Let's see what you've got, team. Hike! Hike!" The dogs took off. They found a good loping pace and settled into the trail.

"Haw!" Nick shouted. "Haw!" His voice echoed through the woods flashing by them.

The dogs didn't turn left. Instead Mischa ran straight.

"Whoa!"

She ignored that command too and kept running until she whipped around a tree and tangled up the lines.

Nick bit back the string of frustration he wanted to let loose on the team. He set the brake and went to untangle the line. "Mischa, this isn't funny." She jumped as soon as he came close, trying to lick his face and play.

But this wasn't play time. Not when so much was on the line. Their livelihood. His future.

The tan and black husky licked his hand and then sat at his feet, pawed at his knee.

"Sure, try to soften me up, huh?"

Mischa started to howl, and the rest of the line answered.

"Yeah, yeah." Nick had to unhook her to undo the mess she'd made of the line, but he kept a firm hold on her collar. Even though Mischa had been mopey in the kennel without Kasha, as ornery as she was acting, he wouldn't put it past her to dart away if he loosened his grip.

She was still bred to run.

But she was also trained to lead, and that she was failing at miserably.

He finally untangled the line and got her hooked back in next to Anakin and the team on the trail facing the right way. "Come on, Mischa. We need this. I know you usually lead with Kasha, but you're perfectly capable to lead this team. And, Ani, you're supposed to help her. What's going on?"

Mischa looked up at him with clear blue eyes and howled.

"Let's try again."

Nick jogged back to the sled, his breath leaving puffy clouds in the frigid morning air. He released the brake. "Hike!"

The dogs shot off down the trail once more. Usually, he would keep them to a trot, but they must've been energized by the fresh snow. It coated the trees in soft layers. Gone was the dreary brown landscape from a few weeks ago. Now they raced into a dazzling white and green world. Nick breathed deep and let the team run. They got off to a bit of a rough start, but they were starting to find their groove.

And he desperately needed them to stay in that groove.

They approached the loop where he would turn them around back toward the cabin. "Haw."

Mischa ignored him again.

"Haw!"

She slowed down.

That's it, girl. Now turn left.

She stopped completely and sat.

What?

"Mischa!"

Of course Anakin, hooked right next to Mischa, followed her example and sat too, and River and Jade right behind them.

"C'mon!" The race was a week away. He fought the urge to punch something and went back to the leads. "Get up, kids."

He finally urged them to their feet. The rest of the line barked and howled. Nick got them headed back toward home and went to the sled. "Hike! Hike!" They surged forward and kept a good pace. There they went. They followed directions at the next fork. Nick relaxed a bit and enjoyed the fresh air. Maybe he'd overreacted. He whistled and they took their pace up a notch. Their paws hit the ground at the same time. They were in sync just the way they were supposed to be.

They approached a sharp turn. "Haw!"

They weren't turning. "Haw! Mischa, Ani, haw!" Instead of left, the leads veered right but were too close to the edge of the trail. The sled was going to hit the big pine tree at the edge of the fork. Nick leaped out and rolled on the ground as the sled tipped. One runner scraped the trunk of the pine and the team stopped.

Nick sat up and brushed the snow off his face. Mischa came over. She whined and nudged him. "Great, Misch. Just great. You're a hot mess and we only have a week before the race. Please—can't you follow *one* simple command?"

She licked his chin. Somehow her neckline broke off. She rolled over exposing her belly, begging to be rubbed. Nick couldn't help it. All the anger and frustration inside cooled.

"I know. You miss your sister." Nick rubbed her belly. "But if I'm going to keep you guys, we need to get this figured out." He tied her neckline in a temporary knot back to the gangline and went to inspect his sled. The one runner's tip had broken off completely.

He groaned. It was going to be a long walk home and a long night replacing the part. With heavy boots instead of his snowshoes, he walked and led the team back to the cabin. As soon as the kennel was in sight, the team sprinted toward it and stopped right in front of the chained stake line just like they were supposed to. "Oh, sure. Now you act like the animals I trained."

One by one, Nick rubbed them down, checked their paws as he released them into their enclosure. He dragged his broken sled and lines to the big shed.

His team was a wreck. And the temperatures were supposed to plummet tonight. All he wanted to do was drown out the mounting stress with some thin crust pizza and sleep. But the dogs would need more straw and still needed food. Nick climbed into the skid loader to move a new bale over by the kennels. He raised the skids and stabbed the top bale. As he pulled the loader back, the bale caught the corner of the one next to it. Nick's heart stopped as the whole stack started to tip. But only the top bale fell and rolled around to the corner of the shed. He stabilized the stack for now. Later he'd rearrange it all and restack the bale that had rolled off. He needed to feed the dogs and get them settled for the night. Maybe a good dinner and sleep would improve their trail run tomorrow.

They *had* to do better tomorrow.

Nick thawed a batch of food from the morning. He fed each dog their soup, but no treats tonight. When he came to Mischa's kennel, she barely lifted her head. Usually she shared with Kasha, but without her sister, the poor thing seemed lost. Nick scooped out food into her bowl. Mischa sniffed at it and then lay down again. She gave him a sad whine.

"Come on, girl. You gotta eat." Nick added straw inside the doghouse then turned to give Mischa a little extra attention and urge her to eat. But the dog's ears perked up and she bolted through the open gate behind Nick.

"No, Mischa! Come!"

She didn't stop. Her tan and black fur disappeared into the woods. He ran after her.

Confounded dog.

❋

After a busy day with back-to-back calls, including a flight to Hennepin County Medical Center in Minneapolis, Jae woke in the middle of the night to the CRT emergency tones once again. She groaned as the dispatcher voice called out, "All emergency personnel respond to fire on County Road 68, Dahlquist Kennel and Dogsled—"

Jae gasped. Nick!

Exhaustion fled with the flood of adrenaline pouring through her. Now fully awake, she threw on clothes and barreled down the stairs to the main bay. Peter was already there starting the fire engines.

"Peter, is Nick okay?"

Peter didn't look at her as he ran to the tank truck and started it. "Don't know," he yelled back. "Ed called it in. He saw it from his place and I haven't heard if he made it to Nick's yet."

Soon other firefighters rushed in and grabbed gear. Jae had none of the fire training. She was useless here. Why didn't she have any fire training?

The helplessness overtaking her almost brought her to her knees.

"Jae, ride with me." Ronnie's brisk command was a God-send. "We'll need all the help we can get."

Yes, something she could do. Ronnie was already pulling out while the firefighters geared up. Jae hopped in the passenger side of the ambulance. The fifteen-minute ride took Ronnie less than ten. One of the fire engines caught up and was right behind them.

As they pulled off the highway and onto Nick's road, flames and sparks shot into the sky above the tree line.

This was bad.

Ronnie swung the ambulance into Nick's driveway. Jae fought to control the panic raging inside. The house was fine.

But the big shed was engulfed in flames. The fire was spreading toward the Quonset dog shed and the kennels. Where was Nick?

Please let him be okay.

There. Ronnie didn't even have the vehicle in park before Jae jumped out and ran to Nick. He stood in the middle of the kennels, holding on to dogs all on leashes. Ed rushed over.

"Nick, go stake these dogs in the front yard. I'll get the rest."

Nick just stared wide-eyed at the fire. It didn't look like anything Ed said was computing.

"Nick?" Jae waved a hand in front of his face.

He turned his stare to Jae, but he didn't seem to see her.

Ed shook Nick's arm. "Nick! Take the dogs to the front yard." The sharp voice helped snap him out of the trance.

"Right."

Ed turned to Jae. "Stay with him. When I got here, he was pretty shaken. He has burns on his hands and arms. I'll get the other dogs into their kennel boxes on his truck." He rushed off with Ronnie on his heels to help.

Jae led Nick to the front yard. The fire roared out of control and he couldn't take his eyes off it. Jae took the leashes one by one from Nick and hooked them onto a line attached between two trees. More trucks and firefighters arrived, clogging up the driveway, adding sirens and flashing lights to the chaos.

Once the dogs were attached to the line and Jae was certain they couldn't escape, she turned her attention on Nick.

His blank stare was scaring her.

"Nick, let's look at your hands."

He stood and kept staring at the fire. "What have I done?"

She only caught his whisper because she leaned in to get a closer look at his hands.

The cuff of his sweatshirt was singed black. Soot smeared his face. Jae reached for his hand. Angry, red blisters bubbled across the back of it. More on his forearms. The other hand had a scrape across the palm.

"We need to treat these burns."

He barely glanced at her. It was like he wasn't even aware that she was there. She gently tugged on his arm to lead him to the ambulance. He followed easily enough but he was not okay. She helped him sit on the cot in the ambulance.

"Talk to me, Nick. What happened?"

Finally, he made eye contact. "Mischa ran away tonight. She wouldn't eat. Then she bolted out of her kennel when I went to add straw." He shook his head. His voice cracked. "I was so mad at her. I was out there for hours on the four-wheeler and I couldn't find her anywhere. I came back to get some warmer clothes but I fell asleep on the couch." He swallowed. The dazed look was starting to edge in again.

She had to keep him grounded. "Then what?" She searched the drawers and pulled out distilled water to clean Nick's wounds and some gauze.

"I heard something. It woke me up. Mischa was on the porch barking. Howling. Scratching at the door. I got up and saw the fire." Nick's shoulders drooped. "What have I done?"

Jae's heart wrenched at the devastation in his eyes. She sank down to the bench right across from him. "It was an accident. It looks like you saved the dogs, right? And the cabin is okay?"

"I'm going to lose it all." His monotone voice sounded so forlorn.

Jae cupped his cheeks with her hands, forcing Nick to meet her eyes. "No, you're not. You are going to come back from this stronger, Nick. I know you. This isn't the end."

"I was on the verge of losing this place already. This *is* the end. How can I race when I have no equipment? The dogs won't listen to commands, and now they have no kennel. I don't have a sled. It's over."

"No." Jae shook her head and scrambled for words to reach

him. To give him hope. "This is...this is just like *Return of the Jedi*. Things look grim as the movie starts with Han frozen in carbonite and Leia gets captured, but they rally and in the end they blow up the Super Star Destroyer and save the galaxy."

"Episode VI?"

"Yeah, *Return of the Jedi.*" She was getting through to him.

"The Ewoks help."

"Yes. They all pulled together and won. They beat the Empire. And just like them, you're going to race again. You've got this."

Nick's gaze cleared and his baritone voice smoothed out once more. "You think I should keep trying?"

She cleared her throat and did her best Yoda imitation. "Do or do not. There is no try."

He released a long, slow breath. "Jae, what would I do without you?"

She lost the accent. She smoothed the lines across his forehead, brushed the singed locks of dark hair off his brows. "I have no doubt you will race again. And you will do amazing."

"I don't have a sled."

"Then we'll find one you can borrow. I'll help."

"That...that might work." Nick breathed deep. His shoulders relaxed. "Thank you."

"It was nothing."

"No, it wasn't. You give me hope, Jae." He tilted his head and frowned. "You know, you sound a lot like someone I know online. A fellow *Star Wars* geek."

Jae's smile faltered. She floundered for an explanation. "There are tons of people who love *Star Wars*. I'm sure it's just a coincidence. I mean, they're classics, right?" Her nervous chuckle fell flat.

"Yeah, I guess you're right." He winced as she started cleaning his hands. His were dirty with soot and blood, hers clean and tiny in comparison.

She was anything but clean on the inside though. Shame flooded her as she cleaned his wounds and wrapped them.

She'd just outright lied to him. Of course, he was in the midst of a personal tragedy. The timing was absolutely awful. And he was finally opening up to *her*, Jae in real life, not Lady-JHawk. He was coming to her for answers, for comfort, to share his hardships. Did she really have to tell him? What if it upset him more?

No. She had to tell Nick the truth. This was killing her. She closed her eyes for a moment and braced herself.

When she looked back up at Nick, his gaze had lost all trace of his earlier panic and now zeroed in on her. His thumb traced her jaw, causing a rumble to roll through her. "Jae."

In that moment, she forgot all words, all thoughts. Everything but Nick. She lost herself in his eyes, eyes locked in on her and filled with so much desire.

"I really don't know what I'd do without you," he whispered.

Before she could put together coherent thoughts, he pulled her close and their lips met. It set everything inside her on fire. Her fingers traced his jaw, the stubble rough against her fingertips. Smoke and desire and heat swirled around and through her.

His kiss was like coming in out of a cold, stormy night and finding the warmth and comfort of home. She wanted this forever. She needed him.

How had it come to this?

A pounding on the ambulance door tore them apart.

"Nick? Jae?"

Oh no. Once again, she kicked herself for missing her chance to tell him the truth.

CHAPTER 13

$\mathcal{N}$ick stared at the bleak view. The scorched ground was a huge blemish on the white landscape. The sheds and kennels were burnt to the ground. Piles of metal siding, fences, and rubble remained on the cement slabs. The trees around the perimeter of his yard were blackened and charred.

Friends and family had helped, and they'd managed to rake a patch of ground and put up some temporary fencing and shelter in a new place for the dogs. Thankfully Tilly and the two puppies Nick had left were fine being outdoors now. Three older dogs went to Ed's. Kasha still boarded with Lena. Nick's vet bill was mounting by the minute.

It was a pain to cook all their food in the house, but at least he had all his dogs to cook for and the cabin still stood.

Nick raked the last pile of debris aside. His blisters and burns hurt like all get out, but he had to get this looking as decent as possible before Mark Bammer came out.

Or maybe he should keep it desolate so the banker would be stirred to mercy and give him an extension.

A car pulled up.

Too late now. Nick leaned the rake against the chimney of the cabin and carefully pulled off his work gloves. The bandages on his hands would need to be replaced again. Later. For now, he finger-combed his hair and walked around the side of the cabin and met Mark.

"Hey, Nick." Mark reached out to shake hands until he saw Nick's bandages. "Ooh. That looks painful."

"Could've been a lot worse."

"True." Bammer looked around the yard and the front of the cabin. "Well, things don't look so bad from here."

If only that were the case. "The major damage is in the back."

"Let's go see it."

Nick led him around the side of the house and stopped by the back deck.

Mark whistled. "I take it back. This looks...bad."

"Yeah, that's why I'm hoping you can give me an extension."

"How did the fire start?"

"One of my straw bales fell over and rolled too close to a heater I had for the shed."

"That's rough." Mark stepped farther into the scorched area. "And insurance?"

"They'll cover the cost of the buildings, but not the equipment inside them, or the custom dog kennels and all the racing supplies, dog food, or other things I stored in them. I didn't realize my policy didn't cover all the upgrades I'd made to the buildings over the last few years."

"But they'll give you something, right?"

"They still need to send an agent out to assess damage, but with Thanksgiving next week and the holiday season, it could be a while before I see any payout. I need that extension, Mark."

"I wish I could help you, Nick. When I heard about the fire, I tried to plead your case for you, but the bank isn't willing to take the risk."

"So what does that mean?"

"The mortgage is still due. That loan has to be paid in full by the end of the year or you lose the whole property." Bammer grimaced. "I'm sorry." He turned and walked back to his car.

Nick stood frozen to the spot even as Mark drove away. He trudged up the back deck steps and went inside. He winced as he pulled off his soiled bandages.

But seeing them reminded him of Jae, how carefully she'd wrapped his hands in gauze, her gentle fingers caring for his wounds. She was the one bright spot in this bleakness. And it confirmed that he needed to set aside anything with LadyJHawk and pursue the real connection he had with Jae.

Strangely enough, she believed in him. Her words echoed.

You are going to come back from this stronger, Nick. I know you. This isn't the end.

They all pulled together and won. They beat the Empire.

Her silly Yoda voice made him smile. If Jae thought he could still salvage something and race next week, maybe it was possible. Maybe he could have a second chance at this. He didn't have to go begging for a job from his parents just yet. But he would need help.

And if anyone could help him now, it would be the man who'd taught him in the first place. Nick headed to Ed Draper's.

Soon they were settled with coffee and a plate of Edith Draper's oatmeal raisin cookies. Nick dunked a cookie into his mug. "What do you think, Ed? Can I still do this? Do you think I can still make it to the Iditarod this year?"

"I don't see why not."

"I mean, I know it's the joke all over town how I attempt these grand accomplishments and races and haven't completed one yet—"

Ed frowned. "Joke? What are you talking about, Nick?"

"Like the fire when I was a kid. Everyone laughed, called me Smoky. To this day, people cook meals for me because they're so afraid I'll set my own kitchen on fire. And maybe they were right with what happened to my shed and kennels. So I've tried to make my own name in the dogsledding world and here I am, attempted the Iditarod twice, didn't even start the first time and had to scratch last year. I finished second to last in the Yukon Quest, made it within a mile of the North Pole and had to turn around. And every time, the news headlines flash my attempts and failures."

Ed chuckled and shook his head.

"See, even you think it's funny," Nick mumbled and stuffed another cookie in his mouth.

"Nick, I'm not laughing at you. And you're not the town joke. You're the town mascot, the hero."

"Huh?"

"Everyone is proud of you. Rooting for you. You put Deep Haven on the map. You aren't afraid to take big risks, put it all on the line. What is it you always say? Burn the ships?"

"Yeah, it's from the Spanish explorer Cortes. When he landed with his men in the new world, he had them burn the ships so they couldn't turn back."

"Exactly. You can't accomplish big things without going all in. And you do. People look up to you for that."

They looked up to him? Really?

Ed sipped his coffee. "I can tell by the look on your face you don't believe me. But what about the thousands of followers you have on that app? You are an inspiration, Nicholas. People don't follow a joke. They follow leaders. Leaders that they want to be like. It's easy for people to talk about doing big things. You actually go out there and do them."

Nick had never thought of himself as a leader. He just wanted to encourage people to get outside and explore God's creation. And the last person he'd pictured following him on social media was Ed Draper, hermit of the woods. "You know about my Instagram following?"

"And your YouTube channel. Yes. I'm not *that* old." Ed set down his mug. "Now what do you need to run the race?"

Right, the race. "Everything. I need a sled, lines, all the equipment. And the last time I took the dogs out, they were a mess. Mischa isn't leading as well as I thought she would."

"Who did you pair her with?"

"I tried once with River. That didn't work out. Then I paired her with Anakin. That was even worse."

Ed picked up a cookie. "There's your problem. You need a stronger dog to lead *with* Mischa. She needs a more serious partner, like Kasha was. Not some happy-go-lucky pup. Anakin and River have only raced for one season."

"But they have so much energy and stamina."

"They don't have the grounding Mischa needs. Their exuberance probably distracts her. They're too young and inexperienced. They'll do better as team dogs in the middle of the line up. But you pair Mischa with one of the more established dogs and I bet she'll do great."

Nick chewed on Ed's advice as he took another sip of coffee. It made sense. He had been thinking Mischa needed energy and cheering up to distract her from missing Kasha. However, a steadier dog could help keep her on track. But he still had a big problem.

"What about the sled? Do you know anyone in the area who would lend me a sled and equipment for the Mush Puppies race? If I can do well in that race and hold out until I get insurance money and some sponsors, I can get my feet back under me. There's even a company rep who wants to meet with me after the race. I think if I win, I've got a shot with some big sponsors and I can buy my own equipment then."

Ed took a bite of cookie and nodded. "I think I know just the sled. And I'm pretty sure the owner would be okay lending it to you."

Hope began to surge again. "Really? Who?"

Ed stood and gestured for Nick to follow him. They walked outside and to Ed's workshop. "What do you think? Will this do?"

There on the workbench was Ed's new handmade wooden sled. It gleamed glossy and bright in the sunshine that poured into the room from the transom window.

"Aw, man. I can't use this. This is too nice."

"Don't tell me you're too proud to be seen with this shoddy, thrown together workmanship."

"No! That's not true. I just don't know that I can accept this, Ed. It's a work of art. What if I wreck it?" he said, remembering the last disaster of a run, the broken runner, tipping over on the curve. How could he take such a risk? He could ruin all of Ed's hard work.

The older man laid a hand on Nick's shoulder. "Nicholas, I'd be honored if you would use this sled. I made it to race. To run."

"Yeah, but—"

"Listen. You've got the team. You've got the drive and the know-how. She's ready to go, if you're willing to take the chance."

A second chance.

To race.

To win.

To beat the odds and get back in the game. Somewhere along the way he'd gotten off track, and here was a shot at getting back in.

Nick ran a finger over the sleek runner. "Are you sure?"

"Kid, I'd bet on you any day. Let's get this over to your place and get those lines set up. You've got some training to do."

❄

On Sunday, Jae walked into church all alone. Nick was training nonstop with Ed to try to salvage his team and get them ready for the race on Friday. She understood the need. She did. But she couldn't deny the very different feel of walking in here without him. People clumped together and chatted in the aisles and among the rows of pews. A bunch of kids were grouped in the back. Families settled into their spots. But where should she sit?

Grandma Doris and Grandpa George probably wouldn't be as welcoming after the way brunch had ended last week. And it was too weird to sit with Nick's parents by herself.

Was it just her, or was it more crowded than last time? Jae didn't see anyone she knew until a bright pink vest caught her eye. Ronnie waved from the left side, where she stood talking with John and Ingrid Christiansen. Finally, people she knew.

"Are you ready to move into your new place?" Ronnie asked when Jae joined them.

"Oh, you found a rental like you were looking for?" Ingrid asked.

"Yup. It happened pretty fast. Boone moved into his new home and I'm taking over his cabin later today."

"That sounds perfect. It will be nice for you to settle into a cute little place of your own. And no Nick today? I have some protein cookies I wanted to give him for the race."

"Since he's using a new sled and equipment and the race is Friday, he's using every spare minute to get the team acclimated to it. He said he and Ed would be worshiping in the woods this morning."

"Good thing God's presence isn't limited to a church building." She winked. "And I hear you were such a help in that call yesterday. Ronnie was telling me how you kept that poor woman calm while she treated her husband."

Jae shrugged. "I was doing my job. No big deal."

"She was eight months pregnant. It is a big deal! Stress and trauma like that could cause preterm labor," Ingrid said. The opening music started interrupting their conversation. "Well, I'll have John drop off the cookies for Nick later and I'll bring by a meal for you tomorrow." Ingrid gave her arm a little squeeze and then stepped into what appeared to be the Christiansen row with John.

A meal for her? She really was one of them now, wasn't she?

"Come sit with us," Ronnie said. They joined Peter and Tiago. "Move over, T, and make room for Jae."

There was just enough room for Jae to squeeze in at the end of the pew.

After the opening song, Pastor Dan took the pulpit for announcements. "I'd like to welcome our visitors today. We're glad you're here with us. And I'd like to give a warm, Deep Haven Community Church welcome especially to my brother David, his wife, Jeannette, and the middle schoolers and leaders they've brought up from the Twin Cities today. They'll be winter camping up here a couple of nights and then head back just in time for Thanksgiving.

"And speaking of Thanksgiving, for those interested, we will have a Thanksgiving prayer service Thursday morning. Just a short time to direct our hearts to the Giver of all good things. Now if you will stand and greet your neighbor, we'll continue with our service."

Jae looked over at the group of fifteen or twenty middle schoolers and decided sainthood must run in Pastor Dan's family. Winter camping? With that many pre-adolescents? Yikes. Just the thought of it sent a shiver down Jae's back. Too bad Nick wasn't here to warm her up. She wouldn't mind cozying up to him as she listened to the sermon. Then again, her mind probably wouldn't be on the passage in Isaiah Pastor Dan was reading and preaching on.

"But now, thus says the LORD, your Creator, O Jacob, And He who formed you, O Israel, 'Do not fear, for I have redeemed you; I have called you by name; you are Mine! When you pass through the waters, I will be with you.'"

Pastor Dan leaned over the pulpit, his voice earnest. "Friends, take heart. God knows your name. Have you ever stopped to think on that? There are billions of people in this world and He knows *your* name. Not only that, He is with you. He didn't say we could avoid the waters and fires and hardships of life. He said He is with us in these trials, and nothing will change the fact that we are His."

Jae reread the words in her Bible, drawing comfort from the image of being carried through the waters, being called by name. Looking back, she knew God's presence was evident in her life, leading her to this point.

She was used to jumping into new places and acclimating. But it surprised her that everyone here accepted her so quickly. Unlike other places she'd worked, the CRT and Deep Haven almost felt like the big family she'd always wanted to be a part of. Maybe this was it. Maybe Deep Haven was the right place to settle down and make herself a home.

Even without Nick here at the moment, she cherished the sense of belonging. Sitting with friends like Ronnie and Peter, a meal coming from Ingrid. This must be what a real home felt like.

As soon as the service closed, Ronnie turned to her. "Oh, by the way, I found some more help to get you moved into your new place today."

"I can't wait. After three weeks of bunking at the CRT, Seymour and I are ready for our own place." The little cabin Nathan had showed her a few days ago was perfect. She had a spot already picked out in front of the fireplace that would be just right to curl up with a book and a cup of tea and look out at Lake Superior.

Ronnie stood and gathered her purse and Bible. "We'll get the team together to help move you right now after church. I haven't been able to get a hold of Nick though. Have you?"

Jae moved into the aisle and toward the lobby. "He wanted to help me move, but I insisted he focus on the team instead. He did promise to bring me dinner later tonight though." And she was counting down the minutes until she could be with him. She missed him. He hadn't even messaged LadyJHawk.

"Good. And honestly, we won't need him. We have plenty of help. I told everyone else to meet us at headquarters in an hour. You have everything packed up?" Ronnie nodded and waved to a lady carrying a baby with curly dark hair.

"Well, yeah, but I didn't have much to begin with. Although my parents did pack up a few more things from storage and the boxes arrived Friday. But really, if Peter has his truck, we can fit everything in it and my car. We won't need a lot of help."

"What about furniture?"

Jae laughed. "That's easy. I don't have any. The place is supposed to be furnished."

"It has the basics. Fine for a bachelor like Boone, but we had something else in mind for you."

Jae stopped walking. "What are you talking about?"

"Not only did I assemble a team of helpers, but you'd be surprised how many people have furniture lying around that they don't want anymore. Ivy and Darek had a loveseat they were getting rid of and it will go great with the couch already there. Lucy and Seb Brewster upgraded to a king bed and were done with their queen. It'll be so much nicer than the full size bed. Issy and Caleb Knight just redid their home office and turned it into a nursery for the baby they're adopting, so they didn't want their old desk and chair." Ronnie ticked the items off on her fingers and paused. "Oh. And Megan has a dining room table. I hope you don't mind mismatched chairs though."

"Mind? Are you kidding?" Jae gaped. "These people hardly know me and they're furnishing my new place? That's…"

Ronnie grinned. "That's Deep Haven for you. I told you. We take care of our own."

She was right. They certainly took care of everything.

Within a few hours, the last box came off Peter's truck.

Cole tried to take it out of Jae's hands. "Let me get that for you, Snowflake."

"Oh no. I'm not going to be denied the satisfaction of grabbing the last box." She slid the box to the end of the tailgate and grabbed it from the bottom.

Oof. It was heavier than she'd expected. Still, she didn't want Cole to see her stumble after refusing him. Jae hefted the box up to readjust her grip and walked up the porch steps with it. She did, however, allow Cole to hold the door for her. Her arms were about to give. She made it two steps inside the door and dropped the box on the new-to-her loveseat.

Megan came out of the bathroom where she'd just hung the new shower curtain. "Is that everything?"

Cole kissed his wife and laid a protective hand on her baby bump. "That's the last of the boxes. And we should probably get you home. I don't want you overdoing it."

She rolled her eyes. "I'm fine. You didn't let me carry anything heavier than my coat. Jae, what else do you want help with?"

Peter leaned against the kitchen counter. "Yeah, if you want furniture set up differently, just say the word."

Jae looked around. The snug little cabin didn't offer many options for changing the layout of the furniture but it didn't matter. The dining room table already had a table runner and arrangement of pinecones and dried flowers, another of Megan's touches. The couch and loveseat faced each other with a coffee table in between. And a small desk was pushed up under the window of the living room.

It was all perfect.

"Everything is great where it is. I can't thank you guys enough." Jae had waited for so long to find a place that felt like this. And she wanted to relish it, to unpack and find a place for everything and maybe catch a nap. So she wasn't too sad when they all said their goodbyes and left.

She brought Seymour in from the kennel she'd set up in the backyard and spent the afternoon unpacking her clothes and toiletries, and making the bed—because, of course, Ronnie had thought of everything. Not only had the Brewsters given her a bed, but also all the queen-sized sheets and comforters they didn't need anymore. She had a full linen closet and kitchen cupboards.

When she came back to the open living area, Seymour sniffed around the stacks of boxes and pawed at one on the bottom. The boxes had been in storage for some time. Jae couldn't remember what was even in them. But with a few hours to spare before Nick arrived and with everything else settled, she might as well go through them too.

The first box held childhood mementos and books. Another was a box of random papers. Ugh. She pushed it aside under the desk to deal with later. Then Jae lifted the lid of the next box. Nestled within some bath and dish towels, she found her grand-mother's onggi. For the first time since that potluck, the sight of the crock brought back warm memories of Omma and Halmeoni making kimchi instead of her cousins' jeers and gagging. Jae carried it to the kitchen and set in on the counter gently. She should get her mother's recipe and try her own hand at making kimchi. Maybe Nick would help.

Back at the desk, Jae grabbed the next box. But Seymour wouldn't stop sniffing the box full of papers.

"C, stay out of there."

He whined and lay down right next to the box.

What was his deal?

"Fine. I'll go through the papers. Most of them can probably be thrown away." She sat in the chair and went through the old training materials and paperwork and worked her way to the bottom of the pile. There was a stack of unopened junk mail.

She pulled out a big manila envelope, and Seymour sat straight up and barked.

"Why are you acting so weird?"

She shook her head and laughed at her dog as she slid her finger under the flap and opened up the envelope. A smaller envelope slid out. Jae gasped. That handwriting.

Matt.

Her hands trembled as she unfolded the plain white paper.

Dear Jae,

Hopefully I'll be able to talk to you about this in person. Hopefully this weird feeling I have is nothing. But this next mission we're preparing for is intense. So if anything happens to me, there are things you need to know—the first thing being how much I love you.

I knew on our second date that you were the woman I wanted to marry. The way you tied on a plastic bib and dug into that huge pile of crab legs still makes me laugh. You are always so willing to do that every day—jump into life and grab on with both hands. I love your exuberance, your passion for others, and your courage. And I've been carrying around a ring for the last two years wanting to ask you to marry me.

But it never seemed to be the right time. Even though we've talked about marriage, I've always felt like I needed you more than you ever needed me. Like you aren't quite ready to jump into this wholeheartedly. I keep hoping every time we're together that you'll finally trust me, and show that piece of yourself you hide from everyone else. I keep hoping you'll let me in. All the way.

I know you're holding back. What I don't know is if that is because I haven't earned your trust yet, or if you simply don't want to be vulnerable and depend on anybody. Maybe it's my profession. There's a lot of risk involved and we aren't guaranteed tomorrow. And while that drives me to want to treasure every moment we do have and put it all on the line, maybe it makes you reluctant to be dependent on me, not knowing if I will come home.

Or maybe I'm just not the guy for you.

All I know is, my heart is yours...if you want it. But if you don't (or heaven forbid I don't make it home), I hope you will find someone worthy of the treasure of your love. I hope that nothing will hold you back from diving into life with that man. I hope that you willingly give him your whole heart. What a blessed man he will be.

I'm still selfish and crazy enough to hope it's me.

All my love,

Matt

P.S. If anything happens to me and Seymour retires as an MWD, I've requested that you have the first opportunity to adopt him. I know you'll take great care of my bud.

With a feather-light touch, she traced Matt's signature as tears blurred her vision. Seymour laid his head on her lap, a small whine escaping him. Jae sank to the floor and held the dog close while she still gripped the letter in her hand.

Matt had loved her. He'd wanted to marry her. He'd even had a ring.

Had she really been so busy trying to show him how capable she was that she'd actually driven him away?

She wiped her cheeks and read the words again.

I know you're holding back.

...don't want to be vulnerable and depend on anyone.

The truth pierced deeply. Matt was right. She did hold back. She hated to be seen as needy. She'd learned never to show weakness.

Because there were times the fear of being helpless made her feel as fragile as the snowflake others called her. She'd learned to fight back. She didn't want to be dependent, at someone's mercy. Someone who might take advantage of her.

But she could've trusted Matt.

Here she'd thought *he* was the one afraid of commitment. But he'd been waiting for her all along. Waiting for her to let down her walls and let him in.

I hope you will find someone worthy of the treasure of your love. I hope that nothing will hold you back from diving into life with that man. I hope that you willingly give him your whole heart.

Losing Matt had wrecked her. Had only reinforced her natural tendency to retreat and hide her vulnerable self. But then she'd found Nick. He'd taught her to live again. To crawl out of her cave and find adventure. Find life. Find purpose.

She'd found her purpose here with the CRT. And she had found that man she could give her heart to. Nick.

But there was one huge thing in their way.

LadyJHawk.

She was still holding back. Still didn't want to let herself depend on him. She was too afraid to trust him.

How dumb was she? Jae had been kidding herself, thinking it was Nick she was waiting on to open up like he'd done online. But the whole time, she'd been doing the same thing.

Holding back.

Her laptop sat on the desk she'd just set up. Jae opened the messaging app and skimmed all the messages she and Nick had sent back and forth.

They might have only known each other a matter of weeks in real life, but they'd been friends for a lot longer. And yeah, maybe she was afraid to tell Nick who she really was, to admit that she was the woman who'd bared it all online.

Because if he knew she was LadyJHawk, he would see the real Jae who held nothing back.

And what if he didn't want that?

She'd been the new girl enough times to know that not everyone would like her, accept her. Even her own family, her cousins, hadn't embraced her. She was too different. And with moving so much, she never knew when she'd need to leave it all behind and start again.

But she didn't want to run anymore. She'd found a home here. A man she loved here, one she could see a future with... here.

Now she needed to take Matt's advice. She needed to tell Nick the truth.

And it might be the hardest thing she'd ever done.

Jae's phone rang and Seymour sat up. She shut the laptop and answered. "Hey, Daddy. I think I messed up."

$\mathcal{T}$he dogs had done better today. They'd run at a good pace and followed almost every command. They were close to being ready for the race. So far, this last-ditch effort to save his dogs, his home, and his livelihood was looking hopeful.

But after the long day out in the cold with the dogs, Nick was ready for human interaction. He was ready to relax and romance the socks off of Jae.

He could see something special, something real developing and he wanted it to continue, but he'd hardly seen her since the fire. And he couldn't wait any longer.

Nick parked in her driveway and grabbed the groceries from the back seat. The buzz of excitement in the air might be a touch of nerves too. Maybe it wasn't a big deal to a lot of guys, but for Nick tonight was huge. He was going all out.

He was going to cook.

Something fit for human consumption and hopefully to show Jae how much she meant to him. He'd practiced late last night after his run. He'd watched a video on the technique. He was prepared.

And still his stomach clenched tight as he rang Jae's doorbell, like an awkward teenager going on a first date.

This was Jae. She believed in him. She stood up for him.

So he had nothing to worry about. Right?

Jae opened the door and he was struck again by how beautiful she was. In her yoga pants and fluffy socks, an over-sized sweatshirt hanging off her shoulder, she was the picture of casual beauty. Her hair cascaded down in long flowy strands framing her face. Her lips smiled and her eyes were bright.

On second look...maybe too bright? And there were pink blotches on her cheeks and neck. Had she been crying—?

"Nick." But her voice was almost breathless as she took one of the bags from his hands and tucked herself under his free arm as he stood in the doorway half inside, half out. The warm air from the cabin escaped out the open door. She settled herself against his chest and leaned into him.

And when a girl did that, he didn't question whether she was concerned about her heating bill. He didn't mind the snow falling down on them. He drew her closer and savored every second. She breathed a sigh that sounded a lot like contentment, and his heart swelled.

See, this would be a great night. There was nothing to be nervous about.

"You must've really missed me." He gave her a light squeeze and kissed the top of her head. He couldn't get enough of her sweet and fruity scent.

"Yeah, I have."

Eventually she pulled away and led him all the way inside her cabin. Nick followed her through the little living area, a desk set up with her laptop and a box of papers, a couch and love seat flanking a coffee table. They set the bags on the kitchen counter. "This is a nice, cozy place you found."

"It's amazing." She pulled out the potatoes and the package of mushrooms from his bag and set them down. "I don't think

I'll ever get sick of that view either." She nodded to the big window that overlooked the lake. The sun was setting, spilling a riot of pink and purple and gold over the water. The softly falling snow added to the ambiance.

But Nick wasn't here for that scenery.

He moved closer, tipped her chin up, and looked into her warm brown eyes. "It *is* a gorgeous view."

She blushed and dropped her gaze. "You're not even looking at the window."

"I'm looking exactly where I want to be looking. And I'm telling you, it's way better than some big, cold lake." He moved in and kissed her lightly. Her lips were soft and giving. She kissed him back, her hands sliding up his chest and wrapping around his neck. The way her fingers tangled in his hair drove him a little bit crazy. He pulled her closer, releasing a low growl as she stoked a deep flame inside.

Then she froze. "Wait. Nick, I...I have to—" She stepped back.

"Right." Nick cleared his throat. "We should slow down a bit. And you must be starving."

"Yeah, but that's not what... Hold on." She looked at the ingredients on the counter and then took out the raw chicken breasts and fresh green beans from the last bag. "When you said you were bringing dinner, I thought you were getting takeout."

Now he was probably blushing. Would she think this was a stupid idea? "I thought we could cook something together. If you're willing to give me a shot at cooking human food, that is. If you don't..."

Her whole face brightened. "You want to cook for me?"

"Well, you were the one who said I could cook. So now we'll see. I have all the ingredients. And I have the recipe printed off right here." He held up the piece of paper from the bag. "So with your help, hopefully I won't burn down your new home and we can have a nice romantic meal. Chicken marsala with roasted potatoes and green beans. And for dessert I made something I already knew." He opened the plastic container, releasing the scent of cinnamon and nutmeg into the air. "Pumpkin cookies. I used these cute doggie-shaped cookie cutters I found."

He was babbling. Yeah, the nerves were getting to him. But the way Jae looked at him, her gaze softening, said he'd made the right choice. A single tear even tipped from her eye and rolled down her cheek.

"Hey, are you crying? I haven't started cooking yet!"

She wiped it away. "I know, but you're just so...just so sweet. I don't deserve this. I still have to—"

"Jae." He touched her lips with his finger and traced them. "You deserve so much more." He moved closer until he remembered how quickly passion ignited with this woman. He should keep his focus on the food and showing Jae how much he cared about her. It took monumental effort to drop his finger from her lips and stop himself from kissing her again. "So, ready to help?"

"Of course, but I really need to talk to you."

"Yeah, let's talk as we get this going. Do you have a cutting board? I need to slice the mushrooms and shallots first." He pulled out all the other items. "The dogs had a pretty good run today. Mischa still isn't leading as well as I want, but she's improving."

"Do you think you'll be ready for Friday?" Jae set a cutting board and knife on the counter and started chopping the shallots.

"I think so." He had to be. If that company was going to sponsor him, they had to place in the top three at least. And there would be other companies there too. The only way he could keep his place and his dogs was to do well in this race.

They kept the conversation to the dogs and the rescue call Jae had gone on last night, as they worked together to prepare the chicken. Soon the rosemary potatoes were roasting in the oven and the savory scent of the shallots, mushrooms, and butter cooking filled the whole cabin. Nick stirred the mixture. His elbow knocked the cutting board, and a small piece of chicken fell to the floor. Maybe Seymour would like a little appetizer.

Where was he? Nick finally spied him under the desk, his head resting on a box. "Here, boy. Treat."

Nick waited for him to come. Seymour lifted his head and looked but didn't budge.

Weird.

"What's wrong with Sey?"

Jae's hands stilled. The tongs she'd been using to mix the salad fell into the bowl. "Well, that's related to what I wanted to tell you." She avoided eye contact and moved to wipe her hands on a dish towel. She walked over to the stove and sniffed. "You might need to stir that first."

Huh? Nick looked down. The shallots were starting to burn. No! He leaped for the wine and poured liquid into the pan. He stirred again, scraping the bottom. Thankfully, he caught it just in time.

Sheesh. Why was this so hard? Everyone else in his family could practically cook in their sleep. All he wanted to do was make this nice romantic meal for the woman he was quickly falling for. "Sorry, I have to keep my focus on this or we'll end up hungry. I don't even have takeout as a backup plan since all the restaurants will be closed by now. But as soon as the potatoes and chicken are done, you will have my full, undivided attention." He flashed her his biggest grin, hoping to cover up his blunder.

"Right." She smiled at him and went back to her salad prep.

Now, where was he? Nick stirred the chicken broth and wine mixture with one hand and grabbed the recipe with the other. Wait. He'd forgotten to add the garlic before the wine. He rushed to mince the fresh garlic cloves. Hopefully it would still taste okay. He threw in the chopped garlic. What else was he missing? The thyme. He added the herbs to the pan and then cream. That smelled right. Smelled good. Now he could add the chicken and let it all simmer.

Jae finished the salad and found dishes to set the table. Nick played a slow country music playlist from his phone and pulled out the candles he'd brought. He set the tapers in the candle holders he'd borrowed from his mom in the middle of Jae's round dining room table. He lit them and straightened the placemats.

Jae looked down at the candles. "Wow, you thought of everything. It's beautiful."

"It's a special night. Your first night in your new place."

"I know. It's all unbelievable. I mean, it's really starting to feel like a home."

The way she said the word "home"—so reverently with a touch of awe—well, it did funny things to Nick. It made him want to create a home of their own. Together. It conjured up thoughts of a big, happy family roasting marshmallows around a fire, pulling up to the Dahlquist family functions with a van full of kids.

Ed was right. Jae was worth the risk.

"Oh no!" Jae gasped, her attention on the stove.

Nick looked. His chicken marsala was bubbling over the sides of the pan. No!

He rushed to the stove and turned the heat down. The sauce that ran down the pan burned and filled the tiny kitchen with smoke.

He was botching this. He moved the pan to a different burner then spun around, looking for something to clean up the spill.

"Hey, it's okay." A small, warm hand on his back cut through the frustration. "Looks like you caught it just in time."

"I'm sorry. I thought I had it all ready—" He reached again

for the recipe. He'd probably forgotten something else. The last part of the recipe was cut off and the ink ran where sauce splattered on it. It was illegible. Great. He pushed his hair off his forehead and fisted it.

He spied Jae's laptop. "Do you mind if I check the website? I've lost part of the recipe."

"Of course." She moved to the window above the sink and cracked it open to clear the smoke.

Nick sat at Jae's desk and opened up the laptop. "What's the PIN?"

"R2D2."

He typed it in. Clever. He'd have to remember that one. He bent down to give Seymour a pat. He was usually a pretty calm dog, but he seemed downright depressed tonight. "What's the matter, boy?"

Seymour looked up at him with his big doggy eyes and whined. Then he laid his head back on the box at his feet.

What was that all about?

Nick sat up straight and stared at the screen.

Wait a minute. He knew this messaging app.

He knew these messages.

That avatar.

LadyJHawk? He blinked, trying to make sense of it all. Stark cold reality sluiced through him.

He looked back down at Seymour.

"C"—as in short for Seymour.

The *Star Wars* references.

The new job-slash-adventure.

No.

It couldn't be. Nick bolted from the chair. "You're LadyJHawk?"

Jae's smile fell. "I...that's what I wanted to..."

In a moment, everything he'd once thought of as intimate and special that he'd shared online was exposed as a cruel joke. "What is this? You've known this whole time?" The whole—

Realization hit. "You knew *before* you moved up here, didn't you? You knew who I was."

She took a step toward him, her hands clasped together at her chest. "Nick. Please. I was trying to tell you—"

"Was I just a big joke to you? You must've had a good laugh over the stupid things I told you about...well, you. Man, I'm such an idiot."

"No! This is just a misunderstanding."

"Oh, I understand perfectly. You've been lying to me this whole time. Hiding yourself. Laughing at me behind my back." Nick grabbed his coat. "I can't believe—"

Jae lunged forward and grabbed for his hand. "I never laughed at you. I've been trying to tell you. And..." She blew out a breath and a bit of fire lit in her eyes. "It's not like you were an open book either. You were talking about things online you could've been sharing with me. You never talked to me about how you felt responsible for my hypothermia episode, how you're on the verge of bankruptcy. You didn't—"

"That's not the point. You've had weeks to tell me who you were."

"Please, Nick. You know me. The real me."

He yanked his hand free of her. "I thought I did. Guess I was wrong about that too."

He turned and marched out the door. The snow that had started earlier was falling thicker now as he sped out of Jae's driveway and left town.

❄

Two days and still not a word from Nick. Jae drove out to his place on Tuesday, but he wasn't there and neither were the dogs.

Her cozy cabin had very quickly become dreary and suffocating after Nick left. The snowstorm last night didn't help matters either. Thank goodness she had her Subaru with all-wheel drive and could actually get to work today when all the schools and many businesses were closed. Because Jae needed to work. She could not slip into that same winter of the soul she'd experienced after Matt died.

But she was on the edge. So she gladly took the on-call shift from Colleen so she and Jack could do some prepping for Thanksgiving.

And what a depressing Thanksgiving it was shaping up to be tomorrow.

Jae grabbed a box of latex-free gloves and another box of gauze pads from the supply room and went to restock the chopper. Even though it was still early in the day, the helicopter bay was darker than usual since the high windows were all covered with snow from the storm. Jae stashed the gloves and gauze in the helicopter and continued the mundane task of taking inventory. After the helicopter, she started in the supply room across from the office.

But the task left her mind with too much space to stew in regrets and replay memories. Sledding with Nick. Roasting marshmallows over her first fire. The sweet way he'd brushed her bangs out of her eyes, his fingers lingering on her cheeks.

They'd had a good thing going before she'd blown it all.

The phone from the office interrupted her depressing trip down memory lane. Good, more work. Jae dashed out of the supply room to the phone and picked up the receiver. "Crisis Response Team. This is Jae."

"Jae. This is Pastor Dan Matthews. I'm looking for Boone. Is he there?" The pastor sounded a little out of breath.

"No, he's actually out cutting down a Christmas tree with Vivien. Can I help you?"

"I think my brother and his youth group are in trouble."

"How so?"

"They missed their check-in last night. My wife and I were at their pickup location with the vans earlier this morning and they aren't there. We've been waiting a few hours. I didn't have reception, so I came down the hill a little farther."

"Yeah, Seb told us that one of the main cell towers in the area is down."

"No wonder I couldn't get through. I'm starting to get worried. This storm wasn't supposed to hit us this far north, and I'm not sure if they were prepared for this much snow. But I didn't want to sound the alarm until I knew more. I was hoping to talk to Boone and see what he thought."

Voices carried over from the bay.

"Pastor Dan, someone just walked in. Let me see if it's Boone. Just a sec."

Jae ran out to the main bay where Vivien and Boone were brushing snow off their shoulders and arms, laughing and stomping their feet.

"Boone! Pastor Dan is on the phone. His brother and that group of kids are missing."

The laughter quickly evaporated as Boone rushed to follow Jae to his office. He took the phone. "Boone here."

Boone leaned over his desk, grabbed a pen and pad of paper, and started scribbling notes. "All right. I'll get dispatch to call the team in and we'll get started on a search grid. Stay there in case they show up. We'll get the chopper up in the air and a team on the ground." He paused. "Be there soon."

He hung up the phone and turned to Jae. "Can you fly in this?"

Jae opened up her weather app and looked at the radar. "If I get the chopper ready now, I should be able to fly, but probably not for long. Maybe an hour or two before the next wave of this storm hits."

"Get the Bell ready then. I'm calling the others."

While Boone called Sabine Hueston, their dispatcher, to

contact the others over the emergency response system, Jae ran to put on extra layers and get her down coat from her locker. She wouldn't be caught unprepared again in the cold.

By the time she came back, a few others were already there. Ronnie, Peter, Cole, and Kyle stood around the Cook County map spread out on the command center table.

"Jae, you're ready to go?" Boone asked.

She nodded.

"Take Ronnie with you as a spotter and in case any emergency medical care is needed. I want you to search this area." He pointed to the map of the county and traced one of the rivers to a chain of lakes and creeks. "They're supposed to be camping here." He circled an area up the Brule River. "And there's an open field right over the hill that they talked about hiking to."

Then he pointed to a service road near a hike-in camping spot. "And this is where Dan and others are waiting. We'll start there. There are fifteen youth and six adults. We don't have a lot of time between these weather systems, so get up in the air and cover as much ground as you can. But be safe about it. If the wind kicks up or that ceiling is too low, come right back."

"Of course."

"Let me know as soon as you spot anything."

Jae and Ronnie ran for the chopper. Ronnie sat in the copilot chair and slipped on a headset. Jae did her preflight check and tried to ignore the churning in her middle.

Fifteen children. Six adults.

Oh, Lord, guide us.

Ronnie gave her an encouraging nod. "Let's find those kids."

Jae maneuvered the helicopter off the pad and out over the blinding white world of Deep Haven. Even with gray cloud cover, Jae needed sunglasses to cut the glare. She flew northeast toward the river Boone had pointed out. Ronnie craned her neck, looking out the front and side windows.

After a few minutes, Ronnie tapped her arm. "There's Pastor

Dan and Ellie waiting at the trailhead." She pointed out the window.

Jae began a back-and-forth pattern over the area Boone had assigned. "Hopefully with the snow, a group of kids in bright winter coats will stick out among all the white."

But they didn't. Two hours later, the wind kicked up and the clouds moved in low and fast. And there was no sign of the missing group.

The helicopter shook, and Jae countered the windy gust with the torque pedals. Her heart was as heavy as the massive gray wall of snow moving toward them. "We'll have to turn back. The next wave of this storm system is moving in."

Once the snow started falling, they couldn't even see out the windows. Jae flew back to HQ and they parked the Bell 429. Together with Ronnie, she moved it into the helicopter bay and joined Boone and Kyle at the command center. "Any sign of them?"

Boone's grim look answered before his words did. "No. But we've organized search teams and we're moving the mobile command center to the trailhead."

❄

Hours later, it was pitch black out and there was still no sign of the missing youth group. Boone organized the team and volunteers into shifts to keep the search going continuously. Jae had finished her shift and had been ordered home for mandatory rest. They wanted her ready to man the chopper at the first light of dawn.

But how was she supposed to face the empty cabin or sleep knowing those kids were out there? Instead, she fed Seymour and let him out for a while but then drove back to the CRT HQ. The couple of hours she tried to sleep in the bunk room were wasted. So she made tea and moved to the office while Boone and the sheriff manned the mobile comm center. Jae blew across her mug of tea and settled into a desk chair. A radio sputtered every now and then with crackly voices of her teammates who were out in the dark looking for the missing group. Jae pulled her feet up into the seat and took a sip from her mug.

Lord, please help us find these kids.

Parents drove through the storm, booked nearby hotels, and gathered in the church, hoping, praying for their children. The thought of all those families waiting at Deep Haven Community Church tore at her heart.

The tea offered little comfort but at least it kept her warm while she was by herself in the huge building. She sipped and prayed. What else could she do?

Jae was about to refill her mug when a ding sounded and the computer screen lit up with a notification of an emergency message.

Message from Interlink Com: *Help. 21 souls. No food. Injuries. Snowed in. Caves near Blue Valley Trail and Lost Lake.*

Jae bolted up in the chair. It had to be Pastor Dan's brother. Surely the mobile command center had gotten the message too. She waited for Boone to respond. Nothing.

Jae called him, but the call disconnected before he answered. She ran to the map of their coverage area on the wall and found Lost Lake and the Blue Valley Trail. The caves must be near there.

Jae noted the coordinates and pulled up her phone weather app. It wasn't loading but hopefully the helicopter systems would have a stronger signal and she could get the bird up in the air. Quickly she wrote the coordinates and a note on the office white board then grabbed her winter gear and one of the handheld GPS units. After typing in the coordinates, she ran to the helicopter bay.

She sent a text message with the coordinates and information to Boone and the team and went through her preflight checklist, while waiting for one of them to arrive and accompany her.

But no one showed up.

The kids were hurt and out of food. And the temps were supposed to drop even farther. They couldn't survive in those caves much longer. Jae was the only one who could fly the helicopter. And maybe it was better she go alone. She would need every seat in it for the group once she found them. Even then, it would take three trips to get everyone. And with more storms moving in, she didn't have time to wait any longer.

Jae was soon back in the air. She fought the northwest wind sweeping down from Canada the whole flight, but the snow eased the closer she got to Lost Lake. The snowstorm might've died down for now, but the temps were falling fast. She needed to get to those kids. She knew firsthand how quickly hypothermia could take over.

Jae flew to the area directly over the coordinates but there was nowhere she could land the chopper. Below was a thick carpet of snow-covered evergreen and bare deciduous trees. The nearby lake had open water. Jae circled until she found a small field. As she lowered the chopper, turbulence knocked against it, but she kept it steady. It would be over a two-mile hike to the coordinates but she would move quickly and keep warm.

She landed the Bell and started her GPS. With the signal strong, she shut down the engines and called the team. Still no answer from command center.

"That's okay." She was layered and she had her equipment. "I can do this. I've been trained for this." Her voice and the wind in the trees were the only sounds in the forest.

She added first aid supplies and protein bars to a small pack and hitched it onto her back. Then Jae replaced the flight helmet with the ugly green hat Ronnie had given her when she first moved to Deep Haven. It kept her head warmer than anything else. And she could not fail this time. She strapped on the snowshoes and hopped out of the helicopter.

A wave of uncertainty hit her. The icy cold that had soaked down to her bones and almost lured her to eternal sleep was too recent a memory.

"No. I can do this," she whispered again into the night. She *had* to do this. This was the best chance at getting those kids back.

With the GPS gripped tightly in her mittened hand and its cord looped around her wrist, she started trekking through the deep snow. Once she reached the tree line, the snow wasn't as high, but she was already huffing, fighting for breath. She followed the signal, winding around trees, moving uphill to get to the other side of the ridge where hopefully the kids were waiting. Her thighs and calves burned by the time she crested the top of the ridge. She leaned against one of the many pine trees to catch her breath.

But when she lifted her eyes, she almost cried. A deep ravine cut through her path. From what she could see, there was no way around it and no easy way across it. She would have to slide down and climb up the other side. How would they ever get an injured person across with sides that steep?

She would just have to find a way. Those kids were depending on her. Pastor Dan's brother was out here. Parents were frantic to hug their children again.

They were all depending on Jae.

She wasn't lost. And so far, she had no signs of hypothermia. She could do this.

With renewed strength of purpose, Jae took a tentative side-ways step over the edge of the ravine. She leaned back to keep her balance and stepped again. Her foot slid and the rest of her body hit the snow. Losing all control, she rolled down the ravine, her scream ripping through the night. When she stopped falling, she landed in a deep drift, something sharp and hard digging into her hip.

Jae lay there, catching her breath, taking stock of each limb, moving first her toes and feet and then her hands and arms. Nothing seemed broken. She'd definitely strained something in her right leg as she landed on a rock, but it wasn't excruciating pain. Slowly she sat up, rolled to her knees, and carefully stood, not sure how she'd managed to make it to the bottom without smashing into a tree. But thank God, she was okay. The only thing she'd lost was a snowshoe, which she found a few feet away.

Now to climb up the steep-sided ravine. She brushed as much snow off her coat and legs as she could, repositioned her hat. Nowhere to go but up now. First, though, she should make sure she was heading in the right direction. Jae looked down at her empty hands. The cord that had been attached to the small GPS device was ripped off and frayed.

Where was it?

She spun around. It had to be here. She frantically dug through the big drifts of snow. No. No. No. No! She looked up the path her body had made as it fell down the side of the ravine. No glowing light or little black rectangle broke up the white ground.

And the snow started falling again.

But she needed that GPS if she was going to get out of here. She dug some more in the pile of snow where she'd landed. She took off her mittens to feel for the hard plastic box. Her fingers quickly lost sensation, though, as she plunged them again and again into the frozen drift. Jae pulled them out of the snow and jammed them back into her mittens. She was losing too much time.

The GPS device was gone for good. And the longer she stood still, the more she could feel the bone-deep shiver start to overtake her body.

No. She would not fail again. She had to move and keep her core warm. GPS or not.

Jae strapped her snowshoes—one now broken—to her pack. She grabbed a slim tree trunk and hoisted herself up out of the ditch at the bottom of the ravine. She reached out to the next closest tree and found a foothold. Slowly she climbed up, moving from tree to tree. She could only focus on the next move. Her body warmed from within as it worked. Eventually she reached the top and collapsed into a breathless heap. Looking up into the sky, she watched snowflakes fall between the naked oak branches and full white pine treetops. They melted as soon as they hit her face and swirled every which way by the wind.

It might be her nickname, but she would not be a delicate snowflake. She had to keep moving with the cold setting in.

Putting her back to the ridge, she headed in what she hoped was a straight path west. If she stopped, she would get too cold. So it was either move and pray she could find the group or stay and freeze to death.

But what if she didn't find them? What if she got lost herself?

She was already lost and it served her right.

The person you need to be honest with first is yourself... Everybody needs help sometimes.

How are you supposed to save lives if you're not honest about your own abilities? It literally almost killed you to ask for help. If we're a team, that means we need to be there for each other and we need to be honest with each other.

Nick and Colleen were right. It had been so easy to wave aside their concerns when she was safe and in the hospital. But out here in the dark forest, the stark reality couldn't be ignored. Jae had a problem asking for help. She had been so worried about being rejected—and now she might die all alone because of it.

Jae trudged through the drifts, frozen tears chafing her

cheeks. She looked behind her and saw her path wound around so many different obstacles it was nowhere near a straight line. Now the snow started falling thick, and even in the shelter of the trees the wind whipped through all her layers. She didn't know which way to turn anymore. And she was shivering hard. Even if they could get back to the helicopter, she wouldn't be able to fly in these conditions. She was lost, cold, and very much alone

When you pass through the waters, I will be with you.

The Scripture whispered through her, the verse in Isaiah.

Then why did she feel so alone?

Maybe because she refused to let anybody get too close. Even God. She might've taken Daddy's advice to be Texas tough a little too far.

When you pass through the waters, I will be with you.

Well, Lord, I sure hope You are, because I've gotten in way over my head and I don't know what to do. And I can really use a rescue.

Colleen's voice repeated in her head. *Decide and make a home for yourself where you are. Here.*

Use the resources around you.

Nick.

Right. She wasn't alone. And she could use the resources around her and make a shelter. Here.

Jae took off her pack and dug a trench with the broken snowshoe. The deep snow was powdery and light, easy to dig, and being small, she didn't have to dig long. The exercise in her arms as well as her legs helped push back the cold and created some warmth. With the all-purpose tool from her pack, Jae cut off full, green spruce limbs. She lined her trench with them. A skinny dead birch branch was quickly snapped off into three pieces and placed over her trench. Jae piled more green boughs on top of them, creating a roof, which she then piled snow on top of.

Her muscles and body were tired. It wasn't the same sleepiness that had overtaken her at Nick's when her body temperature had dropped to eighty-eight degrees. This was the weariness from stress and being awake for too long. She would rest, and hopefully after that she could find her way back to the helicopter or to the caves. Jae climbed into her shelter and ate one of the protein bars. She would sleep a few hours and then see what the new day—Thanksgiving Day—brought.

CHAPTER 15

*N*ick threw a bale of straw into the trailer while snow pelted his face and the wind whipped through his hair. There was nothing worse than being made a fool of. Again.

He stomped through the dark over to the sack with freeze-dried dog food and another of frozen raw meat. Dragging them through the snow, he hefted them into the trailer too.

Like it wasn't bad enough when he'd scraped up the nerve to ask Vivien out in high school. He could still hear Ree and Amelia cracking up about it the next day. They didn't know he was there in the hall around the corner from their lockers.

Can you imagine Vivie and Nick? Together?

I can't believe he got all dressed up and bought flowers.

I would've paid money to see Smoky in a tie.

And flip-flops. Don't forget the flip-flops.

Vivie joined them. *Come on, you two. It was sweet.*

Yeah, but you and Nick? Really?

At least that time, Vivie had kinda stood up for him. And, sure, it had all worked out for the best.

But Jae had played him for a fool. And this time the sting went a lot deeper.

He slammed the trailer door shut. Man, what an idiot he'd been. He'd shared things with Lady J because he knew he'd never meet her in person. She was a safe sounding board. An uncomplicated conversation.

And yeah, he'd kind of been falling for her when Jae came along. Maybe he was a little conflicted when he'd found someone real. Someone on his side. Someone who had believed in him in real life.

But it was all just a big joke. Jae had probably gotten a good laugh at that. It was like the fire that had almost burned down his parents' restaurant all over again. People tried to laugh it off, but it only intensified the burning shame in Nick's gut.

Was he just a sucker for women who liked to toy with his affections?

Nick shoved his hands into his pockets and walked over to the temporary kennel. The snow covered all the evidence of the fire that had taken the big shed, custom Quonset kennel, and the outdoor area he'd built with his own two hands. Maybe he was just a fool to think he could make his own legacy as a dogsled-der. But now it was the only thing he had a decent shot at. If he didn't win the race tomorrow—

No. He couldn't let his thoughts go there.

He should've known about Jae, though. The *Star Wars* refer-ences. The military working dog with PTSD. Hello, her handle? LadyJHawk. The signs were all there, and like a blind idiot he hadn't seen a thing.

But he still had a shot at this race—and he had more on the line than ever.

Nick's phone rang. He answered it as he moved toward his back porch out of the wind. "Peter?"

"Nick, she's gone."

"Who?"

"Jae."

"She left town? In the storm?"

"No, she left in the helicopter. That group of kids from the Cities is missing. We've been searching since yesterday. She missed her shift sign in and there's a note here at headquarters. She flew out there alone. We have a signal for the chopper and it's not far from you."

Nick yanked open the door and ran inside for something to write with. "Where is it?"

Peter gave him the coordinates Jae had written down as well as those for where the chopper was, almost two miles farther.

"Nick, you gotta find her. I don't know how long she's been out there. I don't think she's been gone long, but the signal is weak and it's not moving. Our snowmobiles are getting bogged down in the storm. The trails are buried. Is there any way your dogs can get through?"

Flashbacks of finding Jae frozen on the ground rocked Nick. And trying to find her in the huge expanse of the Lake Superior National Forest now? It would be a nightmare. Even with coordinates. The chopper would just be the starting point. She could be anywhere. In any direction. And the storm would've covered her tracks.

"Nick? Are you there?"

Amid the panic that was crashing through him, one clear thought crystallized.

Seymour.

"Peter, I need Seymour. I'll get the sled and the dogs ready. You bring me Seymour."

"You can get through on the sled?"

"Yeah, being on the back side of the ridge, my trails are more sheltered. Less drifting."

"Right. I'll be there as soon as I can. With the dog."

Peter hung up, and the weight of the whole situation slammed down on Nick. He stood frozen in his kitchen.

Jae. Lost.

She could be alone, cold.

But he remembered her words as they'd sat in the clinic. *I know I wasn't there, but I still say you did the best thing for Grady that you could. You were with him and you prayed.*

And you aren't alone either, Nick. Not then and not now.

And she was right. The truth helped center him and clear his head. He knew what to do. By the time Peter showed up with Jae's dog, Nick had his team ready to go, extra dog food, first aid kit, a satellite phone, and supplies packed. Not sure how Seymour would do with the deep snow, Nick dressed him in two dog jackets and sat him in the sled basket.

"Ready?" Peter looked shaken too.

Nick clenched his jaw, bracing himself against the emotions pounding through him. "Yeah."

"Look, I know something is going on between you and Jae. But you need to put that behind you now. Find her. She's one of ours."

"I know."

Peter grabbed him in a bro hug and stepped back. Nick released the sled brake and stood on the foot boards.

"Hike!"

Hours later, Nick flexed his cramped hands and brushed off the snow piling on his hood. Ice crystals clung to his eyebrows and the tip of his nose. He'd long ago lost feeling in his feet. And the snow was too deep, his trail too narrow to run beside the sled.

No wonder they couldn't get the snowmobiles out. At least among the trees there was a little more cover from the biting wind, but the snow continued piling on. Nick kept the dogs on the sheltered side of the ridge as much as he could, but this trip was taking three times as long in these conditions.

Thankfully the dogs didn't seem to mind the cold and the dark conditions. But he had to stop every hour to feed them and check their paws, wipe the clumps of snow sticking to their bodies, and help break the trail through larger snowdrifts.

When Seymour got antsy, Nick let him run behind the sled. He kept up fine with the team and didn't seem to mind the snow.

They were getting close to the Brule River—probably only twenty miles from Deep Haven as the crow flew, but it might as well be a thousand. It was as desolate as some of the Yukon and Alaska landscapes Nick had raced through.

The dogs were slowing around the curve in the trail. Down on the left side, the trail followed a creek as it cut through the forest. The bank was short but steep, and the icy edges of water looked like jagged saw blades. Only the very middle of the creek had open water rushing downstream. They needed to take it slow.

"Whoa!" Nick tried to whistle, but his lips were too frozen to make the sound.

A panicked yelp broke through the wind.

Mischa!

The dogs stopped. Nick rushed through the knee-deep snow along the gangline until he got to the front.

Mischa had fallen into the creek. She pawed at the slick snowbank for ground. Seymour barked and stood on the bank. Bozwell held Mischa up by the line connecting them, but he was slipping toward the water too as the weight of her dragged him closer.

Nick pulled on the line but Mischa was too panicked and fought against them. Nick slipped, fell to his belly. The breath was knocked out of him as he hit the ground and plunged his hands into the creek, breaking the thin layer of ice on top that hid the perilous water below. The current did its best to drag his dog away. But he wrapped frozen arms around the husky and hugged her middle. With all his strength, he rolled her out of the water and onto the solid bank.

Mischa scrambled off, yelping as soon as her back leg hit the ground. Nick lay on his back in the snow, trying to catch his breath. But he couldn't.

It was too much. Every part of his body hurt. The healed bone in his leg that had broken years ago throbbed again with an intense pain he couldn't ignore.

Surely he was dying.

And for a few seconds, the temptation to slip into the dark pit of unconsciousness to escape the pain overwhelmed him.

Mischa crawled over and licked his face, her cold snout nudging his cheek. She whined. The other dogs barked and gathered around Nick as if they too wanted him to stand up.

You are an inspiration, Nicholas. People don't follow a joke. They follow leaders... It's easy for people to talk about doing big things. You actually go out there and do them.

Ed's words stirred him. And what was it Pastor Dan had said just a few weeks ago?

Throughout the Bible, God chose unlikely heroes....He often chose the weak, the despised, the needy. I wonder if that's because they were aware that they had little to offer while the strong and proud were busy trying to prove themselves worthy.

Mischa whined again. Seymour barked and the others joined him.

Maybe Ed was right. He wasn't a joke. And Nick certainly had nothing to offer in this moment. He was weak and needy all right. But if that's the kind of guy God could love, that God could use—a guy who panicked in a crisis, who was on the verge of bankruptcy, who had spent way too much time trying to prove to everyone that he was worthy—then there was hope. Maybe he didn't need to have some amazing legacy to make a difference.

Right now, his team needed their leader. And he had the whole town rooting for them, praying for them. He wasn't alone.

He had to keep going.

Jae. And the kids. They were still out there.

Nick opened his eyes. *Lord, if You can use weak and needy men, then here I am. Help me find them. Help me to keep going. And no matter what happens, I know You are with me.*

Slowly, Nick rolled to his side and then up on all fours. He took a tentative breath and winced. With frozen fingers, he felt under his coat. He might've bruised a rib, but nothing was broken.

Crawling to Mischa, he checked her over. A deep cut on her back leg was bleeding. She shivered uncontrollably. He made it to his feet and unhooked Mischa's harness from the tugline. But when he picked her up, Nick crashed down to his knees with his first step.

No. He had to get her warm.

The dogs barked encouragement and Mischa licked his face again. He grunted as he picked himself and his dog up and made it three more steps before collapsing.

Nick's arms shook. His fingers were in agony. He dug deep for what minuscule strength he had left and stood again with Mischa. This time, he trudged through the snow and made it back to the sled. After wrapping Mischa up in the cargo basket among the food and supplies, Nick leaned heavily on the sled frame and dropped to his knees. He tried to catch his breath and stop the quaking in his body.

Seymour ran to him, whining and barking.

"Down, boy."

But he wouldn't stop. He pawed at Nick's leg.

"I know. We're going to keep moving. Just…give me a sec."

Using the sled, Nick slowly rose to his feet once more. "Seymour, you have to lead. Go find Jae, boy."

With a bark, the Belgian Malinois bounded to the front of the line.

"Hike!"

The dogs were off once more, but Nick couldn't see anything. The blinding snow cut off all sight. He could only trust Seymour to lead them.

The dogs veered to the right, away from the river.

No. That didn't seem right.

They barked and howled then left the trail and slowly moved deeper into the woods.

No!

But Nick had no more voice and only enough strength to hold on to the sled. They slid down an incline and then back up a hill. The dogs left the trail and stopped. Seymour barked.

He knew something. Nick left the other dogs and the sled and followed Seymour's shadow as he maneuvered around the thick trees. Seymour's barking grew frantic. He sat in the snow by a big mound with—were those spruce branches sticking out of the bottom?

Nick rushed over and found an opening in the snow hill facing away from the wind. Branches stuck out the bottom, and two boots could be seen in the small doorway. Jae! Nick yanked her foot.

"Jae!"

Please be alive. She had to be alive.

He shook her foot again. "Jae!" He peered inside the trench with his flashlight. It was lined well with green branches, the way he had taught them. Jae was tucked in, an even rising and falling of her chest, and a healthy pink glow to her lips.

She roused. "Nick?"

She crawled out of her snow shelter. Seymour jumped and barked. He licked her cheek. "Hey, boy, you found me." She wiped the sleep out of her eyes.

"Are you okay? Are you cold?" Nick ripped off his gloves and touched her cheek. It was warm.

"I'm not cold. The snow shelter was chilly at first, but then it warmed up and kept me comfortable."

Nick grabbed her and held her close. The chill of dread inside melted away and he finally took his first full breath since Peter's call. Jae was okay. *Thank You, Lord!*

Then everything else they'd gone through came crashing in and he stepped back and cleared his throat. "How long have you been here?"

She checked her watch. "A few hours. But, Nick, we have to find those kids. I lost my GPS but I think we're close. I got a good look at the lay of the land in the chopper. I think I know where they are. But...I'm going to need your help."

She was finally asking for his help? Infused with hope and strength from finding Jae, he nodded. "Lead the way, Snow."

❄

Jae looked at Nick, who was checking over Mischa in the sled a few feet away and melting snow for drinking water in the weak daylight. He was probably still mad at her, but for a few glorious seconds she had been back in his arms. Now the snow was picking up again. After surviving in a shelter made from it, she had a new respect for the frozen precipitation.

He handed her a cup of water. "Why don't you drink this? We have some kids to find." He went back to his sled and packed up the burner and pot.

Obviously, he was still hurt. But she would take what she could get. He was talking to her at least. Maybe one day Nick Dahlquist would trust her again, look at her like he used to— like she was the Princess Leia to his Han Solo. But they had a job to do, and together they had a better chance of accomplishing it.

Jae rubbed down Seymour and gave him water. "C, you think you can find those kids? We need you, bud."

He barked.

"Let's go then."

Nick released the brake on the sled, but with all the snow, the dogs had a slow walking pace. They let Seymour run ahead. He seemed to understand that he was looking for something.

Nick used the coordinates Jae had and they headed in that direction.

After a while, Jae shivered again and lost feeling in her toes. Seymour stayed close by her, still leading them, sniffing and listening.

Nick stopped the dogs and yelled over the wind to her. "Are you okay?"

She started to nod and brush off his concern but she paused. No.

That was what had gotten her into this mess. Maybe Nick *could* help. She walked over to him. "I...I am a little cold. I can't feel my fingers."

Nick dug into his backpack and pulled out a couple hand warmer packets. He shook them up and gave them to her. "Ride in the sled and hold Mischa. She could use the body heat too."

Her teeth chattered as Nick picked up Mischa and settled her on Jae's lap in the sled. He wrapped them both in the sleeping bag in the sled and pulled the hood of Jae's parka over her hat. He cinched it tight and then called for the dogs to move again.

Mischa's body shivered too but as the dogs trudged on through the snow and woods, both Jae and Mischa drew from each other's heat and stopped shivering. Jae's fingers thawed, which hurt at first, but then she reveled in the heat from the packets stuffed inside her mittens.

The daylight grew stronger and the snow stopped falling but Jae knew it was only a lull in the storm. Seymour walked in front of the line, sniffing and scouting the trail. He stopped and Nick halted the other dogs. "Whoa." Then Seymour barked and ran ahead.

"He has a scent!" Jae shouted.

Nick nodded. "Hike!" The other dogs picked up the pace and followed Seymour into a thick clump of pine and spruce.

It wasn't long before they heard voices. The dogs barked. A

creek cut through a small clearing they entered. A rocky ledge at the back was topped with snow and more trees.

"Hello!" A woman in a bright green parka waved at them. "Please, we need help!" She came out of an opening in the rock wall and moved toward them.

The sled slid to a stop beside the woman and a young teen boy. They both shivered despite the snowpants and heavy-duty winter coats. The woman's lips were chapped, but tears of relief shone in her eyes. The boy knelt down by the dogs.

"Are you Pastor Dan's sister-in-law?" Jae asked.

"Yes, I'm Jeanette. This is my son, Carter."

"Where are the others?" Nick's teeth chattered as he spoke.

"Just here. In the cave. I can't tell you how relieved we are to see you."

With a small burst of renewed energy, they followed Jeanette and Carter across the clearing. Thirty yards away and cut into the side of a low cliff was a cave. Nick carried Mischa, and the other dogs stayed outside staked on the line. When Carter moved aside the pine boughs they'd used to cover the entrance, Nick and Jae found five more adults and all the students huddled together around a dim lantern. Jae had never seen a more beautiful sight.

"Is everyone all right?" Nick asked as he laid Mischa down. Seymour settled right in next to her.

A man resembling Pastor Dan sat up with a grimace. "I broke my ankle. I can't put any weight on it. One of the boys dislocated a shoulder. We finished the last of our food. But these kids have been troupers and we're so grateful you're here. You're our Thanksgiving miracle."

"That's Dave, my husband. And he's right. You came just in time." Jeannette, still standing by Nick and Jae, dropped her voice. "I'm a nurse, but we need some medical help. I popped that shoulder back in, but we've got the beginning stages of hypothermia here, probably dehydration. I'm afraid Dave's getting frostbite on that foot too. His ankle is too swollen to get a boot on it. We don't have a good way to melt the snow since we ran out of propane for our stoves. We don't have any Firestart either."

Nick nodded and then darted back out of the cave, probably to get water going.

"What happened?" Jae asked out loud, trying to keep it light and not scare the kids any more than they already were.

Dave answered for the group. "We were crossing a river. I thought the ice was thick enough, but it wasn't. My ankle got caught as the ice broke through, and we lost a couple of the sleds we were carrying gear on. The tents and food supply mostly. Then that storm hit. Thankfully we found this cave."

One of the other leaders spoke up. "We went back to the river and ended up retrieving one of the packs. It had the PLB. We used that to send a message but we weren't sure if anyone received it."

"That must've been the message I saw at the HQ. The Personal Location Beacon."

"We're hungry. Do you have anything to eat?" One of the kids stood up and suddenly the cave was filled with chatter and questions.

Nick came back in with insulated water bottles and the first aid kit. He passed them to Jeannette and held up his hands. They quieted. "First I need to contact Headquarters and let people know where we are. Then we'll feed you."

"Yeah!" The teens started talking over each other again.

Nick moved back toward the cave entrance and Jae followed. "Hey, how can I help?"

"Grab the protein bars, the stove kit, and all the dog food I packed. Have Jeanette and the other leaders work on keeping water going. Make sure everyone drinks first and let's get some meds for the injured. Then we'll start hydrating the freeze-dried stuff for the kids but we'll leave the frozen meat for the dogs. Give some to Mischa and sit with her. Make her eat."

He was trusting her with his dog. That meant something, right?

Nick stepped out of the cave and Jae followed. He dug through his pack, pulled out the satellite phone, and called Peter. Leaning in closer, she heard Peter answer clearly.

"Nick! Is that you?"

"Yeah, I'm with Jae. We found them. We found the group."

There was no response.

"Hello? Peter?"

Only static came through and then the call cut out. They tried again with no answer. All other numbers called went unanswered as well.

Something was wrong. They weren't getting through. A deep tremble started inside Jae that had nothing to do with the cold. "Do you think they heard us? Do they know where we are?"

"I don't know." Nick looked around them.

Wasn't he worried? "What are you looking for?"

"I didn't see any wood in the cave."

"Yeah, but what are we going to do? How do we get ahold of the team?"

"For now, I'm going to look for wood. I'll try to keep calling, and in the morning if we still haven't been able to get through, we'll hike back to the chopper. But we need to keep these kids warm and fed in the meantime. I have a feeling we'll need wood to get us through the night. This storm isn't over."

He wasn't panicking. His eyes were clear, determined. Nick's confidence spurred her on and settled the unease. "Then I'll help."

They were in the middle of the forest, but with the heavy snow cover and more coming down, it wouldn't be easy to find fuel for a fire. After handing a package of protein bars, pots, and propane burners to Jeannette, Jae and Nick moved to the trees at the edge of the clearing.

"Should we gather dry undergrowth from beneath the lower branches of the spruce trees?"

"Yeah, but it'll burn fast. We need some thicker logs and branches to get us through the night, but they can't be too green or they could smoke us out of the cave."

Jae spied a slim tree that had fallen against another. It looked like it had been dead a while. "What about that?"

Nick moved slower than usual, probably sore from the fall he'd taken while rescuing Mischa. "That could work." They tromped over to it and together broke it up into smaller pieces they could use. "If we find a couple more like this, they should keep us going for a while. Then we'd better feed the kids."

Maybe it was wishful thinking, but he seemed to be thawing a little bit toward her. He wasn't shooing her away at least.

Nick wandered to another tree and studied one of the bare branches. She trudged through the knee-deep snow over to Nick. "Hey...I wanted to apologize."

Nick didn't look her. He moved to the next tree. "It's fine."

"No, it's not. Nick?" She waited until he faced her to continue. "I...I was wrong. I've been fighting so long to prove to everyone I'm 'Texas tough' and not this wimpy, helpless girl everyone saw me as. You were right. I was hiding part of myself and only showing the part I wanted people to see. The strong part. I've been afraid to accept help. Afraid people would think less of me. I should've told you from the beginning that I was LadyJHawk."

He finally made eye contact. "Why didn't you?"

"That first time I showed up on your doorstep, you practically shut the door in my face."

"Right." He grimaced. "Okay, but what about after that?"

"I didn't want you to think I was a stalker. I mean, I could see why anyone *would* think that after we'd been chatting online for two years and then I moved up here. And I *was* excited to meet you in person. I thought we had the foundation for something special. You were a big part of the reason I moved. And I think I grew afraid that if you met the real Jae, you wouldn't like her as much as you liked LadyJHawk. I didn't want to lose what we had. Online or in real life."

His lips remained in a straight line. His eyes didn't sparkle. But he glanced to the side and then back to her. "Apology accepted." He moved around the tree trunk and pointed up. "I think this is another dead branch we can use."

Okay. Guess that was as good as it was going to get. Jae nodded and pushed back the disappointment lodged in her chest.

Together they lugged the wood they'd collected and brought in the dehydrated food. Once the blizzard started up again and darkness fell, Nick also let the dogs off their lines and brought them inside the cave. The kids all gravitated toward the animals. The dogs helped calm and warm them as Nick started a fire in the middle of the cave. The dogs gladly accepted the attention and rest.

A girl with long blonde braids giggled. "It's like a puppy slumber party."

The adults smiled over the kids' heads at each other. They weren't out of the woods yet, but lines of stress and worry eased a bit as they all helped rehydrate the food Nick brought in and passed it around to the kids who had already devoured the protein bars earlier. Nick even had salt and pepper packed. Everyone shared bowls and cups. Many had to use their fingers, but nobody seemed to mind as the smell of roasted meat and sweet potatoes filled the cave.

"Wow, what is this?" One of the boys took another huge bite.

Jae caught a mischievous glint in Nick's eye as he answered. "Dog food."

Everyone stopped eating and stared at him.

"What?" Some of the girls looked horrified. "Did he say dog food?"

Then the boy who had originally asked shrugged and dug in for another scoop. "Whatever it is, it's the best thing I've ever eaten. I'll have to tell my dad about this."

The girl with the blonde braids spoke up. "Is it really dog food?" she asked Nick.

"It's roasted venison and pork with sweet potatoes and brown rice. I do feed it to the dogs, but there's nothing bad or weird in it. I make my own food for them so I know exactly what they're eating."

Jae settled down with her own portion in one of the plastic bags the food was in. "I've watched him make it. And I've eaten it before. Believe me, you are eating a gourmet Thanksgiving dinner tonight, even if it isn't turkey. These dogs eat better than most humans."

"That's it. Nick and Jae, you can lead the next winter camping trip. I don't know how we'll ever be able to top this," Dave joked from the other side of the cave. But the pain was still evident on his face. He needed medical help. And Nick still couldn't get a call out.

The other adults helped pass out water and organized kids with clean-up duty, but eventually there was nothing more to do, nothing to take their minds off the situation. The kid with the dislocated shoulder and Dave got another dose of painkillers. The storm raged outside the cave wall.

Nick tried again to make a call but it didn't go through. One of the girls scooched closer to River. "Are they going to find us?" Her voice shook. "Will we be okay?"

The other kids all looked to Nick too, scared.

"Hey, we're going to be all right. We have a fire now, right? And everyone ate?"

They nodded.

"The dogs and I have been in worse weather. But we have

249

water now, still some food left for tomorrow. We'll stick together, and we're going to get you all back home. I promise."

A girl in a purple parka and hat inched closer to the fire. "This is the worst Thanksgiving ever."

"When we get back, I'm never going out in winter again," one boy grumbled.

Nick chuckled. "That's too bad. I was going to offer you all free dogsled rides."

The boy's head snapped up. "Really?"

"Yeah. You have experience now. And you know, if you want to accomplish big, cool things in life, it's gonna be hard. A true adventure is bound to have difficulties to overcome. And you guys are doing it. While your friends are back playing video games and hanging out, you've got this amazing adventure you're on. You should be proud of yourselves. I know you're not with your families watching college football and eating pumpkin pie, but believe me—this is a Thanksgiving you will never forget."

Jae watched the frightened looks melt away in the glow of the fire. Nick really was an inspiration.

"Why don't we have one of your leaders pray and then everyone stay close together to conserve warmth and try to get some sleep. Tomorrow, our adventure continues." Nick sat back down and added a small log to the fire.

"Father," Dave prayed over the group, "we know You are the Lord of all creation. We aren't lost to You. Please guide the rest of the rescue team and guide us. Thank You for bringing Jae and Nick to us, like angels in the storm. We always have Your presence to be thankful for. Give us Your peace as we trust in You. Amen."

The blizzard continued to howl, but Jeannette started to hum a praise song and the other leaders joined in as everyone settled in for the night. The kids drifted asleep, curled up close to the dogs.

Jae must've fallen asleep too. A delicious warmth wrapped around her with a familiar spicy scent, almost like a chai tea. It was subtle. The hint of sandalwood lured her back into a dreamworld she was so reluctant to leave.

But a snore intruded her consciousness, waking her enough to remember.

The cave. The kids.

A snap sounded, echoing in the cave. Jae cracked open an eyelid. Nick hunched over the fire, feeding it a thin piece of wood.

The amber glow highlighted his rugged features, the strong jawline, slim nose, beautiful eyes.

Brooding eyes.

He looked troubled.

Jae stayed still, watching. Everyone else must still be asleep. And Jae wanted more than anything to capture the warmth of her dream.

She'd been in his arms. Sheltered. Loved. Wanted.

Then it registered. What was he throwing in the fire?

Jae sat up. Nick's coat slid off her shoulders.

How had his coat wound up on her?

"Are you okay?" He looked over at her, whispering.

She nodded. She watched him feed a curved edge of some sort of finished wood into the fire. The thin wooden strips looked out of place, but also familiar. Like she should know what they were, but they were out of context.

And then she saw a piece of leather lanyard at his feet. It all clicked. And her heart broke again.

No.

"Nick, what did you do?" Even though she whispered, it still echoed off the cave walls.

His gaze avoided hers. "Go back to sleep, Jae. I'll keep watch."

She moved in closer. "But you...you burned your sled? The one Ed made?" She kept her voice low, which was good. Hopefully it meant he wouldn't hear how much his sacrifice had affected her.

"Burn the ships, right? Only this time, it was a sled."

"But—"

"We needed the wood. We already burned through everything else that was dry. And it's coming down too fast to find more wood without risking getting lost in a blizzard."

"Yeah, but...how are you going to race now?"

"It doesn't matter. You do what you have to to survive. Go back to sleep. I have enough to keep this going for a little longer, and it's almost morning."

A different kind of cold set in. "Nick, I'm scared. How are we going to get these kids back if the team can't—"

One of the girls moaned and turned in her sleep.

Nick brought a finger to his lips but kept his gaze fixed on the fire. When the girl settled back down, his voice—even though it was just a whisper—cut through the questions and fear. "We'll be all right. I'll find a way out of here. I promise."

And knowing Nick was watching over them all—and that even here in the midst of the storm, God carried them—Jae lay back down and fell right to sleep.

CHAPTER 16

*J*ae woke to the sound of girly whispers and giggling. She sat up and once more Nick's coat slid off her shoulders. A frigid wind ran down her back. The fire had only glowing coals and embers but there were pots of water from melted snow.

There was, however, no sign of Nick.

The other leaders were awake, and the kids were starting to stir. "Did you see where Nick went?" Jae asked.

Jeannette shook her head. "He left earlier and said he'd be back soon. It's been a while though."

Through the branches of their makeshift door, Jae spied patches of a dark gray dawn sky. He was out there somewhere. Without his coat.

She got up and helped pass out water and the last of the food. The kids fed the dogs too. Not sure about what else to do, Jae suggested they pack everything and prepare to leave whenever Nick got back.

Everything was packed and ready to go, but still no Nick.

Jae put on a brave face for the kids, but she couldn't deny the fear that started to creep in.

When you pass through the waters, I will be with you.

Right. She wasn't alone. God was with them and Nick couldn't be far. She just needed to wait for him. They could depend on Nick Dahlquist.

Just as one of the leaders suggested searching for him, light flooded into the cave and Nick walked in. "Hey, everyone, we have company!"

The group rushed outside to see a bunch of snowmobiles and ATVs crest the hill, come into their clearing, and stop.

"Mom! Dad!" The girl with braids rushed into her mother's arms. After a long hug and a few tears, she dragged her parents over to Jae and Nick. "These are the ones who rescued us, Daddy. They fed us dog food! For Thanksgiving!"

Peter hopped off his ATV and joined them. "Nick, Jae, this is Hamilton and Signe Jones. They run a private rescue team. They helped us track your signal and provided some extra gear. Ham, this is my cousin I was telling you about."

"We can't thank you both enough for saving our daughter." Ham shook their hands. "Wait—Nick Dahlquist? Didn't you do a North Pole expedition a couple of years ago?"

"Yeah. You know about that?"

"I do. And I'd love to hear more about it sometime."

As they started talking about dogsledding, Jae stepped away to find her own dog. She didn't get far before she was wrapped up in a big hug from Colleen. "Are you okay? You had us so worried! What were you thinking flying out here all alone?"

Ronnie slugged her on the arm. Hard. "Yeah, you need to stop doing that."

Jae rubbed her now bruised arm. "I'm sorry. It was stupid of me. I thought I was fine alone. But obviously I wasn't."

"What happened?" Colleen asked.

"I had to land farther away than I realized. Then I had to

hike quite a ways. Then I fell down this ravine and lost my GPS."

"You were literally lost in a snowstorm out here?" Ronnie's eyes were huge.

"Yeah, I was lost for a bit. But I made a snow shelter like Nick taught us, and he brought Seymour. They found me. Together we found the kids."

"So did you kiss and make up?" Colleen asked. She and Ronnie had both heard the sob story after Nick left Jae's cabin that night. "Did you apologize for hiding your online relationship?"

"I've apologized. He accepted, but he's been pretty distant. I...I think I really messed it up. I'll be lucky if we remain friends after all I did."

"You never know." Ronnie was trying to be helpful, but Jae didn't know where she stood with Nick. Their truce might be as close as they got.

But she didn't have any time to dwell on it. The team did a quick assessment on all the kids and leaders and paired them up to ride back in sleds pulled by the snowmobiles or doubled up on ATVs with CRT members.

Boone sent the first group out and then walked over to Nick and Jae. "Hey, can you accompany Jae back to the helicopter?"

It would be a bit of a hike and mean time alone with Nick. He might not want much to do with her now that the group was safe. But she wanted to be with him.

More than anything.

And she was ready to tell him that. In real life.

Jae held her breath while she waited for Nick's answer.

"I would, but I have the dogs—"

Colleen came out of the cave. "Boone, I really think we should get Dave's ankle and the boy's shoulder looked at ASAP. They need the helicopter. It would be torture to try to move them on the snowmobiles."

"All right," Boone said. "Jae, you're going to ride with me back to the chopper and we'll use the baskets to load them. Nick, can you take Colleen's snowmobile back instead?"

Nick, ride a snowmobile? Jae watched the emotions play out on his face but in the end it was a stern line of determination and a curt nod that won out. "Yeah, I can do that. If Peter can take my injured dog to Lena's, the rest can follow me to my place and I'll get the snowmobile back to HQ."

Oh Nick. Her heart squeezed, knowing the courage it took for him to agree.

"Good. I'll let you tell Peter." Boone got on the snowmobile and started the engine. "Jae, let's go get that chopper."

She sat behind Boone and held on to him.

Nick walked over. "If you veer north as you go east, you should avoid the ravine."

Jae wasn't sure what she'd hoped he would say, but that wasn't it. And before she could respond, Nick turned away and Boone and Jae zoomed across the snow.

❄

Nick stood outside the back door of the Trailside Bistro and breathed in the brisk outside air while he could. The dogs were all home, Mischa and Kasha—adjusting to her three legs—had stayed in the cabin recuperating and the others were in their temporary kennel. It had taken so long to get them settled yesterday after the whole ordeal that he'd been up half the night and hadn't had a chance to talk to Jae. He'd tried to say what he wanted online, but it didn't seem to come out right, so he'd deleted it.

Enough with the online games.

He would find her and tell her all that was on his heart. Right after he got himself a job.

And found his phone, which he'd lost somewhere between

the visits to the vet's, CRT headquarters, and Peter's house yesterday.

He pushed his hair back and stretched his neck. Why was he nervous? It wasn't like his own parents would deny him employment. Besides, he was doing all sorts of things he'd never thought he'd do. Like driving a snowmobile home.

It had felt strangely empowering, almost like breaking free of something that had held him hostage.

And if he could get back on a snowmobile, he could figure out a way to cook for humans.

Sure, it would be a big change to be in town every day, working indoors instead of outside. Maybe Dad and Mom could get away this winter for a little bit. If he focused on how it would help them, he could get through this.

And maybe someday he'd earn enough to get back to racing.

He opened the door and walked into the warm air. It smelled like grilled cheese and tomato soup day. From the sounds of it, there was a big crowd in the dining area. Really big. The kitchen was busy too. Antonio was long gone, but his granddaughter Giselle had taken his place. She kneaded dough for fresh dinner rolls while a couple bus boys sipped pop in the break area with Tiger Christiansen, who had a dishwashing apron on. Nick's father was at the helm of the ship, the grill.

"Hey, Dad." Nick watched him flip a grilled cheese sandwich and one of his famous Reubens. "I was wondering if I could work here at the restaurant again. Maybe even learn to cook. But I could start anywhere."

Dad didn't say anything. But that was typical. Greg Dahlquist was a quiet man and disliked quick decisions.

"What do you say, Dad? Can you teach me the ropes?"

"Nope." He flipped another grilled cheese and buttered four more slices of bread.

"What do you mean nope? Won't you even think about it first?"

"Here, have a sandwich." He plated the perfectly golden grilled cheese…Nick's favorite.

"Thanks, but what I really need is a job." Still, Nick took a bite. The buttery bread was toasted to perfection, the cheddar and gouda cheeses melty and creamy. Yeah, his dad made the best.

"You've got a job. Why do you think I gave you the sandwich? You've got to keep up your energy for the race."

Yeah, that one stung. "Dad, even though they postponed the race, I can't run without a sled. So I need work." Nick took another bite.

"Thought your girlfriend was taking care of that for you. You probably have enough for ten sleds by now."

"What are you talking about?"

His dad plated the other grilled cheeses and Reubens and set them under the warmer. He wiped his hands and pulled out his phone. "Well, according to this…" He tapped the Instagram icon on his screen.

"Wait a minute. You have Instagram?" Nick swiped the phone from his dad as the app opened up.

@NixDad was his handle. He didn't have a profile pic or any followers. In fact, he only followed one account.

Nick's.

Which was somehow livestreaming right now. That's where his phone had gone!

Jae's beautiful face filled the screen. She was talking to the camera. "Nick Dahlquist is the kind of hero we all need. The kind who goes out of his way to save others. And now you have a chance to help him. Join Nick's Pack and—"

Wait a minute. The Swedish flag on the wall and the framed newspaper stories behind Jae…she was *here*. Nick dropped the sandwich and pushed through the swinging door to the bistro dining area. The place was packed with everyone from the CRT, all his aunts and uncles and cousins, friends from high school.

And in the middle of it all, Tiago was recording Jae, who stood on a chair in the center of the room.

"What are you—" Before Nick could get the question out of his mouth, hands grabbed him and hoisted him up and over the crowd. A cheer rose as he was passed over to Jae's chair and set down on his feet next to her.

There wasn't much room on the seat for both of them to stand, so he wrapped an arm around her and leaned in close to speak over the chatter and clapping.

"What's going on?"

"We want to see you race, Nick. You can't give up your dream. You've inspired so many of us and now it's a chance to give back a little." She showed him her screen, a crowd-sourcing site with a picture of him with Kasha. The goal was already met and close to being doubled.

What—?

"Is it enough? Ed thought it would be—"

"Jae, it's more than enough. It's…it's…" He swallowed. "Did you get my message online?

"What message?"

"Oh, that's right. I deleted it." He was messing this all up. But this was his chance. He would burn the ships, go all in. "You were right when you said I talked with LadyJHawk about things I should've discussed with you. And the truth is that I'm in love with LadyJHawk and I'm in love with Jae Washington. And I was torn. I didn't know how to reconcile both."

"You…you're in love with me?"

"Every part of you. And even though I've never been one for second chances, I'm learning that they are possible. I've been praying I haven't missed my chance with you."

"Really?"

He drew her close and cupped her cheek. "I might lose the cabin. But as long as I have you at the end of the day, I have everything I need. I can't lose my home when it's right here waiting for me. My home is where you are, Lady Jae."

She grinned with happy tears shimmering in her eyes. "You don't know how long I've wanted to hear that."

Before he could say a word, she kissed him soundly on the lips while everyone around them cheered. She pulled away long enough to shout above the crowd, "All right, Solo, you have a race to get ready for."

❄

The gorgeous winter landscape outside of Silver Bay with its trees covered in a lacy frost, the hills coated in glittering snow, and a clear blue sky overhead made for the perfect winter day. The cold air didn't deter the crowd gathered at the Mush Puppies starting line. Postponing the race had only built up the anticipation.

Excited chatter and barking surrounded Nick as he checked the lines again. Mischa and Ed Draper's dog Captain pranced in place. They were ready to run.

Nick glanced over at the line of spectators. Next to Peter and Tiago were Nick's parents, the CRT team, Ed, and a huge group of Deep Haven natives all there to cheer him on. Some non-Deep Havenites watched too. His newest sponsor, Ham from Jones, Inc., had brought his family to watch. One of the other boys from the youth group couldn't stop raving about the dog food and had convinced his father, an executive at an organic food line, to sponsor Nick too and expand into the doggy treats business. The new sponsorships would be enough to pay off his loan from the bank.

The race was a loop from Silver Bay to Deep Haven and back again so the starting line was also the finish line. And even though most of the runners would take seven to twelve hours to finish, this group was here to stay.

But Nick couldn't find Jae and Seymour.

Peter left Tiago holding on to Kasha's leash by the starting line and came over to finish helping Nick prep. "You feel ready, bro?"

Nick eyed the crowd again. Maybe she would still show up. "Yeah, I think so."

"So this is the new sled, huh?" Peter asked, drawing Nick's attention away from the disappointing view.

Jae wasn't here.

"Yeah. It's amazing. A custom-build a guy out in Ely did. It's made of white ash and Kevlar carbon. It's sleek, light, and super durable." It also came with a custom pack that fit all the necessary equipment. It was nicer than anything Nick had owned before. And he really wanted to show Jae. He looked at his group of cheerleaders. Where was she?

"We'd better make sure you have everything." Peter took a clipboard list and called out the different items Nick needed to have with him according to race rules. "First aid kit?"

"Check."

"Extra batteries for the headlamp?"

"Check."

He called out a few more things. "And last one, the flare gun?"

Nick pulled it out. "Looks like I have it all."

A weird expression crossed Peter's face. "Are ya sure?"

"I think so." Nick riffled through the bag on his cargo basket. "I have everything you called off."

"Do you have room for one more thing?" a sweet voice asked. "It won't take up much space."

Nick slowly turned at the sound. There, dressed in her penguin parka, ski goggles, and neon green hat, stood Jae. "You're here."

She stepped closer and took off her hat and ski goggles. "Where else would I be?"

Nick leaned in and brushed back the long strand of hair framing her cheek. "I don't know. California? Texas. Anywhere, really."

"Nope. I found my home. I'm not going anywhere. And I wanted you to take a little something with you on this race."

"What's that?"

"This." Jae kissed him. Her kisses tasted like hope and desire, sweet and alluring. He couldn't get enough. "And there's more where that came from," she whispered in his ear. "I'll be right here waiting at the finish line. For you."

"Well, then. I'll be right back."

A foghorn sounded. "Five minutes to race time! Mushers, take your mark."

Nick reluctantly let Jae go. She ran off to join the Deep Haven crowd where she stood with Seymour and Kasha and shouted above the cheers. "Go, Solo!"

Nick's starting call rang out.

"Hike! Hike!" Nick, feeling more alive than ever, flew off into the woods with his dogs in the fresh air of a Minnesota winter.

The best adventure was yet to come—and he would be sharing it all with Jae.

❄

CONNECT WITH SUNRISE

Thank you so much for reading *Right Here Waiting.* We hope you enjoyed the story. If you did, would you be willing to do us a favor and leave a review? It doesn't have to be long—just a few words to help other readers know what they're getting. (But no spoilers! We don't want to wreck the fun!) Thank you again for reading!

We'd love to hear from you—not only about this story, but about any characters or stories you'd like to read in the future. Contact us at www.sunrisepublishing.com/contact.

We also have a monthly update that contains sneak peeks, reviews, upcoming releases, and fun stuff for our reader friends.

As a treat for signing up, we'll send you a free novella written by Susan May Warren that kicks off the new Deep Haven Collection! Sign up at www.sunrisepublishing.com/free-prequel.

OTHER DEEP HAVEN NOVELS

Deep Haven Collection

Only You

Still the One

Can't Buy Me Love

Crazy for You

Then Came You

Hangin' by a Moment

Right Here Waiting

Deep Haven Series

Happily Ever After

Tying the Knot

The Perfect Match

My Foolish Heart

Hook, Line, & Sinker

You Don't Know Me

The Shadow of Your Smile

Christiansen Family Series

Evergreen

Take a Chance on Me

It Had to Be You

When I Fall in Love

Always on My Mind

The Wonder of You

You're the One That I Want

For other books by Susan May Warren, visit her website at
http://www.susanmaywarren.com.

ACKNOWLEDGMENTS

Every book has a lot of help from the first spark of an idea to it's release, but this one needed more help than most!

I'm so very grateful for the Sunrise team that made this publication happen. To Susie and Lindsay, who had the tough job of trying to make sense of my first draft and chip away at the rocky and rough exterior to help me find the heart of this story. It was not an easy road, but you believed in me and gave me the tools needed each step of the way.

To Barbara and Rel, thank you for editing and proofreading, finding dropped threads and hunting down those weasel words.

And for my fellow Sunrise authors, Rachel and Andrea, who helped me to keep going, especially through the hardships of the last year—I think we make a pretty great team. Deep Haven has a way of creating lasting friendships. I'm so glad I get to do this with you two!

Thank you to the Air St. Luke's team in Twin Falls, Idaho, for showing me your own Bell 429 and med evac facility. A big shout out to Brandy Bartholomew and all the nurses, medics, and pilots there. Thank you for your service! I hope you'll graciously overlook any errors relating to the important work you do.

I'm eternally grateful for the many friends who encourage me and cheer me on: my Writing Amigas, Julie, Gail, Barb, and especially Mollie for the many texts back and forth and brainstorming sessions when I was stuck and freaking out, my MBT huddles for the much-needed prayer support, my Moms' group (Bethany, Karen, Peggy, Elizabeth, Angela, and Sonja) for kidnapping me and for the game nights and all the laughter and love that remind me what life is all about.

To my sister-friends Linda, Lisa, and Tiara who send me snaps and memes and great Trivia team names, we know how to have the funnest fun.

To the Friends of the Upsala Library who throw the best launch parties and support authors and readers in so many ways.

And my extended family that have loved me all along. How can I ever thank you?

Bless all you readers that help spread the word and share the love of books!

And the biggest thanks goes to you, Jesse, Anders, Evie, Lucy, and Trygg, for putting up with this author-rollercoaster life. You get the brunt of the hardship as I write and yet you cheer the loudest and encourage me every single day. This would be so meaningless without you.

Lord, thank You for doing abundantly more than I could ever ask or imagine. All glory goes to You. Ephesians 3:20-21

ABOUT THE AUTHORS

USA Today bestselling, RITA, Christy and Carol award-winning novelist **Susan May Warren** is the author of over 85 novels, most of them contemporary romance with a touch of suspense. One of her strongest selling series has been the Deep Haven series, a collection of books set in Northern Minnesota, off the shore of Lake Superior. Visit her at www.susanmaywarren.com.

After growing up on both the east and west coasts, **Michelle Sass Aleckson** now lives the country life in central Minnesota with her own hero and their four kids. She loves rocking out to 80's music on a Saturday night, playing Balderdash with the fam, and getting lost in good stories. Especially stories that shine grace. And if you're wondering, yes, Sass is her maiden name. Visit her at www.michellealeckson.com.

CPSIA information can be obtained
at www.ICGtesting.com
Printed in the USA
LVHW031751101121
702989LV00004B/166